"These are wonderful, heartfelt stories—clear-eyed, masterful, and engaging in every detail. Kerry Langan knows the magic of empathy and of smart storytelling, and I know she will fill you with gratitude, as she did me, for the care and grace she has brought to this beautiful work."

Joe David Bellamy
Former member of National Book Critics Circle Board of Directors and winner of Editors' Book Award for novel *Suzi Sinzinnati.*

"With delicate brushstrokes, Kerry Langan paints fine miniaturist portraits of a variety of young, likeable protagonists, all of whom yearn to be seen, heard, and understood as they experience the revelations of maturity and the joy and fragility of life. Kerry Langan's *Only Beautiful* is sometimes humorous, sometimes bittersweet, and always seductive in the best sense of the word. Hers is a new and original voice, and Wising Up Press has done us all a great favor by publishing her lovely and insightful debut collection."

Janice Eidus
Author of *The War of the Rosens, Urban Bliss, The Celibacy Club,* and *Vito Loves Geraldine.*

ONLY BEAUTIFUL

&

OTHER STORIES

WISING UP ANTHOLOGIES

www.universaltable.org

Double Lives, Reinvention & Those We Leave Behind

Love After 70

Families: The Frontline of Pluralism

Illness & Grace, Terror & Transformation

ONLY BEAUTIFUL
&
OTHER STORIES

KERRY LANGAN

Wising Up Press Collective
Wising Up Press
Decatur, Georgia

Wising Up Press
P.O. Box 2122
Decatur, GA 30031-2122
www.universaltable.org

Catalogue-in-Publication data is on file with the Library of Congress.
LCCN: 2009936555

Wising Up ISBN: 978-0-9796552-7-2

For Bob,
"My heart is ever at your service."

TABLE OF CONTENTS

MAKEOVER

Mrs. Turell has new magazines on her coffee table. The covers say things like: "Get Back Into the Dating Swing," "Life After Divorce," and "How to Know if You're Ready To Commit Again."

I've been baby-sitting Gretchen and Andy Turell for almost two years, since before Mrs. asked Mr. to move out. The magazines on the coffee table used to read, "Keeping the Romance Alive in Your Marriage," "Rediscovering Intimacy After Childbirth," and "Holiday Makeover for Your House!"

Now Mrs. Turell is considering using her maiden name, Canfield, after the divorce is final. "But the children," she says to me, "it might confuse them. They've gone through so much already, I don't want to burden them with one more change." She asks me to call her Janet, and lately I've even been calling her Jan.

She looks young for her age, early thirties, I guess. Her blonde hair is almost down to her shoulders and she wears dangle earrings. She's thin, although she always complains about her "saggy tush." I think she's beautiful, like the pictures of women in Vogue, and I wonder what she looked like at my age, fifteen.

The last time he drove me home, Mr. Turell asked me what I thought of his wife. I looked at him and watched as his head rocked slowly from side to side. Maybe he had been drinking. Probably. When I didn't answer, he asked me again: "So, Barbie Baby-sitter, what. . . do you think. . . of my wife?"

I looked out the windshield, watching the road slip beneath the car. "She's nice," I said quietly. He laughed, but it was more like coughing. "Nice," he said, and I couldn't tell if he was serious. He shook his head like he was happily confused, and said, "One thing you can say about my wife—she sure is *nice*." The word sliced the dense air in the car.

Steadying my school books on my lap, I sat perfectly still. He didn't say anything more before we reached my house. Counting out money, he laid the bills one at a time in my palm. I said thanks and got out of the car.

A month later the Turells separated. When I babysit now, Mrs. Turell is giddy, asking my advice about which shoes to wear or the shade of lipstick that suits her best. "Oh, that one," I say, urging her to coat her lips a deep garnet. I'm flattered that she asks for my advice. I only have an older brother, Ted, who barely grunts at me, and Janet is kind of like a big sister now. A big sister who has her own house, beautiful clothes, children, everything except a husband. But that doesn't seem to bother her.

"I'm just going out with the girls. The number's by the phone," she tells me. The girls. She goes everywhere with them: to the movies, out to dinner, shopping. I imagine Janet and her friends at a fancy restaurant drinking white wine from crystal goblets, laughing and talking about cashmere sweaters and handsome movie stars.

"Mrs. Turell's not seeing someone? A new man?" my mother asks.

"No," I scowl and press my lips together tight. Even if she were seeing someone, I wouldn't gossip and be disloyal to Janet.

"Then why does she go out so often?" my mother asks, but I just shrug my shoulders in reply.

"Maybe she's meeting a man someplace and she doesn't want the children to know."

"Don't be ridiculous," I tell her and stomp out of the room.

But tonight, Friday night, there's a man in the Turell's living room when I arrive. He's sitting on the couch reading a magazine, oblivious to Andy who's running through the living room yelling, "Zoom, zoom, zooma zoom. . ."

Janet introduces me. "Michael, this is Barb, our baby-sitter."

"Hi Barb." He nods his head at me and then lowers it as he turns a page in the magazine. He's older than Mr. Turell, with wiry silver coils knitted throughout his light brown hair. It makes me think of tinsel on a Christmas tree. The tip of his nose is oddly pinched, but I try not to stare.

"I'll just be a minute," Janet says, and goes into the bathroom.

"C'mon, Andy," I say, "let's see what's on television."

In the family room, I sit on the black leather couch, Gretchen and

Andy on either side of me. We watch *America's Funniest Home Videos,* laughing at the silly movie clips.

When Janet walks in to say good-bye to us, I check out her outfit. She's wearing a black lace dress with a silver and onyx necklace. She looks taller than usual, and I notice the stiletto black shoes with little silver bows at the toe.

"Wow!" I say. She grins and turns a couple times like she's a model on a runway.

"You look so pretty, Mommy." Gretchen bounds off the chair and hugs her mother tightly.

"Careful, honey, you're pulling my necklace." Janet looks over Gretchen's head and says to me, "We're going to the Shapiros. The number's by the phone."

This is a surprise. Mr. and Mrs. Turell often had dinner at the Shapiros. Mr. Turell and Mr. Shapiro used to play golf together, and maybe they still do.

Janet leans forward, curling a hand around one side of her mouth, and whispers, "Did you like him?"

"Him?" I whisper back.

She points her finger towards the living room, raising her eyebrows as she waits for my answer.

"Nice," I say, tilting my head and smiling, happy that Jan cares about my opinion. I give her a thumbs up and she winks at me and kisses Andy and Gretchen. "Be good for Barb. I want a good report when I get back."

The kids try to talk me into letting them stay up later but I'm firm. I rush them through their baths, their good night stories, their drinks of water. Andy falls asleep almost immediately and Gretchen nods off about twenty minutes later.

It's only nine-thirty. Good. Plenty of time before Jan gets back with her date at eleven. I have the house to myself. One of my favorite things to do is pretend that I live here, that I'm inspecting each of the rooms for a big party I'm going to have. I start in the living room, arranging the magazines on the coffee table so they fan into a semi-circle. The living room adjoins the dining room, a big open room with Scandinavian furniture. The dining table is a little dusty; Jan told me that she couldn't afford to pay the cleaning woman who used to come twice a week. Laying my arm on the table, I move it so the dust sticks to my sweatshirt. Sometimes I actually set the table with china and silverware, even the candlesticks if I'm imagining a really elegant dinner party. I sit at one end of the table and pretend that people are talking happily as they pass the platters of food around. I'm not looking at him, but my imaginary husband at the other end of the table is marveling at how I throw together these chic dinner parties at a moment's notice.

The kitchen is filled with stainless steel appliances. The surfaces shine under the recessed lighting, and I can't resist running my hand over the cool, glimmering refrigerator. The Corian countertop is pale blue, the same color as the floor tiles. It's a "serene, elegant" kitchen, just like the ones in *House Beautiful* magazine. I've described it to my mother many times, urging her to update our ugly brown and beige kitchen, to get rid of the old light fixture that you turn on by yanking on a string. She just shakes her head and says, "Do you think we're made of money?"

I have to wash the dishes by hand at home, but here I carefully load the dishwasher so every dish and glass fits perfectly. Just as I press the power button, the telephone rings. Picking up the receiver, I say, "Turell residence," my voice just a little snobby.

"Oh, really?" someone says, like he doesn't believe me. I know the voice, but it takes a few seconds for my mind to recognize it.

"Mr. Turell?" My voice wavers and I clear my throat. "This is Barb Sheridan. I'm baby-sitting."

"Well, Barbie Baby-sitter, what do you know," he says briskly. "How are you?"

"Fine."

"Good, good. Breaking hearts yet?"

"No." I'm embarrassed because it's a personal question, but also because I don't have a boyfriend.

"Don't worry. Any time now. You're a sweet baby-sitter one minute and a heart stomper the next."

The receiver feels heavy in my hand, and it starts to slip because my palm is damp.

"Where's Jan?" he asks.

My heart bounces in and out against my chest just like it does in geometry class when I know I'm going to get called on. "Out," I tell him.

He laughs once. "I know that Barbie Baby-sitter, but out *where?*"

Running a finger over my lips I say, "She went out with a friend. I think they were going to dinner."

"Where?"

"Oh, I don't know. With some other friends I guess."

I wonder if I should pretend to hear one of the kids crying. Which one? Andy. But Andy never wakes up.

"Didn't she leave a number?"

I realize it will sound too obvious now if I try to get off the phone. "Number?"

He's getting more impatient, but I'm too confused to think. He's sighs, and a feeling, cold and heavy, drops down from my shoulders and lodges in my stomach. "She's at the Shapiros," I say as softly as I can, but he hears me.

"Oh." The line is silent. "She went with a friend, you say?"

"Yes." I exhale loudly, realizing I should have covered the mouthpiece.

"Oh." He makes a couple sounds, not words, more of a sucking sound, like he's running his tongue over his teeth. "Don't worry, Barbie. I'm not going to interrogate you. I get the picture."

"Okay," I say, relieved.

"Tell her I called." I think he's going to hang up, but then he says, "Wait. Tell her to call me. Tell her to call me the minute she gets in."

I close my eyes imagining Janet's reaction to the message. She hasn't given me special instructions about what to say, or not say, to her soon to be ex-husband. I only told the truth, answered questions; I didn't volunteer any information. Still, I worry that she'll be mad at me. That she'll tell me to call her Mrs. Turell again.

"I'll give her the message."

"Do that," he says and hangs up.

In the kitchen, I write on the message pad: "Mr. Turell called at nine-forty-five. Please call him as soon as possible tonight." That way I can just hand her the message instead of saying it in front of her date.

I go into Janet's bedroom, across the hall from Gretchen's and Andy's rooms. It's so much neater now that Mr. Turell is gone. He used to leave his dirty socks on the floor and his tie rack was always a mess. Now Janet has a lot more room for her clothes. In the closet are three hanging plastic sweater cases and two shoe racks. Her slacks and jeans hang upside down on clip hangers. The dresses, covered in plastic, take up a whole half of the closet. I inhale deeply to smell the spicey, cinnamon scent from the lace sachets of potpourri hanging on the back of the closet door.

What I've been waiting to do all night is try on Janet's clothes. I've done this a few times before, putting everything back carefully. I can make myself look so grown-up, much older than fifteen. If my mother saw me, she'd die. Her idea of high fashion is sensible shoes and an all-weather coat.

Placing my own clothes on the king-sized bed, I slip into a burgundy silk dress with double-looped spaghetti straps. It's just a little too long, but it fits fine everywhere else. I've noticed that Janet wears sheer black stockings with this dress; she has a drawer full of nylons in her bureau. Unfortunately, Janet's wearing her highest heels, so I have to settle for little black pumps. But there are pierced diamond earrings in her jewelry box and a necklace with a single diamond pendant. I'm very careful putting the earrings on; I got my ears pieced only a couple months ago and they still hurt sometimes.

Now, the really fun part. Sitting at the vanity, I put on lipstick and blush. I'm careful to use very little, just one coat of "Richest Plum" on my lips and a dusting of "Pink Wine" on my cheeks. I think lavender eye shadow would be wonderful with this dress, but Janet only wears brown. I apply some with the little sponge applicator, careful not to smudge it. There are a bunch of mascara tubes in a little cosmetic bag on the vanity, and I use the darkest one I can find to make my lashes look really long.

Now for my hair. It's reddish-orange, and as if that wasn't bad enough, it's frizzy. I never let myself even wonder what Janet thinks about my hair, Janet with her glossy yellow waterfall of hair. Maybe someday I can ask her to take me to her hairdresser.

I pull my hair back and wind it into a tight bun at the base of my neck, keeping it in place with lots of bobby pins. In the mirror, I'm transformed. I could pass for twenty. Getting up, I walk back and forth across the bedroom floor. You can't get too much practice walking in heels. Standing in front of the mirror, I turn and examine myself from every angle.

I hear something, a creak of some kind or a soft whine. Standing very still, I tilt my head to listen and hear the same sound again. Maybe it's Gretchen; sometimes she gets thirsty and wakes up for a drink of water. Walking into the hallway, I look in the children's rooms, but they're both sleeping. The furnace goes on, making the house sound like it's stretching and breathing. Reassured, I go back to the master bedroom. I decide to change the jewelry, put on pearls. Janet has quite a collection of single and double-strands. I'm deciding which would go better with the dress, regular or freshwater pearls, when I hear his voice behind me.

"Well, well, well. Barbie Baby-sitter grows up."

Turning, I see him in the doorway. He looks amazed, almost happy, but his left eye is squinting and that makes him look confused too.

"I'm sorry." My face is flooding with heat and shame. "I shouldn't have done this. I'll put these clothes back right away." I'm surprised I'm not stammering, but my guilt is enough to drown me.

Mr. Turell enters the room and steps slowly around me, circling me. His overcoat is damp and I wonder why I didn't hear the rain. "Easy, easy," he says slowly. "There's no rush. The Shapiros have the longest, most boring dinners on the planet."

"Still. . ." I begin to remove the jewelry, fingering the clasp on the back of on an earring.

"Don't," he says, almost sharply, but his hand, when he touches my arm, is very light. He stops pacing and stands directly in front of me. His eyes look frightened, but there's something wild building in them; an eerie yellow circle around his pupils expands into the murky brown of his irises.

"Janet, Mrs. Turell, isn't home yet," I tell him, looking down at the blue carpet. I see the little dents in the rug from the heels of the pumps. "She's not home yet," I repeat.

"I wouldn't be here if she was." He sits down on the bed, casually pushing my jeans and sweatshirt over. "Since my wife is out partying, I thought I'd come over and see my kids." Suddenly he stands and pulls back the comforter. How odd it is, the way he's standing there staring at the sheets. He kneels and I have the insane notion that he's praying the way a child does at the side of a bed before sleeping. But, of course, he's not. He runs his flat hands over the sheets and brings his face down to the mattress as if he's trying to smell something.

His back still towards me, he asks with embarrassment, "Do her dates ever stay over?"

I can't answer; tonight is the first time I've met one of her dates. I'm too scared and befuddled to say anything. He stands and then sits on the bed again.

"Well?"

"I don't know. This is the first time—"

"Don't!" he interrupts, noticing that I was slipping off a shoe. He almost stands, but then he sits further back on the bed.

"Andy and Gretchen are asleep,"

"That's okay, that's okay. I just want to take a peek at them."

I nod, like I understand, but I'm so scared I don't think I'm breathing. I watch as Mr. Turell slides his coat off his shoulders. He laughs, startling me more. "Relax, would you? I'm not going to tell, Barbie."

"I'm sorry," I start again. "I was just. . ."

"Trying on my wife's clothes. No big deal. They look good on you. What are you now, seventeen, eighteen?"

"Fifteen."

His face flinches, and he's quiet for a few moments. "Playing dress-up, huh?" He swallows, his adam's apple rising and falling. "Pretending you're a high society princess?"

Shrugging my shoulders, I shake my head yes. Briefly, I think of telling him that Janet told me I could borrow a dress for a school dance, but he could tell in a second it was a lie.

He begins to pull his body forward and stands up. "Why don't you go see Gretchen and Andy?" I say. "I'll change into my own clothes. . ."

I can tell he's not listening. He opens the closet door and looks at the clothes. Running his hands over a blue silk blouse, he fastens the top two buttons. He fumbles through the closet, taking out what looks like a long red kimono. "I got her this for Christmas last year," he says. I wonder if I should tell him that I think it's beautiful, that I love the way the cherry blossoms are imprinted into the fabric, that I understand that it must be terrible to lose a wife as beautiful as Janet.

He walks over to the bureau, studying it for a few moments before abruptly pulling out the middle drawer. When he kneels in front of it, I turn away and stare at the window on the other side of the room. I've opened that drawer also, many times. My hands have run over the satin garments, folded and refolded the nightgowns and robes. I've never had the nerve to try on anything in that drawer, but I've held the soft things against my cheek, rubbed them into my skin as if to bring me good luck.

My favorite item is the deep purple silk teddy with lace across the bodice, but the tiny pink camisole with the skinny straps is also pretty. I know that the drawer also contains tap pants, garter belts, shimmering satin bras in soft pastel colors. I've looked at the Turrells' mail; a Victoria's Secret catalog

comes often. I glance back. Mr. Turell slowly unravels a lavender negligee until it hangs straight. For a brief moment, I consider grabbing my clothes off the bed and running to the bathroom, locking the door behind me. I imagine staying in there until Janet and her date arrive home. But then Mr. Turrell takes a step towards me and says in a heavy, empty voice, "Put this on."

"No," I say immediately. He's crazy, I think—crazy. What should I do? I have to get away from this crazy man.

Mr. Turell doesn't like my answer. He brings his face close to mine, so close I can feel his breath on my face, smell the hard alcohol. "Put it on! Want me to tell Jan what's been going on here, huh Barbie? You're supposed to be watching my kids and here you are trying on her clothes, wearing jewelry I gave her for our goddamn wedding anniversary!"

Grabbing the pendant, he jerks hard. I can feel the clasp break against the back of my neck, and watch as the necklace falls to the floor. Bringing his face closer, his nose almost touching mine, he says in a throaty command, "You do what I tell you—NOW PUT IT ON!"

Covering the bottom of my face with my open palms, I start to cry. I back away until the wall hits me. My tears make everything in the room look drowned, like I'm underwater. But I can tell that Mr. Turell is coming closer. I slide myself down the wall until I'm sitting on the floor, my head lowered to my knees. There's movement in the room but I don't look up.

My nose is running, disgusting snot smeared all over my face and the dress. I stay like that for several minutes. Finally, lifting my head, I open my eyes and see I'm alone in the room. I know instinctively that he left, that he didn't bother to look at his children. Still, I stay seated on the floor. The furnace shuts off and the house is gradually quiet, so silent I hear the spray of rain hitting the window.

Finally, I stand up, my legs wobbly, and remove every item of clothing. My own clothes feel soft and warm, they fit so well. I press a cold washcloth over the stained part of Mrs. Turell's dress and hope it looks okay the next time she wears it. With the same washcloth, I remove the make-up on my face. Scrubbing over my mouth, my cheeks, my eyes, I feel as if I could keep going until I removed my freckles. It's good to keep moving; it steadies me. In the utility drawer in the kitchen, I find a tiny pair of pliers and I do a reasonably good job of fixing the clasp on the diamond necklace. I place it carefully in the top drawer of Janet's jewelry box.

The lavender negligee is swirled into a silk puddle on the floor. Carefully, I fold it into a small rectangle and put it back in the drawer. I walk towards the door but then stop. Sliding open the closet door, I look at the blue blouse buttoned all the way up to the collar. I undo the top two buttons and slide the door shut. As I do, I know I will never enter this room again.

The children are fine. In Gretchen's room, I sit in the dark listening to her breathe in and out for a couple of minutes. Holding her Raggedy Anne doll, I stay there until my watch says it's eleven o'clock, and then I move to the living room and sit on the couch.

Mrs. Turrell and Michael arrive home just a few minutes later. I can tell from the way she rubs her temples that she didn't have a good time. She opens her wallet to pay me, but then Michael offers, "Here, let me."

"Don't be silly," Mrs. Turrell says, "she watched *my* kids." She hands me a clutch of bills that I immediately slide into a pocket. Michael asks me where I live and says he'll drive me home. Before I leave with him, Mrs. Turell asks if there were any calls. The message is on the kitchen table, but I shake my head no. She nods at me as if she understands everything.

LEAD US NOT

Even if he didn't sit in the first seat in the first row, every pair of third grade eyes would still have been on Michael Hoffman. He was smart; he had style. When someone knocked on the door, he rose immediately and swung the door wide open, his foot pointed forward, his head tilted at a jaunty angle.

"Why thank you, young man," the principal, Sister Christina, said the first time she entered. She smiled at our teacher, Sister Serena, and said, "Very impressive."

Sister Serena, a young nun in her early twenties, nodded weakly. Michael Hoffman was the reason she would sometimes retreat to the girls' room and return with red eyes, her hands clutching crumpled tissues. He was the reason she pressed fiercely on the beads of her enormous rosary, rolling the glassy black balls until her fingers must have ached. He was only eight years old, but Michael was more like an adult presence in our classroom.

He had all the confidence that Sister Serena lacked. He was handsome, with wide-set brown eyes and long black lashes. His smile, unlike many of his classmates, had no gaps, his permanent teeth already in. His height was emphasized by his upright posture. There was something intimidating about the width and height of his forehead, more prominent because his hair was short and combed back from his face. It made him appear older than the rest of us; I could imagine him with a briefcase going off to work each morning like my father.

Michael called out the answers before anyone had a chance to raise their hand. And he knew *all* the answers: the capital of every state, every country, how to spell "catechism," how you could use multiplication to double-check your answer to a long division problem. At the end of the first day of school, Sister Serena, exhausted from saying, "Michael, I didn't call on you. Raise your hand. Stop that. STOP THAT!" sent him to the corner where he continued to yell out answers: "ANTARCTICA IS THE SOUTHERNMOST CONTINENT."

During the first weeks of school, he scared me. His voice was as loud and deep as the priest's at Sunday mass. His words were iced with authority. I tried not to look at him, fearful that if he caught my eye, his voice would boom out, "MARY FITCH IS NOT PAYING ATTENTION."

He scared me, but he absolutely terrified Sister Serena. At recess, she stood at the edge of the playground reading a small prayer book. She closed her eyes and mouthed the words silently over and over. She didn't stop until the bell rang and we all walked back into the school. She looked at the round clock on the wall more frequently than any of her students. When the three o'clock bell rang, she sighed loudly with relief.

I walked home every day with Cheryl Mooney, a friend since kindergarten who lived on the street behind ours. We ambled along slowly, sharing our observations about the day. One afternoon, when we reached Kramer's Store, I paused and looked in the window to see a display of tiny dolls called "Little Kiddles." No taller than an inch, each doll had a rhyming name like Tracy Triddle, Lola Liddle, Wendy Fliddle. The dolls came with miniature accessories, colorful plastic tricycles, sailboats, airplanes. Each cost five dollars. Five whole dollars. Gazing wistfully at the dolls, I caught a glimpse of Michael Hoffman in the window's reflection. I nudged Cheryl, who found his behavior hilarious instead of frightening, and she called out, "*Hi-i Mii-chael*," in a saucy tone. Clearly he saw us, but he looked straight ahead, walking past us with a man's full stride.

I liked to go to Cheryl's house after school and my mother was glad to have me there. She spent most of every day cleaning our house, scrubbing floors and counter tops, vacuuming every inch of carpet, dusting and re-dusting the furniture. I wore the cleanest uniform in the school, my white blouse ironed to perfection with pressed seams in the sleeves. I was responsible for making my own bed, but Mother zealously performed every other household chore.

Her quest for order never ceased. She alphabetized the grocery list and wrote down the number of the aisle where the item could be found. The

canned soups in the pantry were more orderly than books on a library shelf. There were no plants in the house because plants required soil which Mother equated to dirt. Dirt in her house? Never. But worst of all was her fixation with my hair. In the mid-sixties, girls were beginning to let their hair grow longer, beautiful locks sliding across their backs. I, however, reported to the beauty salon every six weeks so my pixie cut stayed short and neat. After every visit, I threw myself on my bed and cried. My hair was almost as short as my brother Jim's. I pleaded to be allowed to grow my hair, but my mother was adamant: "Long hair is so messy. It would be all over the house."

Cheryl's mother, Mrs. Mooney, was different. She let Cheryl do whatever she wanted with her hair, pigtails one day, braids the next. Cheryl's dresser top was cluttered with barrettes and swirly ribbons in cheerful colors. A single small black comb sat on my bureau. Mrs. Mooney saw how disheartened I was about my hair and reassured me about my appearance. "You can carry a short hair style off because your eyes are so big, Mary. And what's the name of that model with the short hair? Twiggy? She isn't nearly as pretty as you. In fact, you remind me of a young Audrey Hepburn." Her words, so soothing, helped. I spent as many hours as I could in the Mooney's comfortably messy house, eating snacks with Cheryl while watching television in a family room filled to the brim with framed photographs that hadn't been dusted in months.

As autumn passed, we got used to Michael's calling out the answers. We benefited from it. If we didn't know an answer, we'd simply wait a moment, listen to Michael, and then repeat his answer as if we'd just thought of it ourselves. When we had a test, Sister Serena put Michael's desk in the hall. Within minutes, he'd pound on the door, "I'M FINISHED, SISTER."

"Michael! Sit at your desk and stay there until I come for you."

The rest of us looked around. Was he really finished so soon? We put our heads down and tried to concentrate.

One Friday in October, Sister Serena was ill and we had a substitute. Mrs. Rollins, a short lively woman who smelled as if she took a bath in perfume, stood at the front of the classroom and asked, "Who was the first man to orbit the earth?"

We waited. Nothing. Whispering started. We all looked at Michael who sat upright with his hands folded neatly on his desk.

"No one knows? Children, how could you not know this?"

Cheryl raised her hand and pronounced triumphantly, "John Glenn." It was the first time any one of us had actually answered a question.

That afternoon, the principal came in to observe. Sister Christina slipped quietly in the back door of the classroom and stayed for about twenty minutes. Michael never answered but continued to sit quietly and look as if he were paying close attention. When Sister Christina turned to leave, I noticed the satisfied expression on her face. Mrs. Rollins had no trouble handling Michael. Obviously, inexperienced Sister Serena was at fault.

When Sister Serena returned, it was business as usual. She asked questions, Michael answered. She told him to stop, he didn't. The rest of us were happy things were back to normal.

Shortly after Halloween, the third and fourth grades performed a Musical Review for parents. Most of the songs were from *The Sound of Music*, a movie every nun was absolutely enthralled with. Michael's melodic bass filled the auditorium and helped cover the pitch problems created by the mass of untrained voices. There was a punch and cookie reception afterwards and mothers waited in line to chat with their child's teacher. My mother didn't come. She had planned to spend the day getting the winter clothes out of our storage room and sealing our summer clothes in plastic. "You should be learning at school," she said, "not pretending you're on Broadway." So I stood with Cheryl and ate cookie after cookie, watching Sister Serena nod and smile as each mother moved up the line to speak with her. We were too far away to hear what was said, but Mrs. Mooney got Sister Serena to laugh, a rare sight. Afterwards, Mrs. Mooney joined us and pretended to be stern when she asked, "How many sweets have you two eaten?" She winked at me and picked up an enormous chocolate chip cookie.

With a start, I noticed Michael standing in line with a man, the only father to attend our program. When they reached the front of the line, I noticed Sister Serena's face flush with fear. She started to speak and Mr. Hoffman, at least a foot taller than the nun, crossed his arms and leaned back from his waist. At one point he looked at Michael who shook his head no vigorously.

I felt unsettled. Michael looked as timid as Sister Serena. With his father's hand heavy on his shoulder, they left the line and walked out of the

building.

Turning to Cheryl, I said, "What do you think they were talking about?"

Mrs. Mooney made a *tsk* sound with her tongue. "Poor boy. It can't be easy," she murmured.

"What?" Cheryl asked.

"His mother left them last summer. Oh!" She looked at us with alarm, realizing she had said something she shouldn't have. Sighing, she finished, "Don't say anything about it. Just be as nice to Michael as you can."

Christmas approached and one night during dinner my parents asked Jim and me what we wanted to find under the tree. We had never believed in Santa Claus. My mother thought the whole thing was nonsense.

Jim, two years younger than me, was ready with a long mental list: an Etch-a-Sketch, a Slinky, a G I Joe doll that came with a truck, a paint by number set, a basketball, on and on. My mother got a pad of paper and began jotting things down. When Jim stopped talking, she started a new list, alphabetizing what he had just said.

"What about you, Mary?" Dad asked. "Ready for more Play-dough?"

"Daaa-ad." But as I locked my gaze with my father's pale blue eyes, I summoned courage and announced, "The only thing I want for Christmas is long hair."

My mother stood and started to pile the dishes. "Well, you can forget about that. You know my feelings on the subject." She glared at me before walking to the sink. I knew that later she would pinch my arm and reprimand me for being impudent, for taking my case to my father.

Looking down at my plate, my eyes started to water. I knew my father was looking at me, feeling miserable himself. I stayed there until the tears rolled off my chin and onto the tablecloth that would be whisked off any moment and put in the washing machine. And as much as I loved him, I inwardly railed against my father for not speaking up to my mother. Where was his voice?

I wondered if Michael would stop hollering out answers after his father talked to Sister Serena, but if anything he was more vocal. He didn't just call out answers now, he screamed out lines from TV shows and commercials in a deep monotone: SAME BAT TIME, SAME BAT CHANNEL. HOW LONG CAN A TOOTSIE ROLL LAST? ROGER RAMJET IS OUR HERO. A SLINKY, A SLINKY!!!

Sister Serena. Each morning she started afresh, determined to quiet Michael. She told him that fourth graders didn't act like that. Did he want to go back to kindergarten? Near lunchtime she was threatening to call his father. By afternoon, she was simply pleading with him to be quiet. When she sent him into the hall, she knew she had failed, given up. During these moments, she stopped our lesson and had us stand and recite the "Our Father." With a beatific look on her face, Sister Serena looked up at the ceiling as she recited, "And lead us not into temptation, but deliver us from evil." From the hallway, Michael screamed, "AMEN!"

In early December, I got the biggest present of my life. One morning while my mother was vacuuming cobwebs in the attic, my father came into my room with a triumphant look on his face. "Mary, Mom's agreed. You can let your hair grow out to here." He placed a finger on my collar bone. Of course, I wanted it much longer, to my waist. Still, with it reaching my collar bone, I wouldn't look like a boy. I jumped up and hugged my father.

"Just keep it away from your face," he warned. "If it starts hanging down in your eyes, pin it back. If you don't, she'll make you get it cut for sure."

"Thank you!" I stared into the mirror and imagined how I'd look with longer hair. I resolved to brush it a hundred times a night, to make it look as glossy as pictures in magazines. Mother would see that I was serious about keeping it tidy, and maybe she'd allow me to let it grow even longer. Maybe.

I began going into Kramer's every afternoon after school to look at the display of tiny dolls. I was getting long hair for Christmas, and I hadn't asked for anything else. But the dolls, so compact and pretty, were irresistible. One day when Mrs. Kramer was getting more Christmas lights from the back of the store, I picked up Tracy Triddle on her tiny tricycle and dropped her into my book bag.

As I walked out of the store, I imagined Michael hollering: STOP,

THIEF! SOMEONE CALL THE POLICE! MARY FITCH HAS STOLEN TRACEY TRIDDLE!

When I was safely home, playing on the floor of my closet with the tiny doll with long red pigtails, I was uneasy. Guilt burned at the center of my chest and my hands trembled. Even at that moment, however, I planned to go back to Kramer's the next day and snatch Lola Liddle and her little sail boat. Lola had blonde hair that reached her feet and teeth as white as the lady in the Pepsodent commercial. And maybe next week, or sooner if I dared, I'd scoop up Wendy Fliddle. I felt heat on the back of my neck and my heart began to thunder. I was frightened. And elated, completely elated. The euphoria that came with the fear washed over me and gave my skin a delicious tingle. With a start, I realized that Michael didn't want to yell the answers out in class. He couldn't help it.

Michael was transferring to public school. He wouldn't be back after Christmas vacation. Mrs. Mooney broke the news to me and Cheryl, saying, "Make sure you say good-bye to him before he goes. Tell him you hope he likes his new school." Then she ran her fingers through my hair, an inch longer now and secured on the sides with two Goody barrettes. "You're getting prettier every day, Mary. Soon Miss America is going to have to hand over her crown to you."

At home, I wasn't receiving compliments. In a clipped voice, Mother would tell me that my barrettes were crooked and that if I couldn't keep my hair neat, it was back to the salon for the dreaded pixie cut.

Michael began to call out answers less frequently. Eventually, there were whole days when he simply sat still and didn't utter a word. The room was so quiet I could hear the buzzing of the florescent lights overhead and the hiss from the radiators. The day before Christmas break, Michael quietly stood and walked to the back of the room. He put on his coat, hat, and boots and waited for Sister Serena to notice him.

She turned from the blackboard. "Michael, what are you doing?"

He continued to stand there, an accusing stare targeted at her. Abruptly then, he ran out of the room.

"Michael!" Sister Serena threw down the chalk and raced to follow him. The black folds of her habit flailed about her as she exited the room.

Left without a teacher, we turned our heads to stare at one another and confirm that we had all witnessed the same thing. Then we were on our feet and at the long row of windows. Our classroom overlooked the field behind the school. We weren't allowed to play there during recess, confined instead to the playground. At this time of year, the brown earth was frozen beneath a couple inches of freshly fallen snow.

We saw Michael first, his rhythmic stride carrying him far into the field, his boots leaving prints in the snow. He ran with the easy grace of an athlete despite his heavy clothes. Sister Serena had no coat but I guessed her head would stay warm under her veil. She tried to hurry. Even from our room, we could see the puffs of white about her mouth as she exhaled the winter air.

Michael was almost out of our range of vision. One of the boys began chanting, "Run, Michael, run," and we all took up the chorus: "RUN, MICHAEL, RUN! RUN, MICHAEL, RUN!" We stopped, though, when Sister Serena fell in the very center of the field. Several of us screamed, stunned to see our teacher prostate in the snow.

"WHAT'S GOING ON? I CAN HEAR YOU ALL THE WAY DOWN THE HALL!"

We turned to face Sister Christina. After a moment, Cheryl dared, "Sister Serena is chasing Michael Hoffman through the field. She fell down."

Darting to the window, Sister Christina looked out and took a sharp intake of breath. "Sit down, everyone. Open your readers to the first story and take turns reading a paragraph each." She left the room and none of us had the nerve to return to the window.

We didn't open our readers, but several minutes later, Mr. Banes, the gym teacher walked in looking bewildered. "Okay, kids," he hesitated, "um, how about we sing some Christmas carols. You all know Jingle Bells, right?"

There were plenty of gifts for me under the tree on Christmas Day. I got an Easy Bake oven, a book of crossword puzzles, a copy of *Little Women*, a necklace with a green glass heart to represent my birthstone, knee socks in navy and hunter green to wear with my school uniform, and a beautiful red velvet hair clasp. I knew the last item had been picked out by my father.

It was a wonderful morning, despite my mother waiting like a vulture

until all the presents were opened so she could swoop down and gather up the wrapping paper. She put it in the trash and told us to put our gifts away neatly in our rooms.

I put all my gifts on my bed and admired them. It was quite a haul, my presents covering the entire bedspread. And still I couldn't resist setting a few more items on the pillow. I crawled into the closet and retrieved the dolls from the old shoe box I'd hidden them in. Gathering all the Little Kiddles, I arranged them on the pillow. "Merry Christmas, girls. See," I said to them softly, "we have a new oven. Later I'll make you a little cake." I imagined having a tea party in my closet, munching on my home baked treats with the dolls on my lap.

I remember my mother's gasp from the hallway, how she looked when she first spied the dolls, those first moments when she interrogated me, my sobbing when I admitted I stole them. Worst of all, I remember my father's heavy eyes, his turning his face, his chin on his chest. I knew he wouldn't try to save me.

No one's hair should ever be pulled. It hurts more than a slap to the face, that wrenching of the roots just beneath your scalp. My mother pulled me that way into the bathroom. My eyes were closed but I knew my fate as she opened a drawer in the vanity and removed the scissors. I imagined how the silver scissors glinted in the winter light. The sound—the horrible *queeehh*—as the shears sliced through my hair, and the feeling of my head becoming lighter and lighter until I had to open my eyes and see my almost bald skull in the mirror. I heard my father despair, "Grace, oh, Grace," and walk down the hallway, his footsteps becoming softer and softer and then vanishing.

My hair, more dear to me than my blood, was everywhere,

"CLEAN IT UP! CLEAN EVERY BIT OF IT UP!" Mother yelled. But she couldn't help herself. She knelt and began picking up heaps of it, putting it in the trash can and screaming to my father to get the vacuum.

I ran from the room and out the door, down the street and around the block. It was cold, so cold, and the cold air mocked my naked scalp. Mrs. Mooney answered the door. She covered her mouth for only a second before she took me in her arms. Her voice cracked as she said, "Your day will come, Mary. You just wait and see. Your day will come."

Sister Serena didn't come back after Christmas vacation either. Mrs. Rollins became our regular teacher. She asked me why I was wearing a hat in class and Robert Butler yelled out from the back of the room, "Because she's bald!" The class erupted with laughter and I looked at the empty desk in the first row. I imagined Michael shouting, "LEAVE HER ALONE. YOU'RE ALL A BUNCH OF IDIOTS."

We all assumed that Sister Serena had some kind of nervous breakdown, but then we learned that she went to one of the Maryknoll Missions in Africa. I imagined her baptizing pagan babies or standing in a field of tall and silky yellow grass, mouthing the words in her prayer book.

The public school was a couple of miles away from ours, and to a third grader that was almost as far as Africa. But I prayed for Michael every night, telling God I'd never steal again if he would make sure that Michael was still yelling out the answers, that people were still hearing his voice whether they wanted to or not.

THE COMET

When Tracy, my older sister, started dating Clay, we all shook our heads in disbelief. He was this hot shot corporate lawyer pushing forty and she was singing with The Weeds, a rock band, every night at the Tralfamadore Cafe. Until Tracy met Clay, she used to sleep until noon everyday and get dressed sometime around five o'clock. She celebrated her twenty-first birthday last year by cruising every bar on Elmwood Avenue until they closed at four AM. Then she went to The Cat, a club down on Franklin Street that stayed open after hours. Tracy drank so much Wild Turkey that she fell asleep on the bar and had to be carried to her rusted Mustang and driven home by God knows who. At least she could never remember his name. "He did know how to drive a stick shift, Jake," she told me, as if that made everything all right.

So when Tracy showed up at our folks' house last Easter with Clay in tow, we all did a double take. My father didn't quite know what to say to him. Clay didn't look like the type of guy who could hold his own talking about dry walling, which is pretty much all Pop knows. Tracy must have told him I painted houses, though, because he handed me a card with some guy's name on it and said, "A colleague of mine. He needs a little work done on his summer home up in Algonquin Bay." Algonquin Bay's this ritzy summer place just over the border from Buffalo in Canada. I said thanks and stuck the card in my pocket.

Tracy's usual dates were musicians or bikers with names like Bones and Squirrel. Oh, yeah, and Hammerhead. I stayed away from that one. I hear he's doing time now. Clay wasn't a biker, now or in any of his previous lives, you could see that in a second. He was wearing a pinstripe suit and socks with those diamond things, argyles, on them. He sat in the living room and kept looking around, taking in the surroundings: the worn brown plaid sofa, the pea-green carpeting, the floral curtains that hung to the floor and then some. My mother's sweet, but she's no interior decorator. Last year, Tracy convinced her to take down those pictures of the dogs playing poker. In their place now is a watercolor I did last summer when I took an adult education class at the Albright-Knox Art Gallery. I'd been messing around with paint for years, little landscape scenes, nothing too involved—I think it just sort of grew out of the work I was doing on houses.

The watercolor at my folks' house is of a vase of flowers. The flowers are big; they lean over the vase and look back at you. My teacher thought the color mix was unusual, the flaming reds and jungle greens. She called it "unrestrained" and "raw" and I guess that's good. When I'm painting houses, everything has to be exact. Sometimes a customer will ask my advice about a color, but pretty much I'm just following their directions. When I stand in front of a canvas , though, the only one giving directions is me. More often than not, I'm surprised at what my head is telling me to do, and sometimes it seems as if my arm is moving all by itself with no help from the rest of me. When my mother first saw the picture, she said she always knew I could be an artist, that she knew it when I was in kindergarten and would bring home crayon drawings of our goldfish that she hung on the refrigerator with a Fred Flintstone magnet.

Of course, my mother told Clay that I painted the flowers, and he said he'd noticed the picture right away, that it was a "very strong" piece. Later when we had dinner, Clay asked me if I ever considered getting a degree in studio art. I said no, feeling kind of good and bad at the same time. Maybe he thought I was a decent artist or maybe he thought it was weird that I wasn't in school.

"He could have gone to college," Tracy said. We all looked at her at the same time. She had been pretty quiet through most of dinner. "Jake had the third highest SAT's in his class."

I was surprised Tracy remembered that and I wondered if she was proud of me or defending me. Defending me against what, though? Clay's own education or background? I felt out of sorts all through dinner. What I remember most from that day was the way my mother kept fluttering around Clay, dishing him up her famous sweet potatoes and insisting on giving him second helpings of the lime Jello mold even though he hadn't asked for it. God, who would?

Tracy was cool, though. She didn't treat Clay any differently than she did Squirrel or any of the other guys who followed her around like groupies.

In fact, she barely paid attention to him. But boy, she riveted Clay. I watched him watch her sashay from room to room and look aloof as she smoked her clove cigarettes and read the TV Guide. Of course, she was something to look at, I had always known that. In high school, everybody tried to get me to introduce them to my sister. But she's three years older than me, so she didn't give any of my friends the time of day. I got a little more attention from the girls, though, because of her. I would hear them whisper to each other in the hall sometimes, "He's Tracy Stanton's brother."

Tracy has this long straight blonde hair parted in the middle. She stands out in a crowd. Now lots of girls have these short, military haircuts, but Tracy still looks the way girls did in 1970. Not that I was around then, but I know the look. Tracy burns incense in her apartment and reads Tarot cards. She's got these pictures of Jim Morrison looking tougher than hell on her bedroom walls. What did she and Clay talk about? Did she even know what kind of a lawyer he was? I asked her how they met. She said he came in to hear her sing night after night and one time asked her to sing "Crazy." Tracy didn't know it so she sang "I Need a Lover Who Won't Drive Me Crazy" instead. She has a deep low voice. When you hear her sing, you know she's in charge, you know she's afraid of nothing, nobody. She blew Clay away. He waited until closing and convinced her to go out to breakfast with him. When they got outside the club and she saw the black Porsche, Tracy slipped into the driver's seat and held her hand out for the keys. After that, they were an item.

Clay owned a boat and every weekend he and Tracy went sailing on Lake Erie. Tracy got a dark tan and her hair looked lighter than ever. She stopped singing with the band and moved into Clay's townhouse on Bryant Avenue. I went over after work one day to see the place. The bathroom had a Jacuzzi and floor-length mirrors on one wall. There were speakers in almost every room so you could hear music throughout the place. I wondered if the neighbors could hear Mick Jagger singing "Shattered, Shattered" while Tracy was giving me the tour. We walked into the bedroom and Tracy flopped on an enormous bed in a tall mahogany frame. Her clothes were all over the place and I thought I could smell a faint trace of incense. She seemed happy and yet I wondered what she did all day.

"So," I said, "What now?"

"What do you mean?"

"What are you going to do next?"

"*Do?* Why do I have to *do* anything?" Then she stuck her tongue through her grape Bazooka and blew this huge bubble.

I was surprised, maybe disappointed. All my life I waited to see what Tracy would do next. It wasn't always good, like the time she grew marijuana in our parents' backyard and the neighbor's dog got sick on it, but it was something. Seeing her in this condo just hanging out all day sort of gave me a punch in the stomach, and it bothered me that Clay was making my sister so normal. It wasn't that I wasn't happy for her, I just didn't buy that a person could go from heading a rock band to watching the soaps without missing a beat.

By August she was wearing this rock of a ring and in mid-September we got a postcard from Fiji signed "Mrs. Clay Knoffler." My mother was sad they eloped, but Clay probably figured that our family's idea of a wedding was a back yard party with a lime Jello mold instead of a wedding cake. Not that I was hoping to be best man or anything, but I felt a little shut down by the elopement too. Growing up, Tracy always let me in on the big stuff like where the Christmas presents were hidden, how to fake being sick so you could skip school, and just last year, how to break it to my mother that I was moving out. And now she just runs off and marries this guy without so much as a second thought for me or anybody else.

While they were in Fiji, I met Suzy. She was waitressing at the No Name Bar and Restaurant on Elmwood Avenue, just a couple of blocks from my apartment. I noticed her right away; she was so cute, like a little girl almost with tiny features except for big round brown eyes. She was only about five feet, maybe a little taller, and she wore bright red clogs that clacked against the wooden floor. She was so nice to me when I ordered my burger, asking me how I wanted it done, did I want ketchup, agreeing with me that French fries with the skins still on them are the best. It had been a while since I had gone out with anyone. I got burned really bad last year when Chris, my old girlfriend, dumped me for a bartender working at Peter's Pub. For a long time after, I didn't even look at girls. But when I talked to Suzy, I got that old feeling of excitement back. When she brought the bill, I got my nerve up and said, "Don't suppose you'd want to go out sometime?"

"Okay," she said and jotted down her phone number on the napkin. That weekend, we went up to Crystal Beach, just down the road from

Algonquin Bay in Canada. There's an amusement park there with a roller coaster called "The Comet." It doesn't have all the bells and whistles of these new coasters, no special effects or stuff like that. But at the beginning of the ride, you go up the steepest hill real slow. When you get to the top, you stop for a few seconds, and then BANG! You're going downhill so fast the wind jumps right out of your body. The best part, though, is that The Comet is right next to Lake Erie. After you go down the big hill, the coaster jerks right all of a sudden and you think you're going to land in the lake. No matter how many times you ride it, you always think, this is it, this time we derail and fly into the lake. It used to scare the shit out of me when I was a kid, but it's a helluva ride. I'd take it over Space Mountain any day.

Suzy loved it. We rode it four times, and the last time, when it was dark out and the coaster was lit up, we sat in the very first seat. I liked watching how the wind blew her hair straight out behind her head. She screamed and laughed the whole way and when we got off convinced me to go to the tattoo parlor at the edge of the park and get a snake carved into my upper left arm. I'm afraid of needles, but that night I was so happy, I swear I would've robbed a bank if Suzy asked me to. Later that night when we were kissing, Suzy broke away from my mouth and gently outlined the snake with her finger. "Now you're my Jake the Snake," she said and kissed my neck, that was as high as she could reach. I picked her up and she wrapped her legs around my waist. She leaned forward and slipped her tongue in my ear. My knees buckled, it felt so good, and I almost dropped her.

We left the park and walked down to the beach, taking only a few seconds to look at the dark water before we hit the sand. Suzy surprised me. I had planned on being gentle; she's so little I worried I'd crush her. I never got the chance. Just like ballroom dance classes back in junior high, the girl took the lead. Suzy was everywhere at once, sitting on top of me like a rocking horse, licking and nibbling my neck and my ears on her down swing. I'm six feet, but there was no way I could move or switch position, even if I wanted to. *Incredible*, I thought over and over as I watched her in the night, her hair wild and occasionally draped over my face, her hands on mine and mine on her breasts, so little, so firm, with nipples so bold, I shivered, goosebumps up and down my legs and arms. Afterwards, we slept on the beach for a while, I don't know how long. It got cold and we walked huddled to my car.

We went out every night. Rick, the guy I shared my apartment with, gave me the business about not hanging out with the guys any more. "You're whipped!" he kept saying, or he called me "Loverboy." I was too happy to care.

Sometimes Suzy and I took a jug of hard cider and a bag of chips to the park and had a picnic under the stars. If it wasn't too cold and no one was around, we rolled around on the blanket, laughing low because we were both trying not to make any noise. One night I took her to the Tralfamadore Cafe to hear Tracy's replacement, Yolanda something or other, a foxy redhead with a throaty voice. She talked the songs more than sang them, if you know what I mean. Suzy and I got up and slow-danced. I had to lean way over to hold her, she's so small. We rocked back and forth, back and forth, I felt like I was floating. I was surprised when the song ended and I heard clapping. I thought we were the only people in the room, hell, in the world. Then it seemed as if everyone was clapping for me and Suzy instead of the band. Sometimes, if I close my eyes, I can still make myself feel the way I did that night dancing with Suzy, lighter than air, able to fly.

Tracy and Clay returned from Fiji. They brought all this tropical stuff back with them, seashell necklaces and strange little tribal sculptures that Mom put all over the living room. I told Tracy about Suzy and she said she wanted to meet her, to bring her by. The next day Clay called and invited us both to dinner that Friday night.

When we got there, Tracy and Clay were in the living room dancing to Roy Orbison's "Only the Lonely." That alone flipped me out; Roy's not exactly on Tracy's hit parade. But something else hit me too, the way Clay looked holding Tracy, like a dumbstruck teenager. And Tracy looked, well, she looked like she always does when she's been smoking too much grass. Hard to believe it, but I felt a little sorry for Clay. Before I thought he was changing Tracy's life and it bothered me. Now it hit me that nothing would change her and I hoped Clay wasn't dumb enough to try. But it was clear he was really in love with her. This should have been no big surprise since every guy she ever met was, but I was starting to realize that Clay had deep romantic notions about Tracy. She wasn't just the gorgeous blonde with a killer figure to him. She was his wife, till death do us part or whatever they said in those vows I never heard. Jesus, God help him, I thought as I watched Tracy break out of Clay's embrace without so much as looking at him. She smiled at Suzy and said, "Let me show you the place."

That left me and Clay on our own, and I mostly let him talk.

"Come see the new pool table," he said, and took me into what Tracy had called the entertainment room. It had a huge television, compact disk player, and enormous speakers in two corners of the room. The black leather couch and chairs had been pushed to one end of the room so the pool table could be in the middle.

"Do you play?" Clay asked.

"Me? I've only played a couple times."

"I thought after dinner we might play a game or two. Tracy's quite good."

Where did she learn to play pool? I wondered. Probably in some biker bar. Tracy and Suzy joined us and we sat down. Tracy got up and turned off Roy Orbison and put a different CD in the player. Then Jim Morrison blared out all over the room singing "Don't you love her madly?" Clay went into the kitchen and came back with glasses of white wine and some bean dip and pita bread.

"How did you two meet?" Tracy asked.

Suzy told her I was the cutest guy she ever waited on. I protested, but she pretended to swat me and insisted, "It's true."

"Tracy and I met at her place of employment too, didn't we sweetie?" Clay said looking at Tracy.

"How long have you been going out?" Tracy asked Suzy, ignoring Clay. I wanted to kick Tracy under the table like we used to do when we were kids, but instead I turned to Clay and asked him how they met even though I already knew. Tracy and Suzy continued talking, they seemed to hit it off pretty well. At one point, Clay turned to me and said, "Shall we let the ladies relax while you and I prepare dinner?"

It turned out that Clay was quite the cook. I grated the lemon peel for the pasta and stirred the sauce for the chicken every now and then.

"Jake, the other day I met the Chair of the Art Department at Buffalo State College. I chatted with him a bit about their program and told him I knew a talented young artist."

I stopped stirring the sauce and looked at Clay. Did he mean me or did he really know some talented young artist? Clay looked at me, obviously he was waiting for some kind of response. I sort of nodded my head.

"I'll be representing him in a legal matter, so I'll probably get to know him a bit. Do you think you'd like to meet him?"

I was excited, I have to admit. Nobody in my family went to college, that's probably why I never even gave it a thought, despite the SAT scores.

"It's expensive," I said.

"Well, it's a state school, so the tuition might not be as high as you think. And of course, there's financial aid. No one is supporting you presently, so you'd probably qualify for a good sum. And loans aren't so terrible, Jake. That's how I did it. For both undergraduate and law school."

"Really?" I figured Clay was probably born wearing his argyle socks.

"Really." Clay smiled. I started to loosen up and relax. Then Clay said, "Why don't you give Bert a call? His name's Bert Warner. I'll write his number down. I told him you might call."

"Thanks." I held the piece of paper in my hand and looked at the loopy numbers Clay had made with his pen. "I'll probably be too nervous, but thanks."

"Don't be nervous. Just call. He'll probably want to see some of your work, so call and make an appointment."

Tracy and Suzy walked into the kitchen and made noises about how hungry they were. Suzy looked a little bit dazed so I figured Tracy had probably given her some pot. Clay and I picked up the bowls and platters and headed for the dining room.

During dinner, we mostly talked about sports, the Bills losing the Superbowl again and the start of hockey season. Clay's firm had a box at the Auditorium and he thought we should all go see a Sabres game. Tracy said she didn't want to go, that she hated hockey. I knew this; hockey bored her to death. Football was Tracy's game. Clay turned to me and Suzy and said, "Hockey is too violent for Tracy. I really shouldn't subject her to it."

I almost choked on an olive. I didn't think that someone who had gone to see "The Terminator" five times would find hockey too violent. Tracy read my thoughts; she winked at me but put her hand on Clay's and said, "You know me so well, babe." I wondered why she was lying about something so stupid; would Clay really have cared that she was bored by hockey? I could understand her telling Hammerhead that our father was an underground narcotics cop when she wanted to get rid of him, but this just seemed strange. Clay looked happy, though, with his arm around the back of Tracy's chair, and it was none of my business anyway.

After dinner, we played pool, men against the women. Clay and I didn't stand a chance because Tracy was so good. She couldn't miss. Clay

was really proud, he kept calling her, "My pool shark bride." She didn't pay attention to him. She didn't pay attention to any of us. She just leaned over the table and looked real intense as she sank ball after ball.

We left about eleven and walked back to my apartment. "Tracy is beautiful," Suzy said. "Why didn't you tell me that your sister is so beautiful?"

"Yeah, almost as beautiful as you." We stopped at the corner of Bryant and Delaware Avenue and kissed a long time. "What do you think of Clay?" I asked.

Suzy put her finger to her lips and looked away for a second. "He's really nice," she said. "But I think he's in over his head."

"Yeah, I know the feeling."

Suzy put her arm around my waist and we crossed the street. "We're swimmers, Jake," she said.

School was hard. Along with the art classes, I had to take history and psychology. It had been a while since I had studied for a test or wrote a research paper and it took time to get the feel of everything. My art teachers were tougher than the ones in the adult ed classes. They told me to work on my perspective, on my use of light, on my dimensions. Sometimes I wondered if I was doing anything right.

I was surprised when one of my paintings, a portrait of Suzy from the back with her legs up on a coffee table a couple of feet from a television, got honorable mention in the annual student exhibit. My folks, Clay and Tracy, and Suzy came to the show. Ed Tomkins, one of my teachers, came by and introduced himself. He told my parents that I had great potential. I was a little stunned. He had never said that to me, but maybe that's what he said to all the parents. I prayed that my mother wouldn't bring up the pictures of the fish on the refrigerator and she didn't.

Tomkins continued on down the hall, talking to other families. Clay slapped a hand on my shoulder and said, "Look out art world. Jake Stanton has arrived." Then Suzy stood next to the painting and we all laughed at being able to see the front and back of her at the same time.

"Is this Suzy?" somebody asked. I turned and saw Gloria, a friend from my watercolor class. She came over and said hi to everyone. Then she hugged me and said, "Congratulations, Jake! You deserve it!" She looked at Suzy and said, "He kept telling me about this idea he had of painting you from the back." Gloria laughed a little and Suzy smiled and sort of raised her eyebrows.

"Well," Gloria said holding out her hand, "It's nice to meet the front of you." Suzy shook hands with her and said, "You too." Things were quiet for a moment, maybe a little awkward, and then Gloria reached over and patted my arm. "See you in class Monday." She turned to look at everyone else and said, "Nice meeting you all." She disappeared into the crowd as we were saying goodbye to her.

No sooner had Gloria left than Tracy started in on me. "Quite a fan you got there. If she was giving out the prizes, you might have won."

"Cut it out," I said. I was embarrassed, especially with Suzy standing there. Gloria was just a friend. But then Clay chimed in, "You didn't know college would be such a good place to meet women, did you Jake?" My dad chuckled and Mom told Suzy not to pay any attention to this nonsense.

"Don't you worry, Suzy," Tracy said. "You and I will go out cruising the bars without these two guys cramping our style."

Clay widened his eyes, amused, and said, "Them's fighting words, don't you think, Jake?"

I looked at Suzy. She was still standing next to the picture staring at nothing in particular. I went over and put my arms around her. "I only cruise with Suz," I said, trying to sound funny. We went across the street and had chicken wings at J.P. Bullfeathers Wine Cellar. Clay ordered a couple bottles of champagne which was kind of silly with the chicken wings, but fun. We all got a little drunk and went home early.

Later that night, in bed, Suzy woke me up. I heard a small voice ask if I liked dating a waitress. I pulled her on top of me and circled my arms around her back, holding her tight. "You bet," I said.

"You're meeting all these new people."

"So?"

Suzy looked up at me, resting her chin on my chest. I could barely see her in the dark, but I smoothed her hair back from her face with my hands. "Your life is changing. Mine is the same," she said.

I reached over and turned on the lamp next to the bed. "Suz, we have the same life. If you're happy, I'm happy. If you're sad, I'm sad. School's not going to change that."

"I run when I get scared, Jake," she whispered. "There's a guy in Boston still wondering what happened to me."

I stopped breathing for a few seconds. "You met me, that's what happened. And you're staying right here." I didn't relax my arms until I heard her breathing get so regular I knew she was sleeping. For days after, I looked at Suzy differently. I was scared. I kept imagining her telling someone, some guy, about a painter she used to know in Buffalo. It got to be too much. I convinced her to spend every night with me. I wanted to know where she was when I woke up every day. Suzy kept her apartment, but really she was just there to grab a change of clothes. Rick was working the night shift, so it worked out pretty well. I had to leave for school before she was up and she had to work until after I got home, but the nights were ours.

In late spring, I had a painting job over on Lancaster Avenue. School was over for the term and it actually felt pretty good to be on a ladder again. It was a good job; it would take months to paint this three-story Victorian house two basic colors and three trim colors, and the yuppie owners were paying me big bucks. I was only about half a mile from Suzy's restaurant, so we got together for lunch most days. One day, though, Clay's Porsche pulled up and he asked me if I'd "lunch with him at the club." I didn't know what club, but I knew my jeans and football jersey were not the right gear. Clay just said, "Oh, dressing down is all the rage there." We drove down Delaware Avenue and he turned right into what looked like a driveway, but it wound around and around and came out at this tall stone house. Clay gave the keys to a guy at the front door and we went in.

I was self-conscious, that's for sure. There was more silverware on the table than I could possibly use and I worried that my jeans would leave dirt on the chairs covered with white fabric. A few people were dressed sort of like me, but there was nothing even close to a hamburger on the menu. I let Clay order first, the garlic shrimp over linguine, and then said, "I'll have the same." I started to worry that I might be allergic to shrimp. A couple of years ago I got sick as hell on some clams, and that would be awful, getting sick in this swanky place. Then I realized that Clay looked pretty sick himself. His face, usually so tan, was stark white. He was sweating a little and seemed really fidgety. He kept playing with his cigarette lighter, this slender square of gold with the initials "CMK" on the lid. I kept trying to think of something to say, but I was too nervous to come up with much beyond "Nice place." Clay wasn't much help. I asked him if he ate here often and he just nodded his head.

"Clay, is anything wrong?" I had a strong hunch I already knew.

"Tracy's left me," he said.

Bingo. "Where'd she go?" Please, God, not back to Bones, I thought.

"She left a message on the answering machine that she needed space." Clay finally slipped the lighter into his pocket. He put his hands together on the table. It was an effort for him to keep still.

"Oh," I said. "I'm sorry." And I was. But I wasn't surprised. Tracy has always come and gone as she pleased and this thing with Clay lasted longer than I would have guessed. Still, it was too bad. I thought for a second of Suzy. If she left me, I'd probably shave my head and drown my sorrows in Rolling Rock. Or at least I'd go up to Crystal Beach and ride The Comet all day by myself. I rode it seventeen times in one afternoon back in high school when I got cut from the baseball team. But the amusement park wouldn't be open for another month or so, and anyway, Clay didn't look like the type of guy who'd get a thrill out of a near miss with Lake Erie.

"Will you talk to her?"

"Tracy? Me?"

"Yes. She's singing at the Tralfamadore Cafe again. I keep trying to talk to her, but all she says is 'Not *now*, I need some space.' I'm too embarrassed to go back in. I'm worried she'll have the manager stop me at the door."

"I thought the Tralf got a new singer. What's her name, Yolanda something or other." I thought of the redhead and then I remembered dancing that night with Suzy.

"Yolanda Bliss. Actually she started all of this."

The shrimp came and I looked at it suspiciously. "Yolanda started this? What do you mean?"

Clay asked the waiter for a glass of Chardonnay. "Tracy wanted to go there one night. After she heard Yolanda, for days she kept complaining about her voice, and why did they hire her, and why did people go hear her and on and on. It was clear she wanted her job back."

"You don't want her to work?"

"I don't mind in the slightest. I got back from an overnight trip last week and she said they had hired her back. All she had to do was let the band

know she was interested and Yolanda was history. Two days later, I got the message on the machine."

It made sense. Tracy never could stand someone else being the center of attention. I didn't think she could sing at the club and be someone's wife. Tracy would be coming home near dawn most nights and she was bound to meet other guys at the club. Clay had been one extended party, but she was tired of it, entertainment room and all. But just leaving a message on the machine, that was cruel, even for Tracy.

"Clay, I don't think she'll come back." He was staring at his food and blinking his eyes really fast. I worried that he might break down in the middle of the restaurant. "I'm sorry," I said.

He nodded. I ate a couple forkfuls of the pasta and we left. Clay didn't say anything on the way back. He pulled into the driveway on Lancaster and left the ignition on. He sat there dazed, looking out the front window.

"I don't think it will do any good, but I'll talk to Tracy. I'll try to find out what's going on with her." But I knew it would be useless. Even as I was telling Clay this, I knew it was a lost cause. I didn't tell him what I should have, that he was better off without her. That breaking hearts was something of a career for Tracy and he was probably lucky to get out now.

He nodded and looked at me. I could see he didn't have any hope either. Then he shook my hand and said, "Good luck, Jake. I wish you and Suzy all the best." He sounded so serious. Then he told me to stick with school. I watched him back out of the driveway. It hit me that he had been a pretty decent brother-in-law. The next time around it could be Bones or Squirrel. And you can bet they wouldn't be taking me to lunch at the club.

I had a hard time painting that afternoon. My strokes weren't even and the paint looked streaked. I went home at five and waited for eight o'clock to come. That's when Suzy was done with the dinner shift and I couldn't wait to see her.

I called my folks to see what they knew about Tracy. I realized Clay hadn't told me where she was staying, if he even knew. Mom told me Tracy was staying with a girlfriend and looking for her own apartment. "It's too bad," she said. "Dad and I will miss Clay. Did you know he took Dad golfing a couple weeks back? He was always so thoughtful. I wish Tracy would have given it a little more time. The first year of marriage is the hardest. Remember that, Jake." I told her that later that night Suzy and I would stop in at the Tralfamadore and try to talk to Tracy.

It was only after I hung up that I saw the message tucked part way under the phone. Gloria had called, something about an art students party. I thought it sounded like fun but then I realized that Suzy must have taken the message because Rick and his brother were on a camping trip. I felt a few butterflies in my stomach. I guess I was a little worried that Suzy might be upset about Gloria calling. I went to the refrigerator and got a beer, sat down on the couch and watched the clock. Eight o'clock came and went. Eight fifteen, eight thirty. I couldn't stand it. Where was she? Maybe she wasn't coming. My heart started pounding so hard I had to move. I grabbed my jean jacket and headed down the stairs and out, up Elmwood Avenue.

There were people everywhere, out taking walks because it was warm and still light out. There were little tables set up outside of all the restaurants and bars so the sidewalks were really crowded. My sneakers pounded against the pavement and each slap of rubber seemed to echo, "run when I get scared, run when I get scared." My chest felt heavy and I wondered if I was too young to have a heart attack. I ran three blocks before I saw her. I stopped and my breath kept coming out fast. Suzy was walking up the street towards my apartment, towards me.

She looked happy, relaxed, weaving in and out of the crowds. She was in her own little world, looking up at the sky, almost smiling, not noticing the people all around her. I was so relieved I was trembling. And I was so happy just looking at her, just knowing that of all these people on the street, I knew her better than anyone. I wanted to run up to her, but I couldn't. I just stood there, watching her, waiting for her to see me. Hoping that when she did, I wouldn't still be crying. I would love to paint all of this, but I know I could never capture the feel of the air on my face, or the feeling of wanting to rise into the air and fly over the people on the streets to Suzy. "Jake!" she yelled and her arm shot up in the air. She started running towards me, her hair flying out behind her head. I lost sight of her for a second, but then she dodged around a couple of girls wearing Walkmans and came straight at me. I thanked God that I wasn't going to have to spend the next couple of days riding a roller coaster. Because something tells me, I would've hit that lake for sure.

A WORLD TRANSFORMED

Angie spoke quickly, repeating what Sister Michael Marie had said to her that day about the length of her skirt. Her mother set aside the *Time Magazine* she was reading and listened, her eyes expanding as her daughter spoke. Sister had kept Angie behind in the hall after the other students had filed into the classroom and explained, quietly but firmly, that even if miniskirts were in fashion, this was still a Catholic school. Mrs. Reno, turning her gaze away from Angie, pressed her fingers to the skin above her lips and said, almost as a question, "Well, Sister understands you're not wearing mini-skirts, just that some of your skirts are a little short."

She looked at Angie, hoping for her affirmation, and Angie felt herself glow with recognition, a warm yellow light building deep within her chest and flowing into her arms and legs. Earlier in the week, her mother hadn't taken Angie's part when she fought with her brother Tony, two years older, about whether they'd watch *Bewitched* or basketball on television, hollering at both of them that if they couldn't share the TV, she was going to throw it out. And she'd been too busy to help Angie study for her geography test only yesterday. That's what she told Angie, but then Angie spied her simply sitting in the dark living room smoking a cigarette, the sliver of orange light at the tip growing suddenly brighter and then almost disappearing. But today, Angie felt herself to be correctly at the center of her mother's world in a way she hadn't been perhaps since her father moved out of the house last year and married Penny Stockton's mother.

"Saturday," her mother said after hearing Sister Michael Marie's observation. "We'll go shopping first thing Saturday morning." Then she went to Angie's closet and made her hold various dresses, jumpers, and skirts up against herself, telling her which she could still wear and which to set aside to give to her cousin Theresa.

"You have gotten tall, Ang," her mother said, running her closed hand around one of Angie's long dark braids and bending to kiss her cheek. Angie almost jumped back at her mother's touch, but then she stretched up and wrapped her arms eagerly around her neck. Mrs. Reno looked at their reflection in the bureau mirror and sighed, disengaging Angie's hands. "I don't know why the school doesn't switch to uniforms like everybody else. It'd be so much cheaper." She walked out of the room.

Angie leapt up, stretching out her arms in a silent pantomime of celebration. "Hooray!" she whispered. She wanted to ask her mother where they would shop, if they would go to the stores at the Waverly Plaza where they had gone as long as Angie could remember, or if they would go to the brand new Southview Mall, thirty or forty stores with no doors, just open fronts that lined the wide corridors. There were places to buy food, and you could take your pop and sandwich to little stone benches next to pretend plants and small reflecting pools filled with shimmering pennies. Angie found the mall so protective and comforting, all of these things going on under a single roof. She had been there only once, but some of the girls in her class went practically every Saturday. They met outside Spencer Gifts and spent the afternoon going from store to store.

It seemed so sophisticated, the independence these girls had, some of them already wearing make-up and fishnet stockings. If Angie went shopping at the mall, maybe her mother would buy her fishnets to go with at least one of her new outfits. She thought of herself walking into the classroom, a floral dress skirting the middle of her thighs, her legs slim and lovely in white, or maybe even yellow, fishnet stockings. Janet Longburne had every color you could imagine, red and even turquoise. The other girls would exclaim over Angie's hose, maybe even the very popular Margie Shallock, who had slumber parties Angie had only heard about. And from across the room, her used-to-be-best friend Penny Stockton would wonder what the fuss was about and turn her head to see Angie at the center of a group of girls. And this time, it would be Penny who would be left out. She wouldn't say anything to Angie, of course. Angie's mother had forbidden her to talk to Penny, and so she'd remained quiet those few times Penny had tried. The girls hadn't spoken to each other since last year in fifth grade.

It made her father sad that the girls were no longer friends. "It shouldn't be like this," he told Angie when he saw her on Sundays. "You girls went to kindergarten together. You were best friends."

More than that, Angie and Penny used to tell people that they were sisters. They stayed over at each other's houses on Friday nights and imagined together what it would be like if their two families lived together in one house.

Angie missed having a best friend, but she was determined to be angry with her father whenever he mentioned Penny. "You'd rather be her father than mine!" she'd accuse him, inevitably starting to cry.

Her father would rub her chin, a new silver ring on his finger now, and patiently explain, "Now you know that's not true. You're my girl, you'll always be my girl. I just wish we could all be together."

"Mom too?"

He would sigh at the question that wouldn't go away. "Honey, we've talked about that. Sometimes it doesn't work out the way you hope."

Once Angie had asked him, "If Penny's father hadn't died, would you have stayed with us?" She thought his death in a car accident was the cause of all their problems. Penny's father had died and her own had moved in with the Stocktons. He'd left her and her brother and their mother, and now he had a new family. Her best friend had stolen her father.

"What's done is done," Angie's father said about the accident. "We've got to make the best of life."

The day before the shopping excursion, Angie came home after band practice and found her mother grading papers at the kitchen table. She was always, it seemed, grading papers. Her mother taught third grade at Angie's school, Our Lady of the Rosary. After much fighting, Tony had transferred to P.S. 42 last year when their mother took the teaching job. He didn't want to go to a school where his mother could keep on eye on him and his friends would make fun of him for being Mrs. Reno's son, even though his mother wasn't really Mrs. Reno any more.

Now Angie stood silently in the kitchen, wondering if it was safe to interrupt her mother. She hadn't said anything when Angie opened the door, so that could be bad, but she hadn't yelled or been upset about something either. Her mother sat with her chin propped up in one hand, a thick red pencil in the other. She wasn't wearing the pink frosted lipstick she wore to school and that Angie liked. Her hair, cut short now, was laced with silver, and the new gray hair rose coarse and wiry over the smoother, darker hair beneath. A fat round juice glass filled with an orangish-brown liquid and ice cubes sat on the table. Angie knew it was from the bottle stored in one of the upper kitchen cabinets because Tony occasionally took it out and stole sips. It used to be that the bottle only came out at Christmas; her mother and father had cocktails while Angie and her brother drank ginger ale with maraschino cherries. But last month, Tony had been upset to find a new, unopened bottle in the cabinet; he couldn't break the seal and have it go unnoticed.

Angie never told her father about the drinking because her mother had impressed upon her and her brother that nothing that went on in their house was "Any of his damn business." Angie kept the secret like it was her high card to be played at the right moment. When her mother was especially angry at her, raging and shouting, she'd think, *I'll tell Dad about the drinking and he'll come and get me. He'll leave Penny's house and we'll go away together somewhere. And we'll never come back.*

A cigarette in a red tin ashtray burned at Mrs. Reno's elbow. Angie looked at the long ashes and wondered why they didn't drop off; they stuck out over the ashtray like a tiny gray snake flecked with black and white. As always, the smoke caused Angie's eyes to burn, but she stood as close as she could to her mother.

"Mom?"

"Hmm." Her mother kept her head down, marking a piece of paper with perforated edges on the left side where it had been torn from a spelling workbook. The red pencil was raised and lowered as she moved her hand down the page, putting a small red cross next to correct answers and a large check mark made with a wild sweep of her arm next to mistakes.

"Can we go shopping at the mall to buy my clothes?" Angie spoke fast, the speed of her words meant to indicate her strong desire.

"We'll see." Her mother turned the page over and continued grading the paper.

"Please?" Angie stood with her hands raised and tightly interlocked, as if the pressure of her palms could sway her mother.

Her mother looked up at Angie and frowned, the little lines running into her top lip becoming more deeply creased. She picked up the cigarette and brushed the ashes against the side of the ashtray, the snake evaporating into little splashed particles. Putting the cigarette to her lips, she blew the

smoke out in a slow coil, the last of it coming out her nose. "I said *we'll see*."
She picked up the next piece of paper from the pile and poised her pencil
over the top of it.

Angie left the kitchen and walked down the short hall to her room,
letting herself fall heavily on her bed, hopeful and scared her mother could
hear the bed bouncing from the kitchen. When her mother didn't call to
her, Angie looked at the books on the shelf over her bed and pulled out her
autograph book, a small rectangular volume with a yellow vinyl cover filled
with different colors of bright paper rounded at the edges. The book was
two-and-a-half years old, a birthday present for her ninth birthday. Angie
flipped through the pages looking at the things written by her parents, some
friends, and a couple of aunts and uncles. On an aqua blue page, her mother
had written, "Always be as sweet as you are. Love, Mom." In the corner
of the page, her mother had drawn a tiny daisy, the center a little smiling
face. On the page immediately opposite, Aunt Regina had written, "2 good
2B 4gotten." Angie paged forward and found the stupid message written
by Tony on a dark red page, "Angie: Why don't you go play in traffic? Hate
you, Tony." Angie smiled now remembering that her parents had made Tony
apologize and clean out the garage for writing it.

Angie fanned more pages, looking for the one she knew was there,
a pale orange piece of paper toward the center of the book. "To my best
friend," it read, "Remember Mrs. Greco in kindergarten, Remember Sister
Ambrose in first grade, Remember Mrs. Roberts in second grade, Remember
Sister Margaret Mary in third grade, Remember Mrs. Collins in fourth grade,
and ALWAYS ALWAYS REMEMBER ME! Love, Penny." Penny had drawn
two stick figures of little girls holding hands with her name and Angie's
beneath them. Angie studied the stick figures, the funny straw hair Penny had
drawn to make look like pig-tails, and the smiles that extended to both sides
of the faces. She stretched the book as wide as it could go, until she could see
the white thread stitching, and slowly tore the orange page out, saddened to
see it leave a small ruffle along the inseam of the book. It would be hard to
remove it without scissors, and scissors could ruin the binding. Angie closed
the book and returned it to the shelf. The orange page she held for a moment,
wondering what to do with it. She took down her copy of "Black Beauty" and
tucked the orange slip into the back cover.

The next morning, Angie woke early and took her bath. She put on her nicest underwear and her good slip with the tiny pink rose sewn into the top front of it. Angie put on the dress she had worn last year on Easter, a navy dress with a white sailor tie that she thought was cute but too young for her, just like the navy tights she also put on. Angie thought about being in the dressing room at a store, coming out to model the outfits for her mother and the saleswomen who would help them.

"She's so cute!"

"What an angel."

"She looks good in everything she tries on."

Angie would smile modestly at them, secretly filled with enormous pleasure, while the saleswomen continued to compliment her. From behind the curtain in the dressing room, she would hear her mother tell them that Angie was in sixth grade, an A student. They would exclaim over her again, nodding at her as she made her entrance in the next outfit. She thought of herself and her mother leaving the store laden with boxes peeking out of cheerful shopping bags, maybe blue, no pink, she thought, pink bags would be best. It would all be so wonderful, and maybe, no, more than maybe, *definitely* this would be the day, the event, that would bring a return to her old life. She didn't know how her father would fit into it all, but at the very least, her mother would be her old self today and from now on. Angie continued imagining her day at the mall until her mother called her to come out and eat breakfast. Tony was already at the table pouring Lucky Charms into his bowl.

"Well, don't you look nice," her mother said as Angie sat at the table.

"Mom, can we stop at the record store?" Tony asked, pouring his milk over the cereal so it splashed onto the vinyl tablecloth.

Angie jerked her head quickly towards her mother, letting out a small cry. "He's not coming!"

"Eat your breakfast." Her mother pushed the carton of milk in front of Angie and looked at Tony. "Do you have money for a record?" she challenged him.

"Mom! He's not coming!" Angie felt her cheeks slowly sail up in front of her eyes and the bottom of her face disintegrate into curved folds of skin.

"Look, do you want to stay home? Huh? Quit whining and eat your breakfast."

Angie lowered her face to her cereal bowl, feeling her tears cross the sides of her lips, and watching them drop finally into the small chipped ceramic bowl. This was supposed to be the day that would correct everything, but her brother would ruin it.

Tony picked up his bowl and drank the milk he couldn't reach with his spoon. "You're buying her clothes. Why don't I get anything?"

Angie's mother picked up her coffee cup, blowing the steam across the top. She took a sip of the coffee and put the mug on the table, a pink smudge on the porcelain where her mouth had been. Angie was happy that her mother was at least wearing lipstick, but she was dressed in her old brown corduroy pants and a tan sweater badly frayed at one of the elbows. She was already putting on her sunglasses, heavy dark ones with thick black frames that looked like they were made for a man. Angie realized that in her fantasy, her mother had looked like one of the mothers on TV, like Samantha on *Bewitched*, wearing a sleek, short shift in a bright shade like red or green. And she thought her mother would carry a big leather purse with a long shoulder strap and a large gold buckle as they traveled from store to store under the high, sheltering ceiling of the mall.

"Why don't I get anything?" Tony asked again, louder now, having mistaken his mother's silence as an admission of the inequality of the situation.

"Because you can't wear records to school!" she hissed at Tony, her face moving directly in front of his. "You want records, ask your father."

Angie's stomach did a violent twitch. She wanted to run to the bathroom, but she was too scared to move. Despite her fear, there was a mountain of anger within her at Tony for making her mother talk about their father.

The last time her mother had sounded so angry about her father was last summer when Tony invited him to his team's final baseball game. The whole Stockton family had come with him to watch the game and were already in their seats by the time Angie and her mother arrived. Angie's mother had led her across the field and they sat in the opponents' bleachers. They'd left before the last inning.

The next day, Angie's mother had made her call her father at the Stocktons to ask him for money for her Girl Scout dues. Penny had answered the phone and Angie had panicked, not knowing how to ask for her father. If she said, "May I please talk to my father?" Penny might have said, "You mean *my* father?" and she wouldn't have been able to stand it. Her mother was in the kitchen waiting to hear Angie demand the money, the ice cubes in her drink clinking together with an insistent, nasty sound. When Angie hung up the phone right after Penny answered, her mother had shouted at her while Angie cried into her hands.

"What's wrong with you! Don't you even know how to talk on the phone?"

Angie had heaved sobs and wasn't able to speak for several seconds. Then she said, in halted chokes, "You. . .you. . .you said I couldn't talk to Penny."

Her mother had thrown her glass into the sink, the sound of the fractured shards ringing against the ice, and left the room. The next day, she gave Angie an envelope with three dollar bills, and told her to get a receipt so she could submit it with the other household bills that month to Angie's father.

Now Tony and Angie sat tensely at the table, waiting to see if their mother would say something else about their father. Angie realized that Tony was as worried as she was, no longer kicking his leg under the table, but she was still mad at him for causing the whole thing. Their mother picked up her mug and walked to the kitchen sink, rinsing it out and putting it quietly in the dish drainer. "Get in the car," she said, and Tony and Angie exchanged relieved glances.

Of course Tony got to sit in the front so he could push the buttons on the radio. Angie sat in the back, watching out the window, praying they would get on the expressway and drive the ten minutes or so to the mall, but she was not surprised when her mother drove only five blocks to the Waverly Plaza.

The Plaza was shaped like an L with rows of vertical aisles for parking stretching from the longer side. It was crowded and Mrs. Reno had to park towards the end of a row. Angie watched as her mother looked in the rear view mirror and smoothed her hair with her hands. Then she took out her lipstick from her purse, moving the thick pink crayon over her lower lip. She curled her upper lip to meet her lower lip and checked the mirror to see that the lipstick was on correctly, touching her lips with her index finger to smooth the outlines.

"I'm going to go play the pinball machines," Tony said to his mother while he reached for the door handle. There were a few pin ball machines outside the entrance to Avery's, the five and dime store located near the corner of the plaza.

"Don't wander off any place else. I'm not going to go looking for you."

"Well how long are you two going to be?"

"I don't know. If you get done before us, come to the back of Rafferty's."

Angie moved forward on her seat, feeling a rush of nervous hope. Rafferty's was a nice store. If she wasn't going to get to go to the mall, at least her clothes would be from a nice store. Maybe all was not lost yet. It was still an opportunity for her mother to be nice and to realize that she liked being nice. She wondered, though, if Rafferty's sold fishnets.

They walked in the clear, slightly cool morning sunlight between two rows of parked cars toward the stores. Angie started to skip, happy that they were here to buy clothes and not food. The cleats on the heels of her brown tie shoes scraped against the gravel parking lot and she stopped immediately, certain her mother would complain about how much her shoes cost.

"See you later." Tony sprinted off, the sound of quarters hitting against each other in his jacket pocket. Angie watched him run, the soles of his sneakers chewing against the asphalt parking lot.

Her mother opened the tall glass door and they stepped inside Rafferty's. It was a different world, a world transformed from the one just outside. A musical rendition of "Up, Up and Away" was piped throughout the store and the air was heavy with perfume. The white tiled floor was slippery and smooth, Angie's cleats now making a soft, dignified *click* against it. The first glass counter contained make-up and hair accessories. Oval mirrors rimmed with gold were set up at various spots on top of the counter and cosmetic samples were arranged in neat piles next to them. The saleswomen wore elaborately teased hair in a variety of short and long styles and had extended nails painted in pearly whites and pinks, their fingers and wrists laden with rings and bracelets. A woman spraying perfume on the wrists of customers wore a huge necklace with the peace sign shaped like a tear drop.

Angie's mother put her hand on Angie's back and guided her past the perfume woman, down the aisle and past the escalator, to the very back of the ground floor of the store. Angie's pulse quickened a bit and she shivered with excitement. They were in the Pre-Teen Department surrounded by mannequins in sporty or fancy clothes. One mannequin was already wearing a yellow and orange striped two-piece bathing suit, the bottoms like little shorts. Another wore a long-sleeved lime green dress dappled with enormous pink flowers and, *yes!* matching pink fishnet stockings. Several loops of tiny love beads were placed over the collar of the dress. Angie looked at her mother to see if she had noticed the mannequin. She could picture herself in the ensemble, walking into the school yard Monday morning, and Margie Shallot running over to her and exclaiming, "How pretty!"

But Angie's mother went straight to the back wall where dresses were hung in a long row, circular wheels of white plastic with sizes painted in black arranged intermittently on the rod. Only one saleswoman was present, a young, pretty woman with very long and very straight dark blonde hair tied back with a flouncy yellow ribbon. She was much younger than the women at the cosmetics counter, Angie noticed. She wore a dark green pantsuit, flared widely at the ankles, with a yellow blouse to match the ribbon. She smiled brightly at Angie and her mother. "Do you need help finding anything?"

Angie smiled at her, at the familiarity of the scene. It wasn't just as she had imagined it, but she was willing to settle for it, especially if the end of her fantasy, leaving the store while clutching pink bags filled with beautiful clothes, was borne out.

"Just browsing," her mother answered quickly, and surprisingly softly, her head not raised enough to look at the saleswoman's face. Puzzled, Angie looked up at her mother and noticed that she still wore her sunglasses. They were lowered on her nose so she could peer over them.

Her mother stood in front of the rack of dresses, moving a few steps to the right to the size twelve's. She looked at each one: plaids, stripes, flowers, solids. She pushed the hanger forward to see the next as she studied and rejected dress after dress. The heavy metal hangers made small clawing noises as they were pushed over the shiny silver bar.

"Those are too big, Mom."

Her mother continued to push the dresses, stopping finally to look at a dark brown one with short sleeves.

"That's too big, Mom. I wear a ten."

Her mother took the dress off the rod. Angie thought it was horrid, an ugly color, an ugly style with those itty bitty sleeves.

"It won't fit, Mom."

"Her mother held it up against her. "How do you know?" She ran her finger down the front of the dress, satisfied that it hung to Angie's knee. "Sister talked to you about the length of your dresses."

"No one wears them this long, Mom."

"You're growing fast and I can't afford to take you shopping every time you sprout an inch." Her mother reached into the neck of the dress and found the tiny white tag with the price written on it. She held the dress out towards Angie and said, "Go try it on," while she looked about for the dressing room.

Angie didn't take the dress. She looked at it, pulling her upper body backwards in distaste, and said pleadingly, "But Mom, it's so ugly."

With her index finger, her mother lowered her sunglasses to the bottom of her nose, glaring at Angie while she pushed the dress against her. In a deadly still voice, teeth locked together, her mother said, "*Try—it— onn.*"

The saleswoman hadn't heard what Angie's mother said, but she sensed the situation. She walked over and lowered her head, trying to meet Angie's eyes. "Would you like to try that on, honey?" she asked, her voice so nice, so gentle, Angie wanted to cry. She nodded her head, her chin almost bumping against her chest, and followed the woman to the tiny room with two cubicles, each hidden behind a bright psychedelic curtain with orange, yellow, and pink swirls. Angie pushed the curtain of the first cubicle and entered the small room. There was a tall, rectangular mirror on one wall and two clothes hooks on the opposite wall. She pulled the drape shut just as her mother entered the corridor, her loafers visible to Angie beneath the curtain.

She removed her sailor dress, which looked very pretty now in comparison with the brown dress, and put it on one of the hooks. She took the brown dress from the hanger and unzipped the back, careful not to catch the fabric in the zipper. Angie held the dress by its hem and slid it over herself, her arms finding their way into the short sleeves. She pulled the dress down in front and looked at herself in the mirror. The dress was huge, comically huge. Even her mother would have to admit this. It hung exactly at the top of Angie's knee, but it circled around her waist without touching it. She looked as fat and round as a cupcake. Angie started to laugh; two people, she thought, could fit in this dress. Relieved, she pulled the curtain back, anxious to have her mother see the ridiculous sack dress.

Her mother looked at her appraisingly.

"Perfect fit, huh, Mom?" Angie joked, hoping for at least a minor concession on her mother's part. She wondered if the green and pink dress were available in a size twelve. Even if her mother would make her wear it too long, it was pretty enough that it might not matter.

"Turn around," her mother said.

Angie turned and faced the wall, feeling her mother move in quickly behind her. "Silly," she said, "it would help if you zipped it up."

The fabric moved about Angie for a moment and, nervous, she looked at herself again in the mirror. She couldn't deny that the appearance of the dress improved, slightly, but it was still floating around her waist.

Her mother stepped into the cubicle and put her arms on Angie's shoulders. She pushed them back and said, "Stand up *straight*! You hunch over like an old woman."

Her mother looked at Angie's reflection in the glass and said simply, "There. Perfect."

Angie looked at her mother and opened her mouth. "Mom, it's too big. All the kids will laugh at me."

Her mother opened her purse and took out her wallet. "Don't be so dramatic, Angie," she said, sounding tired. "When I was your age, I never got a new dress, let alone one from a store. Hurry up and change. I have to go to the post office before we go home."

Angie stopped pulling the curtain shut. "Is this the only dress we're buying?" she asked, shocked.

Her mother gave a curt laugh. "What did you think? I was going to buy the whole store for you? C'mon, get dressed. We have to hurry."

Her mother walked out of the corridor and Angie changed quickly. She was eager to take the brown sack off. It made her feel like a fat eight-year-old. She resolved to never, never wear the dress. It could hang at the back of her closet for a million years and she wouldn't even look at it. Or she would wear it and damage it right away. Rip it somehow and tell her mother she was pushed by some bully in her class. Then she thought of her mother insisting that she call the boy's mother and demand payment for the dress. She knew she would have to wear the dress and she thought of trying to walk unobserved into her classroom, taking her seat before anyone noticed her ugly outfit. At lunch time, however, she'd have to walk with her class to the auditorium where the students ate their brown bag lunches at long, naked tables. Penny would see her in the dress, staring curiously before she averted her eyes. Angie blinked back her tears, asking herself, *why did I ever want to go shopping?* She thought with longing of lying on their living room floor, her head propped up with a worn corduroy couch pillow, watching the Saturday morning cartoons.

She walked out of the dressing room and handed the dress to her mother. While her mother took it to the cash register and paid the pretty saleswoman, Angie walked to the mannequin in the bright flowered dress. Her lips felt big, the lower one starting to protrude, and the flowers became slowly fused as she felt her eyes fill with water. Her mother came and stood next to her.

"Where do they get these colors?" she mused. "That would show all the dirt. And long sleeves are such a pain to iron."

They walked through the store, the sleek, shiny surfaces drifting past Angie, out of her reach now, not meant for her. They stepped outside, back into the dreary concrete world of the parking lot.

"Oh, I forgot," her mother said, stopping on the sidewalk, her voice pleasantly teasing, "I have a surprise for you. While you were changing, I bought these."

She reached into the bag and produced a pair of brown nylon knee socks, an exact match for the dress. "Won't they be pretty with the dress?"

Angie felt a catch at the back of her throat and she struggled to catch her breath. Her sobs came more quickly, though, and it was difficult to inhale. "Do I have to wear them?" she sobbed, not looking at her mother, but holding her gaze on the awful socks.

One, two, and then a third slap, all on the left side of her cheek. It was so abrupt, her mother's hand flying like a little bird. She didn't bother to see if anyone was walking by or watching.

"YOU THINK YOU'RE TOO GOOD FOR ME, JUST LIKE YOUR FATHER!" she shrieked. "Well, if you don't like it, *get out*! Go live with him and the Merry Widow and your little friend, Penny! You think it's a picnic for me being stuck with you two ingrates? I can't even go out of the house for fear of running into someone I used to know."

Angie swung her head around frantically, at the sidewalk behind them, at the parking lot, watching the people watch her and her mother. Some averted their eyes and continued walking, and a few, including a father holding the hand of a small girl, stared at them. Angie's mother turned to face the parking lot, jerking her head so quickly her sunglasses fell mid-way down her face, resting there for just a second before falling to the ground. Her face exposed, Angie was shocked to see that her mother's fierce glare had been replaced with a furtive watchfulness, her head lowered almost to her shoulders and looking about with small, taut movements. Her mother raised her hands to the outer corners of both eyes, like blinders on a horse, as she bent to retrieve the glasses. She stood, her glasses on her face again, and paused at the edge of the sidewalk, saying in a flat voice, "Find your brother."

Angie looked up and saw her mother slide a single finger under the right side of the glasses, holding it for a moment behind the right joint of the glasses. Her mother stepped into the parking lot and strode across it to the car, the white Rafferty's shopping bag hitting the side of her leg as she walked.

Angie held her stinging cheek and walked carefully down the sidewalk, in front of all the stores displaying jewelry, fabric, shoes, signs advertising meat specials in the butcher's windows. She didn't want anyone to see her crying, so she looked down at the shoes of people passing her: sneakers, sandals, loafers, suede moccasins with fringe around the ankles, a pert pair of red pumps holding slender feet wrapped in white fishnets, the design now reminding Angie of a baseball diamond repeated over and over. She wanted the walk to last forever, one foot in front of the other, on and on. But she was in front of Avery's already and she could see Tony standing with another boy as he leaned back and pulled a lever with his right hand, releasing a ball so it shot to the top of the machine, descending now through a series of bumpers and bells, the chimes ringing out and the lights blinking on and off, on and off. The ball had barely settled into the slot at the bottom before Tony pulled the lever again and the second ball soared.

TRYING SO HARD

My mother looks so butch with her hair cut like that, buzzed short so it sticks up in tiny dark spikes. She thinks it's funny when people tell her she looks just like me, her thirteen year-old son, but now I'm letting my hair grow out. But still, we're both chubby, especially in the legs, and we both wear wire-frame glasses.

I act like I'm cool with this whole lesbian thing even though my father asks, "How's Wonder Woman?" when he picks me up every Sunday. They divorced last year, after my mother told him that she faked every orgasm since their honeymoon. Some things I wish I didn't know.

At first I thought my mother was going through a phase, that she was trying out lesbianism like I was trying out roller blades. But when she went camping with Sandy, a school bus driver with a personality that ran every stop sign, it hit me that my mother felt the same way about girls that I do. Except she's getting dates and all I can do is stare at Kendra Mackelby's chest in math class.

In a few months, I'll graduate from Highland Elementary and go to Marshall High. I spend a lot of time wondering how different it will be, if the girls will be different, if they'll stop hiding their breasts behind their books when they walk through the halls. Both my parents keep telling me that I can talk to them about anything, anything at all. My father's idea of a conversation is a fifteen-second monologue where he says, "Don't worry about it. Things will work out, sport," regardless of the topic. He's a little insecure about his own sexuality since Mom's conversion; I don't think he has any advice to offer. There's no way I'll talk to my mother about girls because I know that she knows exactly how I feel about the opposite sex, and that embarrasses the hell out of me. A guy's mother shouldn't have a gage on his hormones; it's just not right.

Today, we're having supper at a little diner with Mary Ellen, a woman who helped Mom pick out a plant at the garden shop last month. "She's dying to meet you," my mother has said every day for a week. My father tells me the same thing whenever he's dating someone new. This power I have, deciding whether or not to like a parent's latest significant other, is my chief source of fun. When my folks were together, they almost never asked for my opinion on anything. Now, they're tripping over themselves serving up their latest date to me on a silver platter.

Dad's last girlfriend was a toothy receptionist who seemed to think everything I said was hysterical, even when I said the pizza we were eating tasted like wet cardboard. So when she asked me what I wanted to be when I grew up, I said, "A serial killer," so I could roll my eyes at Dad when she almost laughed herself under the table. Mom's dates are out to prove that they can talk about "guy" things: sports, rock music, TV shows like *South Park*. What they don't get is that the big GUY thing is girls. They never ask me about girls.

I should give today's date, Mary Ellen, a break. She's trying so hard, ducking her head whenever she asks a question, like she's afraid of me. She should be. Mom's last girlfriend was history after I declared her neurotic because she spent the entire night picking fuzz off her sweater. She thought she impressed me with her knowledge of MTV, but Mom told her the next day that she didn't think they had a future together.

"So," Mary Ellen says, dipping her chin towards the table so her back is humped and her neck disappears, "what do you like to eat?"

Before I can even open my mouth, my mother says, "Give him a burrito and he's the happiest kid on the block. Right, Chris?"

I jerk my shoulders wondering if after dinner I'll ask Mom how she can date someone with such poor posture. Or maybe I'll complain about Mary Ellen's hair, which is a terrible orange and cut like someone put a bowl on her head. She's thin, though, and I wonder if that's what attracts my mother to her. I like skinny girls too. At home I wear weights around my ankles, hoping they'll slim my legs down. Mary Ellen looks like she's been munching on nothing but rabbit food her whole life.

There's got to be a better way to spend a Saturday afternoon than meeting your mother's girlfriend. Ron Bielman and Tim Wilcox, two guys in my class, said they were going to take the bus over to Carnegie Avenue today. Ron's brother works at a store called "The Lube Tube," a shop filled with sex gadgets. You're supposed to be eighteen or older to get in, but Ron's brother is alone during the lunch hour and Ron brings a different guy with him every couple of weeks.

Not that he's going to ask me to go with him; he doesn't say hi to me and I sit right next to him in homeroom. I was in the bathroom once when Ron was telling a bunch of guys about the stuff in the shop.

"They sell every kind of condom imaginable," he said, "even condoms in different flavors that you can eat."

"Eat?" Jimmy Colfax sounded confused.

"Yeah. And there's all kinds of lotions and cards with naked women on them, and blow-up dolls." He started laughing in that closed, throaty way, and I knew he was about to say something dirty. "You can get a blow-up doll that's a blonde or a brunette," he said, winking at Tim.

"Who cares what color her hair is?" Vince Fennelson asked.

"Well," Ron said as he leaned back until his head rested on the mirror, "it depends on where the hair is."

Then there was a lot of high-fiving and whistling, and Ron noticed that I had been washing my hands for five minutes.

"Got a problem?" he said loudly, so his voice bounced off of the tiles.

I shook my head no as I wiped my hands on a paper towel. When I went back to class I looked at Kendra Mackelby and wondered what color her hair was down there. The hair on her head was light brown; it never occurred to me that she might not match.

We're all eating hamburgers and I watch as Mary Ellen puts ketchup on both sides of the meat. She eats her French fries with her fingers, taking little bites and then licking the salt from her fingertips.

"Are you going to go to camp this summer? Your mom told me you really liked boy scout camp last summer."

Last summer was a million years ago. I thought it was great that I got to start a fire and sleep outside. Now I wouldn't be caught dead wearing a screaming yellow kerchief around my neck and geeky shorts that had all kinds of pockets for special little hunting tools.

"Chris has outgrown camp, haven't you honey?"

I pretend to be chewing so I can't answer, leaning my head ever so slightly sideways to make a non-committal response. Thumbs up or thumbs down on Mary Ellen, I wonder to myself. It's not like I can nix every one of my mother's dates. Sure, when she first started going out, I thought that if I hated them all, Mom would give in and take Dad back. But now I know that those two are splitsville for good. And Mary Ellen is better than most of my mother's "friends" as she calls them. If only Mary Ellen didn't make herself look like a little old lady leaning over the table like that.

It's like she's reading my mind. Pushing her chair a little closer to the table, Mary Ellen arches her back the other way, just for a few seconds. But it's long enough for me to see her two nipples straining against her navy t-shirt, two symmetrical flowers with very round, hard centers. She relaxes her shoulders and hunches again, but it's too late. I'm harder than cement, the front of my jeans a painful straight jacket.

"Are you feeling okay, honey? You look warm." My mother turns to look at Mary Ellen. "When he was a baby, he had terrible fevers. It seemed like I was sticking a thermometer up his little butt every other day."

Well, that's enough embarrassment to relax my body, but I can feel that my face is a hard, bright pink. My mother starts talking about running across the street to the pharmacy for some aspirin, and I almost shout, "I'm *fine*, okay? I'm fine."

But then Mary Ellen arches her back again, lifting and separating, and my body answers. It's like we're playing Simon Says and she's the leader. I'm getting turned on by my mother's girlfriend. It's too much to handle, and I know I've got to distract myself somehow.

"So how long have you lived in Cleveland?" I ask Mary Ellen, surprising and delighting both women, despite the saliva I've spluttered onto the table.

"Oh, about five years."

"Where did you live before that?"

"Chattanooga. Do you know where that is?"

"Sure. *Chattanooga Choo Choo, won't you choo choo me home,*" I sing. The look that passes between my mother and Mary Ellen is nothing short of ecstasy. My mother's eyes fill out to meet the wires of her glasses and she looks at me proudly, hoping for more conversation.

"Uh, excuse me. I need to go to the restroom." I get up, happy that my shirt hangs almost to mid-thigh. As I take the first few steps, I can hear Mom half-whisper to Mary Ellen, "You're doing *great*!"

I don't have to go to the bathroom, and it's a good thing, because I couldn't if I wanted to. My penis, not my heart, feels like the very center of my body, and it's throbbing with a sad ache I know all too well. When I'm home and excited, lying on my bed with the cover over me, I try to imagine Kendra Mackelby's face, her Hard Rock Cafe t-shirt. But now, as I close myself in a stall and shut my eyes, all I can see are Mary Ellen's beautiful flowers, their centers reaching out to breathe. It's silly, but I almost feel as if I'm cheating on Kendra, a girl who has spoken to me exactly twice, the first time to tell me to get out of the way of the pencil sharpener. But I can actually imagine Mary Ellen's chest naked and I spend several moments thinking about her very white skin. Does she have freckles on her chest like she does across her nose?

Before you know it, Mom's face is a part of my fantasy, and I can hear her saying again, "his little butt," over and over, and I open my eyes. The erection retracts immediately, and, I can't help it, I start crying. I can see the tears dropping off my face and landing in the toilet. Stop it! I command myself, but it takes a few minutes to keep that choking feeling from welling up in my throat. Walking out of the stall, I'm grateful that no one's in the bathroom with me. In the mirror, I look like I've run a marathon; my face looks like beefsteak and I'm sweating.

Lapping water from the sink over my eyes, my cheeks, my chin, I think I feel something. I learn forward, pulling my face as close to the mirror as possible, and it's there, just below my right nostril, a tiny black hair. Very gently, I touch it, afraid it will vanish, turn out to be a speck of dirt. But it stays, a firmly rooted hair, and what's more, it looks like there's an even tinier one sprouting beside it. I rub my fingers over and over the skin above my lip and finally walk out of the men's room and towards our table.

When I'm only half-way across the room, Mom and Mary Ellen look up. My mother's hand is resting on Mary Ellen's and they're both looking at me with such shiny eyes, eyes full of fragile hope. As I come closer, I smile and say, "Not talking about me, I hope?" They laugh and shake their heads no, share guilty smiles. When I suggest we all go to a movie, my mother puts her arm around my shoulders and says, "Sure, honey, what do you want to see?"

I wriggle out from under her clutch and say, "*Mo-om*," but she keeps smiling. She smiles at me and then she smiles at Mary Ellen. Carefully, I take a peek at Mary Ellen, and she's beaming ear to ear, kind of nodding her head like she approves of me and my Mom. I count the freckles on her nose—one, two three, four, there are four all together, and I think that's enough.

MAN TALK

Because my father died in a plane crash when I was seven, Mother trotted out her brother, Uncle Jack, whenever some male rite of passage was about to occur. Not the usual male rites of passage, mind you, the big two-wheeled bicycle, the birds and the bees lecture, the keys to the car on prom night. No. Those were reserved for more conventional (and less affluent) families. I was a "Cameron Man" as Mother was fond of reminding me, and this meant legacies of all kinds to which I had to live up. Technically, I wasn't a Cameron Man since my father's last name was Renwick, but, alas, he was dead, and my mother fell back on her own family's traditions and customs to instill in me. And there was good old Uncle Jack waiting in the wings to make sure I toed the line.

That's absolutely untrue. He wasn't waiting in the wings. Mother was shoving him onto my stage with both hands. She insisted that he partner me in the father-son golf tournament at the club every summer, and that he teach me to swim, to ride horses, to row. Although Uncle Jack did all of these with a pleasant enough attitude, I knew Mother was behind it all.

I eavesdropped on a phone conversation between her and Uncle Jack when I was thirteen and about to leave for boarding school. Standing in the hall next to her slightly ajar door, I listened to a woman who knew how to get what she wanted:

"Jack? This is your sister, Margaret."

Reinforcing her blood relationship was always Mother's opening attack. Then she said, "Charles is about to leave for Philby Prep and he needs a word or two."

She was silent for a moment and I imagined that she was twisting the telephone cord around her diamond-laden fingers as Uncle Jack sputtered questions about what "a word or two" meant.

"*You know*," she said coaxingly, "what's expected of him, how to get along, what sports he should go out for."

I gathered Uncle Jack tried to protest because Mother fairly shouted, "Jack! The poor boy doesn't have a father. Do you mean to tell me you don't have a mere hour to spend with your nephew?" Cringing, I wondered how many times Uncle Jack had heard that before.

It must have worked, because she resumed her society tone, restrained and tolerant, as if she were the one doing the favor. "Splendid. Pick him up at eleven-thirty this Saturday. I know he'd enjoy lunch at the club or Chumley's." Chumley's was one of Mother's favorite seafood restaurants; I think she ordered the shark.

She hung up the receiver heavily and I sprinted back to my room and waited for her to appear. She entered, an aura of victory about her.

"Darling, Uncle Jack wants to take you to lunch this Saturday and discuss Philby with you."

"Darling," I sassed back, "I don't think that's quite right. I think you are making Uncle Jack take me to lunch on Saturday and he'd rather be sleeping off Friday night's hangover."

"Oh, you," she said, standing there, tall and imperial in an elegant black Halston dress, her hair swept into a chignon at the base of her neck, although it was only Wednesday night and she wasn't going anywhere.

She reached over and rumpled my hair. This was supposed to be an affectionate, motherly gesture, but it was always a bit too rough to qualify for that in my book, the rings on her hand somehow snaring and yanking my hair to their very roots.

Uncle Jack was Mother's youngest brother, still a bachelor at thirty-six. He did something at a bank, although was scant with details whenever anyone asked him. It didn't really matter what he did because he was, after all, rich. What he really did, it seemed, was be seen about town with the most beautiful women in Baltimore and then be written up in the newspapers. Some of his dates were society women, but most were not, and this upset Mother; she did so want her eligible brother to settle down, literally, with the right Junior Leaguer and spawn Cameron heirs.

He arrived an hour late that Saturday to take me to lunch. "Darling, here's Uncle Jack," Mother said as he entered the study, prompting me to

stand and shake hands as was the habit in our family. As I did, I noticed that his silk tie was stained, a smudge of egg yolk or something, and he wasn't wearing a suit as I was. He had on a navy blazer and gray flannel slacks, but he was clearly dressed for a more casual occasion than Mother had led me to believe this would be. She had made the cleaners rush my dark blue suit for our outing.

Uncle Jack was freshly shaven though, and his dark blond hair was still damp from the shower. As always, I noticed the scar, about an inch long, on his cheek, just in front of his left ear. He had fallen from his bike while racing down Hedgeford Hill when he was nine. The scar was the only thing marring his appearance, which went beyond handsome. He had the trademark slate blue Cameron eyes, but his nose was shorter than most in our family, straight and noble. His jaw jutted out in a manly square, with a mischievous cleft in his chin.

After we shook hands, he punched my shoulder and called me, "Chuckie!" to which my mother and I both winced.

We headed out the door and my spirits lifted. At the end of the drive sat Uncle Jack's pride and joy, his sleek black Jaguar with the convertible top. The car was in the auto garage being fixed for something or other most of the time, and I had never before ridden in it. Although it was late summer and there was a decided chill in the air, we rode topless, the hair on our heads lifted to comic effect. There was a somewhat close call at an intersection when I wondered if Uncle Jack was going to acknowledge the red light or decide it was optional. He stopped late, stepping on the brake with such force that the glove compartment opened and a plastic bag full of marijuana bounced onto my lap. He didn't notice as he fought with the gear shift, ready to burn rubber as soon as the light turned green. I replaced the bag silently.

He took me to Vander's, a pub that served hamburgers and chili on stained white crockery. The little square tables, black boxes rimmed with chrome, had large, heavy sugar jars with domed steel lids and bottles of ketchup gummy at the top from the cap being removed and replaced over and over. Motown music thundered from the juke box, almost drowning out the sound of sizzling grease on the grill. The waitress, a red-headed woman in her forties, called "Jackie!" to my uncle as we filed through the tables to take a seat in the back.

Uncle Jack drank three beers with lunch and I had a Coke. At one point, when I was about to ask for a second soda, he tipped his beer bottle and poured me half a glass. He didn't say anything about it, but I smiled my thanks. We both ate hamburgers and French fries, and I watched, fascinated, as Uncle Jack squeezed mustard on everything. I mean *everything*. Every French fry was coated with thick yellow paste, and it slid over both sides of his hamburger. He ate a few small bags of potato chips and was disappointed to learn the bar was out of peanuts. He had to settle for pretzels which he crunched until they must have been goop in his mouth. Years later, after smoking a particularly satisfying joint, I would remember this lunch as I frantically searched my apartment looking for any available munchie. That day with Uncle Jack, however, I only ate half of my burger. When I was about to take a bite, I noticed the web of gristle holding the meat together and lost my appetite. I was my mother's son, after all.

"So," Uncle Jack pronounced, "Philby."

I nodded as I swallowed a French fry. "We don't have to talk about it. I know Mother put you up to this."

He looked up at the ceiling and let out a long, slow whistle. "You've got her figured out, good for you, Chuckie."

"Chuck," I said. "Charles or Chuck, please." I wiped my mouth on the paper napkin and placed it folded at the edge of my plate.

"Chuck, yeah, Chuck. Be firm about that. I was Jonathan until my eighteenth birthday when I laid down the law."

I sat up a little straighter. "Really? You've always been Uncle Jack."

He drummed his fingers on the table, matching the beat to the Supremes. "Sometimes your mother still slips. Well, she doesn't slip, she does it on purpose. She says '*Jonathan*', and I know I'm in for it." He lifted his glass and drained the last of the beer.

I had swallowed that first half-glass of beer in a minute and Uncle Jack ordered himself another, filling my glass almost to the top and showing me how to get a good head. I was moderately drunk, which meant I was as euphoric as only a thirteen-year-old boy can be in such circumstances. Later, I would brag to my friends about getting drunk in a bar in broad daylight.

"Was Mother always like this?" I asked Uncle Jack.

He smiled, little lines branching out from his eyes, and the cleft in his chin deepened. "Pretty much," he answered.

"She always talked that way, walked that way?" We both laughed at my rhyme.

"From the cradle." He pulled out a packet of Salems from his jacket

pocket.

"How old was she when you were born?"

"She was," he said slowly, thinking, "she was nine, yeah, that's right, she was nine."

"What was she like then?"

He shook his head then rested it on his upright hand. "The first important thing I remember was her debutante ball in Newport. The summer house was full of a million guys in tuxedoes and there were girls everywhere running around in those puffy dresses. There were all these people bringing in food, food, and more food." He exhaled a raft of smoke and set his cigarette on the edge of the table. "I got in trouble for running through the garden and squirting everyone with a water pistol." He laughed out loud. "That was the only debutante bash I ever had any fun at."

He raised his hand and caught the waitress's eye for the check. "Actually, when your father was alive, she was happy. And she was more relaxed about society stuff." He counted money from his billfold. "When your father died, she really dove back into it. It helped her, I guess."

He was telling me something interesting, important, and later I would try to reconstruct his words. At that moment, however, I was worried because, in my hazy drunkenness, I didn't quite have the sense of my feet under the table. I tapped them against the linoleum to make certain they were there. Assured they were, I then asked, "Was Mother nice to you?"

Uncle Jack smiled ear to ear and blinked. "Was she nice to me?" he quoted back as if it were a riddle. "In her way, I guess. She was so much like my own mother, up on form and duty and all that crap, but she did look out for me."

"How?"

Uncle Jack moved his head a bit to the right and looked suddenly alert, his eyes locked into an enthralled stare, but then I realized he was watching the pool game going on behind me. "Well," he said, blinking his eyes again and turning towards me, "she tried to keep me out of trouble." He smirked, knocking the cigarette ashes against the side of the table so they fell to the floor. "Hell, she's still doing that."

I laughed, but I didn't know why. I did know that I wanted Uncle Jack to think I got the gist of whatever he was saying; I didn't want him to think I was still some kid. We were sharing a moment of some kind, but I wasn't sure what it was about. Still, we were two men having a beer in a bar on a Saturday afternoon. That counted for something.

At dinner, Mother wanted to know everything. I told her about Vanders, about the hamburgers, and especially about the mustard, I couldn't resist, and I could see she was visibly shaken by this. Not that she suspected that Uncle Jack smoked pot; it was the poor display of table manners that upset her. But she said, trying to convince herself, "That was sweet of Jack to take you to Vanders. He knows how to entertain a young man. You don't really like the club, do you Charles?"

I didn't mind it, but I agreed with her.

But, of course, what she really wanted to know was how Uncle Jack had "counseled" me about Philby. I hesitated as I lifted a forkful of carrots to my mouth. The truth of the matter was Uncle Jack and I hadn't discussed Philby. Oh, he did tell me that he liked it and that I'd have a lot of fun there, but that was it. The mainstay of our conversation, such as it was given my first encounter with inebriation, was Mother, and I could never have admitted that to her. I knew I wasn't prepared for the litany of questions she was drafting in her mind, and I looked somewhat frantically about the table, as if some other sibling might miraculously appear to distract Mother, but as I was an only child, none did.

I set down my fork and gave Mother my full attention, something I rarely did at least in an acknowledged way. "He thinks I'll do fine there."

Mother smiled fully, stirred by this. "Of course you will, darling. What else did he say?"

She leaned forward, as if she were inspecting my plate, making sure I had eaten all my vegetables. When I didn't answer, she raised her face and I was forced to meet those slate blue eyes straight on.

"Mother," I said, stalling for time, and something hardly appropriate leapt into my mind, and I blurted, revealing how nervous I was, "a lot of what we discussed was, you know, man talk." Flushed, I looked down and lifted my fork to spear some baby peas.

Surprisingly, Mother uttered a faint, "Oh," and leaned back in her chair, her own arms resting on the arms of the chair. I stole a glance at her and realized, amazed, that she was pleased, more than pleased, proud somehow. What had I said? I had to remember it for future occasions. Man talk. Mother liked that Uncle Jack and I talked man talk. I would remember that.

But what did she think we talked about? I attended the progressive

St. Mark's Academy, so she knew that I knew everything there was to know about sex, drugs, every social ill from which money was protecting me. Man talk. Somehow it made Uncle Jack more responsible in her mind, it seemed, and that was a good thing. It was my first realization that all of Mother's efforts to couple me with Uncle Jack were meant as much for his benefit as my own. What better way to induce maturity in a reckless younger brother than to bind him to a fatherless nephew? Oh, she was brilliant, killing two birds with one stone. I worried that she would call Uncle Jack and thank him for whatever it was he supposedly said to me, but I was to learn that whenever I uttered that magical phrase, *man talk*, mother would stop prying and joyfully accept that Uncle Jack was somehow doing his Cameron duty.

During my first year at Philby, close to summer break, I went into the school library and found the old yearbooks. I estimated that Uncle Jack had been at Philby from 1978 through 1982. He didn't distinguish himself much that first year; his only photo in the book was the standard freshman shot. His sophomore yearbook showed him on the rugby team, however, one of the taller players in the second row, his hair cut ridiculously short, his expression exceedingly confident, fun. He and the guy next to him had their arms raised and their hands joined in a victory gesture. In the junior picture, he was front and center, co-captain of the team. That year the school had won their division in rugby, the first time in seventeen years, beating our worst rival, Amberson. Uncle Jack and another guy were holding a big trophy with some gold Greek-like runner at the top. The small black print under the photo told of the team's many triumphs, concluding with the big game, and specifically mentioned the "rough and tough Number Eight player, Jack Cameron."

I stared at the photo and felt a prideful swelling in my chest. The next time Mother got Uncle Jack and me together for "a word or two" we would discuss rugby. Eagerly, I opened the senior yearbook, fanning the pages to find the rugby photo. When I did, I scanned the faces, read the caption, but Uncle Jack was nowhere. I went to the senior section, found the "C's," but there was no sign of him. Odd, I thought, as I put the books back.

I went home two weeks later and mentioned Uncle Jack's absence from the senior yearbook to Mother while we ate dinner. She stopped eating and looked at the center of the long table. I was seated just to her right, but she seemed to have forgotten I was there.

"Mother?"

She jerked her chin at me, but I could see she was still lost in her thoughts.

Then she spoke cautiously, her knowing manner abandoned. "Uncle Jack didn't tell you about that when you had your, er, man talk?"

I shook my head, my heart starting to sink.

She leaned her head slightly in my direction, rubbing her finger gently back and forth against her lower lip, and all but whispered, "Uncle Jack got in a bit of trouble at the start of his senior year. A school boy prank. He and a few other boys pushed the headmaster's car into the pond, and, unfortunately, it was quite ruined."

I raised my shoulders and started to laugh.

"Charles! Please! It was anything but funny."

Mother looked down and concentrated on the rare beef on her plate, stabbing at it with a ferocity that made me wonder if she realized the cow was already dead. She looked at me and her pupils seemed to dilate, the black depth of the ocean overtaking the blue surface. "He didn't tell you about this when you had your man talk?" she said with such wonder in her voice I broke out into a sweat. She was saying those words with such familiarity now, like another Cameron tradition had been launched. God, what had I done? I shook my head no.

"Well, I don't expect he would," she said briefly, and my chest relaxed. "It's nothing to be proud of. Jack understands that. As he should. But certainly," she said with emphasis, lowering her head to mine, "he told you to *avoid* such hijinks."

"Yes," I said, recovered now as I reached for my milk, "he did say that. Said the school was pretty tough on pranks."

Mother nodded, her head moving up and down with taut motions. "It was a dark day in the family when that happened, let me tell you. Well, if Jack doesn't want to talk about it, don't mention it to him when you see him Saturday."

"Saturday?"

Mother smiled, glad to change the subject. "Yes, darling. He wants to hear all about your first year at Philby."

No, mother wanted him to hear all about it. But anyway, it would be a great to talk about rugby with him.

Elsie, our housekeeper, came in to clear the dinner dishes. Mother waited until she left to say, "We never did believe it was Jack's idea, although he insisted it was, and he was the only one to be expelled. A couple of the other boys were, well, they were quite. . . common."

She said "common" as though it were the most distasteful word in the King's English. "Ah," I said, making fun of her, "and you think it was one of those common boys who lured Uncle Jack along and then dumped the blame on him."

Mother confronted my taunting with indignation. "Yes," she said abruptly, "that's *exactly* what I think. Jack was just too much of a gentleman to set the record straight. And there is some dignity in that, remaining silent under an accusation. At least that much can be said." She looked expectantly towards the dining room door to see if Elsie was returning with the dessert.

I fumbled through a maze of feelings. I didn't know whether I should rail against Mother for her implicating the other boys because of their lack of status or believe with her that Uncle Jack had been lured along. She interrupted my mental struggle. "That's why, Charles," she said firmly, "*you* must conduct yourself as a consummate gentleman at school." Mother nodded her head slowly at me, her chin lifting and lowering with a graveness appropriate for funerals "There have been four generations of Camerons at Philby and, except for that mishap with Uncle Jack, every single one of them distinguished himself academically and athletically." Elsie entered and Mother immediately stopped speaking.

We had dinner at home that Saturday, myself, Mother, and Uncle Jack. Over leg of lamb, Mother made less than subtle inquiries about Uncle Jack's position at the bank, his romantic life, and whether he was going to assume her position on the board at the Baltimore Public Library.

"You really do need to become more involved in civic service," she told him. "The Camerons," she said, her voice rising, an often rehearsed speech about to spill forth, but Uncle Jack stopped her.

"The Camerons," he said, mimicking her, "have always stuck their noses in other people's business."

Mother protested, but it was clear Uncle Jack wasn't going to assume her position on the Library's board. She relaxed over dessert, listening tolerantly, even suppressing a few smiles, as Uncle Jack told boyhood stories about sabotaging some of Mother's dates. He had told one of her early suitors that insanity ran in the family, and another that their father was going bankrupt any day.

"I could have killed you," Mother said to him, and I knew there was truth in that statement. She rose from the table and said, "I'll leave you two men alone. I've got to meet with Edith Winslow about trustee elections for the Museum."

As soon as she left the house, Uncle Jack pressed the intercom button and said, "Elsie, two cold ones, and I don't mean root beer." When Elsie brought the two bottles of Heineken, she appeared almost frightened, but then Uncle Jack kissed her on the cheek and said with gusto, "Atta girl. If anybody asks, I drank both of them." Elsie retreated from the room, glancing back at me with a look that tottered between concern and amusement.

"So," Uncle Jack said, removing his dinner jacket, "I guess your mother wants us to talk about Philby."

I was gulping beer so fast, my throat felt cold and and pinched. "She said you wanted to hear about it." I smiled, warming to the feel of another man talk session where Mother would be the target of our worldly musings.

"Sure I do," he said. "Of course I do. What do you think of the place?" He pushed my beer away from me, saying, "Slow down."

"I think Philby's terrific."

"Yeah?" He looked pleased and interested. "Yeah," he said wistfully, "I liked it too."

"I'm on the rugby team."

He punched my shoulder. "So I hear. What position?"

"Wing." This wasn't nearly as impressive as Number Eight, but it was only my first year, after all.

"Did you beat Amberson?"

"No," I said, deflated. "They creamed us. David Lazlo, our fly-half, had a bum ankle and couldn't kick anything. Next year."

"Lazlo?" Uncle Jack pushed his chair back and looked up at the ceiling. "What did you say his first name was?"

"David. Why?"

"There was a Lazlo in my year too. At Philby, that usually means the same family."

"Oh," I said, wanting to get back to rugby talk.

"Hey, is Mr. Albertson, the Latin teacher, still there?"

"No, I don't think so. I've never heard of him. They don't make you take Latin anymore."

Uncle Jack laughed and he glanced fondly at the ceiling. "Albertson was a sweet old guy. Told me I had the worst pronunciation he'd heard in thirty years."

I reached for my beer and, practicing restraint, took only one full swallow before setting the bottle down again. "Do you ever go to any of the alumni weekends?"

He seemed surprised at my asking. "No," he said, smiling wryly, "I'm not certain I'd be welcome given the circumstances under which I left."

I had anticipated our talking about this, our laughing about the headmaster's car in the pond, a tale I could take back and brag about at Philby. Yes, Mother had said not to bring it up to Uncle Jack, but what did she know? Looking at him then, however, so suddenly quiet, dejected, I realized Mother was right, and I changed the subject.

"The guys are great," I told him.

"Yeah? Good," he said, and he seemed to relax, drinking from his own beer. "They were great when I was there too."

"I've been invited everywhere this summer." I told him about the invitations I'd gotten to spend time at various summer homes stretching between Maine and South Carolina. Distinguished families, every one of them. Mother was quite pleased, and insisted that we reciprocate by having my friends to the Newport house for the fourth of July weekend.

Uncle Jack listened carefully as I ticked off the names of my buddies: Pierce Drexel, Merse (short for Emerson) Hotchkiss, Chip Ellsworth, Clay Pendleton, and Andy Preston.

He rolled his eyes and belched silently into his closed hand. "Sounds like the Social Register crowd."

"Well, yes," I said, proud and embarrassed by the distinction.

He turned his head slightly to look at me from the corner of his eye, to appraise me. "You know, this is your chance to shake some of this off."

"Shake what off?"

Uncle Jack leaned back slowly in his chair and raised his hands to indicate the room. "This," he said, as if it were obvious. "This house, weekends in Newport, the Cameron curse." Despite his words, he didn't seem angry, simply tired.

"What do you mean 'curse'?"

He was surprised that I didn't understand, and I realized I was letting him down in some way.

"Do you know what *predestined* means?" he asked.

"Sure." We were Presbyterians, how could I not?

"Well," he said slowly, expectantly, "doesn't it drive you crazy?"

"What?"

He looked at his watch. I think he had decided I wasn't worth whatever education he was trying to give me, but I persisted.

"What?" I said again, this time more forcefully.

He looked at me and his mouth hung open for a second before he spoke. "That you don't get to live your own life," he said softly. "Everything is decided for you."

"I'm living my own life," I said defensively.

"You think so?" Uncle Jack said, ready to disprove me.

"Yes, I do," I said, and I recognized Mother's regal tone in my words.

He put his elbows on the table and crossed his forearms. I could tell he was trying to decide whether or not to proceed. "Well tell me this," he said finally, "why aren't you visiting David Lazlo this summer?"

What a stupid question, I thought. "Because he isn't my friend."

"Oh, why's that?"

"What?"

"Why isn't David your friend. You play rugby together, don't you?"

"I play rugby with a lot of guys."

"And you have a lot of friends. What's wrong with David?"

"Nothing. Nothing's wrong with him. We're just not friends. *Okay?*" I asked sarcastically, making him see that he was making a mystery out of nothing.

"Okay, sport." he said, and he swallowed his beer noisily, making it sound like water slipping down a drain. He looked at his watch. "I've got to get out of here," he said.

"I know what you're getting at," I accused, angry at his wanting to run off. "You think I don't associate with David because he's not rich, or cultivated, or connected."

Uncle Jack stood. "Who says he's not?" he asked indifferently. He looked at me still seated at the table. "You?" he said as if he were feigning surprise.

I stood, angry that someone who didn't know me, not really, was making such judgments. David and I weren't friends. That was all. Simply that. I couldn't be friends with everyone in the entire school, could I? Despite these reasonable thoughts, the words I hurled at him were, "You're one to tell me who to be friends with. *I'll* never get kicked out of school."

He smiled and shook his head, laughing lightly. He shrugged his shoulders, and said, "You're right, Chuck. It'll never happen to you." After he left, I went to the window and watched his Jaguar slip out of the driveway and into the night, wondering what on earth I was going to tell Mother this time.

Over the summer, I nursed my anger at Uncle Jack. He was so clearly in the wrong, attacking someone so much younger than himself who had done nothing, nothing whatsoever I told myself, to deserve it. I visited all my friends, had a great time, told myself what a great group of guys they were. And they were. This added to my anger. I felt I was protecting them from Uncle Jack's reverse snobbery. But I finally had to admit to myself that he hadn't attacked me that night. He'd been very quiet, simply offering a different view.

Then we got word that Uncle Jack had eloped with a decidedly not Social Register type, and was in London. He found work there with a newspaper, although who knew if it was a real job? The icing on the cake was that Uncle Jack and his wife, Maria, were happily expecting their first child. Mother, of course, all but laid down and died. She suspected Uncle Jack had been tricked into getting married by the prematurely pregnant Maria. But in the end, without his permission, Mother sent out wedding announcements to the press and anyone else who mattered. She sent Maria pieces of family china and crystal, and, with some reluctance, I'm sure, a cameo and seed-pearl ring that had been in the family for more than a hundred years.

But Mother couldn't help being encouraged by the reports she got back from friends visiting London and some distant cousins living there. Uncle Jack was a hard working, loving husband, and Maria was a perfect wife, beautiful and smart. I overheard Mother say to someone on the phone, "Yes, it's true love. I'm thrilled."

Mother went to England frequently. I wondered what Uncle Jack thought of that, but it must have been okay, because she kept flying over, coming home with stories of how precious her new nephew was, what a wonderful wife Maria was, such a good influence on Uncle Jack. I was surprised by the apparent change in Uncle Jack, but I was even more surprised at the change in Mother. She retired from a number of her committees and spent more time at home simply reading or sewing. On one occasion, she even referred to her old crony, Edith Winslow, as "that busybody." Mother began visiting me at Philby with an almost embarrassing regularity, I took some teasing for it, and every couple of months or so, she crossed the Atlantic for an extended visit with Uncle Jack and Maria.

The Philby graduation was a spectacle. Held outdoors in the east orchard on a cloudless, sunny day, all eighty of us watched our parents from the stage. Mother cried just a bit when the Headmaster called, "Charles Cameron Renwick," and read off my awards, highest honors in history and French. It had taken twenty-one years, but, in Mother's mind, the smudge on the Cameron name at Philby caused by Uncle Jack had finally been cleansed.

Afterwards, there was a reception on the south grounds. Families visited with one another and servers began setting down plates of food far better prepared than anything served to me here in the last four years.

I noticed that a few tables over a slender man with thinning blond hair appeared to be watching me. He held a Panama hat against his chest, every now and then fanning his face with it. I didn't know him and yet there was something oddly familiar about him; perhaps I'd seen him at a big game weekend or something. He was sitting next to David Lazlo, and I was reminded of that conversation with Uncle Jack three years ago.

The man realized I caught him staring at me, and he smiled shyly, waving his hat slightly. He stood and walked over to an oak tree a few yards away, and I understood I was to come over. Mother was off photographing everything for a scrapbook she was compiling for me, so I did. The man introduced himself to me as David's father. We shook hands and I started to tell him who I was, but he stopped me.

"You're Jack Cameron's nephew." He smiled openly now, and shook my hand more vigorously before he released it.

"You know Uncle Jack?" I asked.

He nodded. "I sure do." His eyes scanned the orchard and looked

back at me. "Jack was one of my best friends when I was here. I've been to your grandparents' house many times."

I looked about the orchard also, but I couldn't determine who he was searching for. Mr. Lazlo started to speak again, his voice hushed, almost lost against the noisy backdrop.

"Jack did something for me that saved my life. And a few other guys' lives too. You're his nephew. I want you to know."

"Oh?"

"He took the rap for a trick we pulled on the headmaster."

I lifted my head and our eyes met. He seemed embarrassed, but determined to hold my gaze. "Yes, I heard about that."

"You didn't hear it all," he said quickly, knowingly. "I know Jack, and I know he never told anyone the whole story." He glanced around, and I instantly understood that he was worried about Mother recognizing him. She didn't seem to be nearby, so he continued. "There were four of us in on it," he said, raising four bowed fingers. "All of us here on scholarship, the penny poor boys they called us, except Jack."

"The penny poor boys? How rude. I'm sorry," I said, as if I were responsible.

He laughed, pressing his handkerchief to his forehead. "It was true. We didn't have a penny to our names. And we would have been booted out of here at the first hint of any trouble." He raised a closed hand with an outstretched thumb and gestured. "You see, it was such a big deal for me and the others to be here. It was the first shot our families ever had at prep school and Ivy League, all that. If I had been bounced out, you can bet I would have been the last Lazlo here." He looked over towards his table, and smiled. "And now, here I am at David's graduation, thanks to Jack."

David was talking with whom I guessed was his mother. He didn't seem to be aware that his father had left the table.

Mr. Lazlo leaned forward on one foot and spoke into my ear. "It wasn't even Jack's idea, although," he laughed, "most of the ideas were Jack's. But he was just in for the fun on that one. Still, he told everyone he pushed the car in by himself." He lowered his head and half-closed his eyes. I thought he had finished talking, but then he breathed in a great gust of air and said, "And we let him. We stayed quiet. All these years. . .and I never contacted Jack. I never told him. . ." He didn't finish.

I struggled to find something to say. What would Uncle Jack want me to say to this man? I stammered and then said, " I'll be sure to give Uncle Jack your regards. Did you know he lives in London now?"

Mr. Lazlo's face lit up, and he said, "Jack's in London? Well, good for him. Yes, please give him my best regards and my thanks. It's too little too. . . late." His voice died with his last word.

I rested my hand on his forearm briefly. Mother at this point was heading our way, and I asked Mr. Lazlo to pose for a picture with his son. He hesitated, but I whispered, "It's okay." Mother clearly didn't recognize him as she held the camera in front of her face and called, "Smile!" Before the shutter clicked, Mr. Lazlo raised his son's arm in the air with his, and I realized why there was something so familiar about him.

I wrote to Uncle Jack about what Mr. Lazlo had told me and enclosed the photo. I also said that I hoped Uncle Jack could forgive me for what I had said a few years ago, blaming it on an excess of youthful pride. Then I went for broke and wrote him about my man talk deceptions with Mother, and how kind he was to have spent all that time with me when I was growing up.

Two weeks later, Uncle Jack phoned me and we spent some Cameron money talking trans-Atlantic for a couple of hours. Life in London suited him. He was writing a regular column for a financial paper and enjoying being a father and husband. When he told me that the only drawback was being separated from his family, from Mother, he must have heard me gasp because he laughed out loud.

"She's probably the only reason I'm not in prison now. Let me tell you, marriage, fatherhood, all that jazz gives you a different perspective."

I said good-bye, promising I would come over at Christmas just as Mother looked in my room.

"Who have you been talking to for so long?" she asked.

"Uncle Jack," I said. Then I added, sitting up on my bed, "He wanted to set me right about Princeton, make sure I knew what was expected of me."

Mother stood framed in the doorway, and I watched her fill to the brim with surprise and happiness. Her expression quickly changed, however, to one of sisterly approval and pride. "Well, be sure to do *exactly* as Uncle Jack tells you, darling," she said to me with an admonishing confidence, as if she knew every word he had said to me.

MEMPHIS, TENNESEE

I've always been real proud of my feet. They're sitting up there on the dashboard of this old Firebird as we drive through the desert. Lou's flooring the gas, but we're only going about seventy; that's as high as this heap will go even on a good day. My feet can feel the vibrations from the rattling engine and the buzz from the radio as Lou keeps turning the dial trying to find a good song.

It's not just that my feet aren't too long and they're narrow with high arches like a ballerina's, though all those things help. It's the toes, really, that I've always, since I was a little girl, been convinced were something special. Those five pink buds on the right foot are identical to the ones on the left foot, even down to the way the pinky toes stand almost sideways. My big toes are really big, the pillow of skin behind the nails spreads out evenly on both sides and the curve of the nails is so friendly, it's like they're smiling at me. The big toes are the mother toes and they're each balancing four tiny toe children on their hips. And the smile never leaves the faces of those big toes; carrying around four little ones never seems to tire them out or make you think that those toe children are any burden at all.

We've been driving for five days straight and we're hoping to make Las Vegas tonight. I've never been there, but Lou says he's got a couple connections in the casino business. He'll get a job bartending in one of the clubs and maybe I'll be a cocktail waitress, and that will set us up good for a while. Until Lou gets itchy and wants to get back in the car and drive to Montana or Dallas or God knows where. I can't keep up with Lou's plans. Three weeks ago we were headed for Miami, but half way there, he changed his mind and we ended up in New Orleans. I think he likes the getting there part better than the being there part, and we can't stay in any one place for too long. That's the way it's been since I met him almost a year ago in Nashville. My girlfriends bet I didn't have the nerve to go up to him at this dive bar, but I showed them all, and two weeks later I was in the car with Lou heading out for Kansas City. He kept singing some song about crazy little women in Kansas City, but I don't think we saw any.

Lou's six or seven years older than me, past thirty. I should know more about him, but he doesn't talk too much. But he sings along with whatever's on the radio and you can learn a lot about a man by the way he sings, how much of himself he puts into it, the kind of music that makes him happy. Lou was born way too late; he should have been a fifties rocker with Buddy Holly and the Big Bopper, those guys that shout a song out. When they're on the radio, Lou throws his head back and makes the strangest faces as he hollers along. He closes his eyes and scrunches up his face; if I didn't know better, I'd think he was in some kind of pain, but he's having one great time. When he's really into a song, popping his cheeks to doo-wop, bee-bop sounds, and making ridiculous noises, he doesn't even mind when I laugh at him. A man who will let you laugh at him, even now and then, is a good one.

I decided a long time ago that Lou is smart, although he still hasn't picked up that I'm pregnant, probably two, two and a half, months along. Or if he suspects, he's not saying anything. Sometimes, he's the strong, silent type, especially when he and Elvis are singing a serious song. I don't like to eat around Lou for fear I'm going to be sick, and it's getting harder to sleep in the car at night. It feels like the ground beneath the car is waving up and tossing me onto some beach that's not there. When I put my hands on my stomach, it's like I swallowed a tiny apple whole. Depending on whether I'm sick or not, it sometimes feels like a green crab apple, and other times a sweet red one, but it's my apple, mine and Lou's. It's a hard bubble just below my belly button and it's pushing with all it's might saying: "Hey! I'm here! What are you going to do about it?"

What can I do? After a year of riding around with Lou, I know that if I even hint about us maybe getting hitched in one of those chapels in Vegas and raising a couple kids, he'll pull over to the side of the road and leave me out here alone in the desert. He'll drive off singing "The Wanderer," and I'll probably die of heat stroke waiting for someone to come by and give me a lift, but to where? Every day I look for some little sign, anything, that

I'm wrong about this, that when I tell Lou I'm knocked up, he'll turn to me with a mouth shaped like a little boat, up at the corners, and say, *"Why, Mona, why didn't you say so! We got to make some plans. When will the little guy be here?"* Yeah, I fantasize that Lou will get excited that he's going to have a son, but I already know it's a girl. I look at my stomach and I just know that there's the softest, sweetest little girl in there just dying to be the apple of her daddy's eye. And I know she's going to get her heart broke just like me.

The reason I keep my feet up on the dashboard is that I remember my friend Cindy's feet swelled when she was pregnant. Of course, that wasn't until the eighth month, but I'm not taking any chances. Lou might buy that I want to lose a couple of pounds and that's why I'm not drinking beer anymore, but he'd notice elephant feet in a minute. So I keep them raised and tell him I'm trying to get my legs tan through the glass. He laughs and tells me not to get a sunburn.

Today has been one of the toughest days because I felt too lousy to eat breakfast at that truck stop we were at this morning. Walking into the restaurant, I thought I was going to keel over from all the fumes coming out of those trucks' asses, but I made it into a booth. The thought of bacon and eggs was enough to gag me, but I chickened out on ordering what I really wanted, ginger ale. Too obvious. I drank some water and told Lou I was still full from the hotdogs we ate last night. Now it's past lunch time, but Lou wants to keep pushing as long as we can, maybe not stop until dinner. We've got some twinkies, and I'm nibbling on the doughy part, leaving the cream filling. If I don't toss my cookies all over the car before we hit Vegas, it'll be a miracle.

Lou finds a station coming in pretty good and jacks up the volume so he can sing along with Chuck Berry to that song about Memphis, Tennessee. He's slapping his leg with his free hand, and tapping the accelerator to the *"booomm, booomm, booomm, boom—boom—boom"* sound of the guitar, and the car races forward and then jerks back with the beat. It makes my stomach swell to the bottom of my throat, but the music is so nice I can't resist flapping one of my feet up and down in time with Lou's hand. Momma and baby toes are all in on the action, and we go down the highway like this, bopping to the beat. When Lou sings that part in the song about Marie being only six years old, his voice sounds so sweet, and then he closes his eyes and tilts his head like he's really talking on the phone to some long distance operator.

It's all I can do not to break down bawling on the spot because

I'm hoping this is it, that sign I've been waiting for. I'm hoping I'm seeing something in Lou that maybe I missed before. I take my feet off the dashboard and lean back, my hand searching for that little apple beneath my stomach. Lou is slapping his leg hard now for the final guitar chords, and in my mind I imagine our happy life in Memphis, me, Lou, and our little Marie.

ETERNAL YOUTH

They say that of all the senses, smell is the one that can trigger memories of the past most easily. I believe it. When I was twenty, I was one of the perfume girls at Sheffield's, one of the nicest department stores in Toronto. Scents of all kind were a big part of my life then. Every week, I sprayed some new fragrance on the customers. Honey had the standard golden color of most perfumes, but it came in a little glass jar shaped like a bumble bee; you opened the lid by unscrewing the bee's wings. As clever as that was, the perfume itself smelled a little too much like bug repellent for my taste. It didn't do well. Sunlight was a big seller. It was a topaz-colored fluid, a browner gold than usual, and it had a spritely, open-air scent. I was supposed to say, "Would you like a ray of sunlight?" and then wave the bottle in a circle before squirting a customer. I only did that when a supervisor was walking by; I didn't want the customers to think I was nuts. My favorite perfume of all was Rain Forest, a deep emerald elixir that came in a concave-shaped bottle painted with little gold vines everywhere and a beautiful long-beaked bird with fuschia and yellow feathers. It smelled like overgrown grass in August after a strong rain.

Not every one wanted to be sprayed with perfume. Women looked past me, avoided my gaze, suddenly becoming engrossed with the floor pattern or reaching into their purses to locate their car keys. I would call out to them, "Would you like to try. . ." but they'd say "No thank you," so abruptly that I'd stop talking mid-sentence. That kind of rejection can get to you after a while, so I learned not to hound the women who quickened their pace when they saw me. Other women stopped, eager to see what I was selling, and I sprayed their wrists, telling them to wave their arms a bit so the alcohol evaporated before they sniffed. Otherwise, the scent was too potent. For every ten bottles I sold, I got a teeny, tiny sample bottle. I would have preferred a commission, but it didn't work that way at Sheffield's. As it was, I was always worried that if I didn't sell enough perfume, I'd be out of a job.

Nancy, my friend who sold Coach purses, always came to see me before she left at six o'clock. She usually had a date and, like everybody else who worked at the store, couldn't afford to buy the things we sold. I looked around to make sure no one was watching and then sprayed her wrists and the back of her neck. In return, she would talk loudly about how wonderful the scent was, trying to drum up business for me. She wasn't the only one getting something for nothing. Every now and then, I snuck over to the Estee Lauder counter and Lucille, a woman who'd been at the store forever, gave me a mini make-over. We couldn't get away with that too often. There was always the risk of Billy Sheffield, the boss's son, lurking about. He cruised the store trying to look important, making sure everybody was doing their job. I could usually tell when he was around because he sucked on eucalyptus cough drops all day. Every January, he went to Arizona for two weeks for his health. No one missed him.

One day I saw him leave early through the employee exit, so I walked fearlessly over to cosmetics. Before I asked Lucille if she could do my eyes with pearl-gray eye-shadow and black eye-liner, she raised her wrist and said, "Smell."

The jasminey scent with the spicy, clove undertone filled my nose up to my brain. I recognized it, but didn't know why. It wasn't a perfume that I promoted. Without warning, a picture formed in my mind and I got that spooky deja vu feeling. A corner of my brain started to reel and it was like I was watching a miniature movie. I remembered myself in a bedroom standing next to a bed I was too short to see over. The bed had a white chenille spread and I was reaching up, rubbing my hand back and forth over the fleecy lines that felt as soft as talcum powder. There was a woman standing in front of an open closet, her back to me, the zipper on her dress waiting to be pulled up. Her brown hair stopped at the bottom of her neck and flipped up at the edges. I think it was night time, and the room was swimming with the fresh scent of perfume, of this same scent on Lucille's wrist. I assumed that the woman at the closet was my mother, but, in my mind, I only saw her from the back.

"What is it?" I almost demanded of Lucille.

"Shangri La. Nice, huh?" Truth to tell, Lucille was wearing too much of it, but it was a nice scent. Not as obvious as most of the fragrances we sold, lighter, more secretive.

"Where did you get it?"

She lifted a curved hand to one side of her mouth and whispered, delighted with her deviousness, "Ormonds," a store just around the corner, Sheffield's' biggest competitor.

"They've just reintroduced it," Lucille said. "It hasn't been sold for over fifteen years."

"Fifteen years?"

"Yeah. Ormonds ran a promotion the first day they were selling it. Half off."

The hanging fluorescent lights seemed to give up extra rings of hazy blue glow, and my left eye began to feel strained, a pinching just behind it.

"Want me to do you?" Lucille asked, unaware of how dislocated I felt. I distracted myself from the feeling by getting up into the long-legged make-up stool. I sat facing Lucille, my back to the customers passing by.

I didn't know enough about my mother. My father died in Vietnam when I was two, and my mother left me with my grandmother a few years later. I was almost five, ready to start kindergarten. We were living in Auburn then, a little town in upstate New York. I remember sitting in the back seat of a car, my clothes stacked in plastic laundry baskets next to me and some stuffed animals on the floor. The blue vinyl seats smelled like spilled nail polish and a slight spatter of rain hit the windows. There was a band-aid taped awkwardly over the valley of skin between my thumb and index finger, and I remember tugging at the edges of it. We didn't go to the laundromat, however, we went to my grandmother's house even though she wasn't home from work yet. When we got there, my mother made me macaroni and cheese, my favorite meal. While it was baking, the wonderful aroma of milky cheese and slightly burnt bread crumbs filling the house, my mother took out a camera from her purse and told me to stand by the fireplace. She took three pictures, calling out to me to smile each time. It took me a long time to eat the macaroni and cheese because I had to wait for it to cool. My mother seemed nervous, sitting in a caned-back chair and bouncing her the soles of her sandals against the rug. She got up and went to the window every time she heard a car. I wondered what we were doing at my grandmother's when she wasn't home, but I didn't ask. After I finished eating, my mother told me to lie down on the couch. I did, and almost immediately fell asleep as I usually did after eating a big meal. The last thing I remember is my mother's hand gently brushing the bangs from my forehead and the scent of Jergen's hand lotion, a rich, almost cherry-flavored smell. When I woke, there was a different hand stroking my forehead, my grandmother's, and the fruity scent of Jergen's had been replaced with the pristine waft of rose milk. Grandmother was seated on the edge of the couch and she looked down at me proudly; I was her only grandchild. She asked if I had a good nap and whether I was hungry. She seemed sad, her eyes locked in a dead stare that didn't really see me. She ran her forefinger down my nose and tapped the end of it. "Don't you worry, pumpkin," she said, "you and me are going to be just fine."

I knew instinctively that my mother was gone. I didn't cry. I felt confused more than abandoned, wondering where I would sleep in that big house and whether there was someone for me to play with in the neighborhood. My grandmother brought me into the kitchen and fed me Graham crackers and milk, and she told me she was going to put up a swing set in the yard. It preoccupied me until evening when reality set in. Sitting in the bathtub, my lips started to quiver and I cried with the heartbreak of an adult. It frightened my grandmother and that frightened me more. She added more bubble bath to the water, crystals a harsh pink color that smelled so potently feminine, motherly, until they dissolved in the water and relaxed into just another soapy scent. I cried until I got the hiccups and my grandmother got me out of the tub and into bed. She sat in a chair next to my bed until I fell asleep, her words sounding in my ears as I drifted off, "Don't you worry, Linda. We're going to be fine. *Just fine.*" When I think of those words now, I realize how fiercely determined she sounded.

When Lucille finished with my make-over, I walked around the corner to Ormond's and found the fragrance department. There were bottles of Shangri La everywhere on little tables. The first thing I noticed was that the perfume was lavender, that muted, romantic shade of purple. The bottle itself wasn't that impressive, just a simple glass cylinder with a gold cap, but the label was lovely, the word "Shangri La" written in an exotic, Arabic-like style, short, thick letters in cornflower blue ink against an ivory background, an elaborate pink rose dotting the "i".

None of it was familiar to me, but then a young woman about my age with a very short haircut came up to me and said, "Would you like to visit Shangri La, land of beauty and eternal youth?"

How could I say no to a fellow perfume girl, especially one made to spout such a goofy line? I smiled at her and held out my wrist. She was impressed when I waved my arm for the alcohol to evaporate with no prompting from her. Then I sniffed my wrist and waited for the memory to bob up. It surfaced immediately, bringing something new this time; the woman at the closet, my mother presumably, was leaning over to put on stockings. I think she wobbled a bit as she adjusted a clasp on her garter belt. In the store, my own legs started to wobble and I said apologetically to the woman, "It's beautiful, but I can't afford it." She nodded her head like she understood, and I said, "I'm the perfume girl at Sheffield's."

"*Ohh*," she said, smiling widely. "Wait here."

She returned with a couple tiny samples of the perfume. I thanked her and told her Sheffields was pushing Moon Mist that week and that she should come by so I could return the favor.

Since my grandmother's death the previous year, I shared an apartment a couple miles from the store with two other girls. That night, I put the perfume sample on my night stand. I thought if I smelled it every night before I went to sleep and every morning as soon as I woke up, I'd piece together the memory and maybe it would tell me something about my mother. Aside from my own few recollections, all I knew about her I'd learned from my grandmother.

Grandmother. She had nurtured her anger at my mother through the years and often told me that if anyone asked, my mother was dead. While growing up, I had all kinds of questions which my grandmother didn't want to answer, but she did acknowledge a few things over the years. She told me my mother had a hard time recovering from my father's death, and was reluctant to begin dating again. When she did, she discovered that she was very admired. "Could have had her pick," was how Grandmther characterized it. There was one man in particular, James, who was insistent on being the only man in Mother's life and, unfortunately, he was the one my grandmother cared for least of all.

For starters, he was black. He had also been in Vietnam. My grandmother somehow felt this had something to do with my father's death. I don't know how. Like, maybe if James had died in Vietnam, her son would have come home instead. My father's military portrait hung in our living room, and I knew that my grandmother carried around the newspaper clipping of his obituary in her wallet. Every year, on the anniversary of his death, she had a special mass said for him. Growing up, I didn't know who was more of a ghost to me, my father or my mother.

My mother's dating James was a disgrace to my grandmother and, she argued, to my father's memory. I do remember the fights she and my mother had, my grandmother's hand slapping against the table, each of them shouting at the same time. My grandmother's high card was me. How could my mother disgrace her own child? Hadn't I gone through enough losing my father, and now my mother wanted to confuse me and lay me open to who knows what kind of abuse from people who also disapproved. My mother protested vehemently. If her husband's death had taught her anything, she said, it was that wars were fought because people didn't realize they were all alike. To this, my grandmother sneered. She said that she was nothing like Hitler, thank you very much, and my mother screamed back that James wasn't Hitler. My grandmother told me that she never in a million years believed my mother would leave town and marry James, but then she came home that day and found me on her couch and she didn't so much as blink an eye.

It's funny. James was in my life for such a short time, but I'll never forget him. I knew him for less than a year, but I felt I understood everything about him, and he understood me. He used to ring the doorbell over and over and my mother would let me run to answer it. Before he even stepped in the door, he held out two closed hands, but there was always candy in both. One time he brought me a paper parasol that I broke from opening and closing it too often. Another time he reached in his pocket and took out a few Mexican jumping beans that we watched jump off the window sill onto the floor. His voice was as deep as Brutus's in the Popeye cartoons, but it wasn't scary, it was funny. He laughed a lot, his "heh, heh, heh's" spilling out in sets of three over and over. And I remember that he called his car, an old blue station wagon, Maybelline. I thought it was the most beautiful name I'd ever heard, but I didn't understand why a car had a name.

I think my fixation with scents started with James. When he squeezed me around the waist and lifted me in the air, I breathed in his rich, sweet, smell, like grape jelly. I told him, "You smell like peanut butter and jelly," because I never ate jelly without peanut butter, and he said, "Yeah? You smell like Rice Krispies," or he'd say, "You smell like root beer." It was something different every time.

Young as I was, I had the strange knowledge that my grandmother wasn't the only one who didn't like James. Mother and James took me once to the soda fountain for ice cream and we sat in the cool vinyl booth for a long time, but the waitress never came over. We finally left and bought ice cream at the supermarket, taking it home to eat. Another time, James came with my mother to see a nursery school play in which I had a bit part, and the seat next to him remained empty even though people were standing in the back of the room and sitting in the aisles.

I started to carry a sample of Shangri La in my purse, taking it out to sniff several times a day. Then, two weeks after Ormond's promotion, Sheffield's followed suit and I was spraying it on customers. For days, I was surrounded by the scent, and pieces of the puzzle started to fall into place. I remembered more and more details about that memory, waking up one night with such a start, my breath stolen from deep within my chest, when it finally all came together. I still think about it. The thing about trying so hard to remember something is that once you do, you can't make it go away. No matter how hard you try, it'll always be there, following you around like some starving dog. So, for the rest of my life, I will remember this:

My mother is adjusting the clasp on her garter belt and I'm standing by the bed, reaching high so I can pat the mattress which rises above my head. The chenille ridges on the bedspread almost vibrate against my fingers as I run my hand back and forth faster and faster. My mother is humming a song, I don't know what, and replaces the cap on a perfume bottle. The smell of the perfume casts a pleasant feeling of anticipation over the room- James is coming over. There is a loud crash as something shoots through the window, blowing pieces of glass onto the bed and the floor. I watch the rock fly across the gray carpet, blending in with it, and my mother turns around in slow motion and shrieks. Her face is something horrible, like someone scared to death in a movie. I lift my hand from the bed and am confused when I see the blood dripping from me to the white bedspread. When my mother sees it, she hesitates for a moment before running to me, grabbing my other hand, and taking me into the bathroom. She sits me on the side of the sink and runs my hand under cold water that stings. She digs at my hand, making it hurt more and more, and I cry out and try to jerk my hand away. Finally, I feel my skin open up and she removes the glass, throwing it into the waste basket. The cold water doesn't bite as much now, and I realize that I can't smell the blood any more. My mother presses a towel against the cut, finally taping a large bandaid over it. She is mumbling under her breath, and I can't make out what she is saying, but always, later, when I remember this night, I hear her say that my grandmother was right.

What does blood smell like? At the time, I thought it smelled like a strange red berry with no sweetness, instead a mineral odor like the nickel I had sucked on once in church while waiting for them to pass the offerings basket. Now, as I went to work each day, I remained haunted by the smell of blood. I asked myself why the scent couldn't evaporate from my mind like alcohol from perfume.

"She made her choice," my grandmother said all those years. I grew up thinking my mother preferred James to me and I tried to hate her. Hate her as much as my grandmother did and seemed to think I should. But I always had my doubts. You read about parents who abandoned their children showing up later at graduations or some other public place, watching their son or daughter secretively, anonymously, grieving for the choice they made however many years ago. I always believed that my mother would do that, or that she would have done it if she had the chance. Shortly after she left, my grandmother retired and we moved to Toronto and lived with her friend, a woman I called Aunt Selma, until we got our own place. I was eleven or twelve when I first worried that my mother was looking for me but didn't know I was in Toronto. I wondered if she and James had gotten married, if they'd had children. But my grandmother, despite all her opinions and prejudices, was kind to me, and I liked living in a big city.

When my friends asked about my parents, I told them they had gone to Vietnam together and had died there, that my mother had been a nurse and my father a solider, and they were both dead. I could almost believe it myself. Once, when my grandmother listened to me repeating this story to a neighbor, she looked at me directly and put her arm around my shoulders saying, "Yes, they're dead." She patted my arm as if she were comforting me. Afterwards, whenever she mentioned my mother, she said things like, "Before she left with your father for Vietnam," or once even, "I wish I'd saved that letter she sent me from Saigon." I didn't challenge her—what difference did it make? I had come up with the story she liked, and, in her mind, she changed history. She was happy knowing her daughter-in-law, like her son, had given her life for her country.

My recollection of that night so long ago bothered me for weeks. It made things messy, opened doors that had long been shut, locked. I asked myself all kinds of things. Had my mother left me with my grandmother out of fear of further violence, violence that could hurt me? I couldn't forgive her for choosing James's' over me, but the thought of her wanting to protect me ate away at me, softened me. And what if she had tried to find me all those years, but couldn't? What if she were still trying to find me?

My performance at work, such as it was, suffered. I didn't sleep well at night, and I was tired during the day. I shifted my weight endlessly from one foot to another and hardly called out to the customers. One afternoon, Billy Sheffield caught me slouched against a display counter, one of my shoes slipped off, and he told me to straighten up and fly right or else. I hurried back to my position on the floor and realized a woman in her mid-forties had witnessed the reprimand and was now smiling at me sympathetically. I raised my bottle of Tulips, which smelled curiously more woodsy than flowery, and she politely held out her hand.

"Oh, that's nice," she said.

"It's available at counter three for just twenty-four ninety-five," I told her.

She smiled at me and I scanned her face, her clothes. She was a pretty woman with dark blue eyes and dark lashes. Her eyes were close together in that way that can be attractive. She was dressed in a polyester jacket and slacks. I knew right away that she couldn't afford the perfume.

"Maybe another day," she said and thanked me.

I saw that woman many times over the next several days. Sometimes getting on the elevator, other times just browsing the main floor. Always, she smiled at me, and one time, when I caught her eye as she just entered the floor, she waved at me as if we knew each other.

It occurred to me that I was the reason she was in the store so often. She was about the right age and her coloring was similar enough to my own. I had a couple photos of my mother, but they were so old, they had a non-descript quality about them. This woman seemed interested in me and I began to look for her each day. More often than not, I'd see her. She never came over and spoke with me again, but it was obvious that she looked in my direction every time she was in that part of the store.

The gamut of emotions I felt that week flung me up and down, left and right. Was I at last going to be reunited with my mother? Would I be disloyal to my grandmother by forgiving my mother for having left me all those years ago? I imagined what a perfume named Forgiveness would smell like, a neutral, honest scent that wouldn't be too strong or too weak.

On Friday afternoon of that week, the elevator bell sounded, and I watched the customers step out from the cubicle. I saw the woman; she was more dressed up than I had seen her previously. She wore a black, probably rayon, suit with a pink blouse that had a bow in the front. Her hair had been cut into a stylish bob and she looked younger. Our eyes met and she walked towards me. My heart beat became irregular and everything in the store became silent. I couldn't hear the people walking past me, the sales women talking, the music that was usually piped all over the main level.

As soon as she reached me, my ears flooded with the noises of the store and I strained to hear what she was saying to me. She was holding her hand out, introducing herself. Should I hug her? I was so confused, more so when I saw that she was already backing away, lifting her hand to say good-bye.

"Wait! Who did you say you were?"

She smiled and stepped forward again. "I'm Karen Tiffen. I was just hired as a part-time perfume girl, evenings and weekends."

"Perfume girl?"

"Perfume woman I like to call it," she said and winked at me.

"You were just hired?"

She shook her head yes and smiled broadly. "Mr. Sheffield hired me on the spot. Told me he thought I could increase sales with women my age."

She was kind, and I realized I must have seemed remote. "I've seen you in the store a lot lately," I said, trying to recover and sound friendly.

"You noticed," she said, nodding her head eagerly. "I was trying to get familiar with the whole store." She turned her head about, taking in the main level. "I thought it would help with the interview. I'm hoping," she said, glancing towards the accessories counter, "that I'll get to work in a real department before too long."

I nodded my head. My throat felt like a jar with a lid being clamped on it. "Good luck. Nice to meet you. What did you say your name was?"

"Karen. And you're Linda," she said reading my Sheffield's name tag. She waved and walked out of the store.

I had to find my mother. The encounter in the store made me realize that if I did nothing else with my life, I would find her. I went to the public library and looked at all the phone books. There was no Marie Salyers in any of the directories I looked at, but, of course, if she had married James, she'd have a new last name. Or would she? Was my mother a feminist? I didn't have a clue. And I didn't know James's last name, probably never did.

I talked with the reference librarian, a woman about thirty who asked me lots of questions and wrote things down as I spoke. I told her I couldn't afford to hire anyone to look for my mother, I had to do it myself. She suggested that I telephone veterans' associations in the Auburn area and ask about James's whereabouts. The library had a collection of phone books on microfiche, and the librarian helped me find a huge list of numbers.

I spoke to at least thirty people before speaking to a man who thought he remembered James.

"Big guy with glasses?" he asked me on the phone.

Glasses? It was too long ago to remember. I told him all I could, that James was a tall black man, well over six feet, that he'd fought in Vietnam in the late sixties, and that he lived in Auburn just after that. I explained that he was a friend of my mother's, but that didn't seem to matter to him. I wanted to tell him that James smelled like jelly, but that was crazy. Then I heard a low murmur at the other end of the line, and the man cleared his throat hesitantly.

"Say," he said, "is your mother a white woman?"

"Yes!" I shouted, excited, realizing I had failed to tell him the most helpful piece of information of all.

"Sure, sure," he said. "James Williams. I remember him and your mother at a VA dance. They sure shook up that little town." He laughed and

I felt peculiar, like he was laughing at me.

"How can I find out where he is now?"

The line was silent a moment and then the man said, "Oh, he's got to be listed somewhere. The VA keeps tabs on people. Give me your number and I'll call you back."

He didn't call back for two weeks and I gave up hope. Maybe this man was like my grandmother, maybe he too had disapproved of James and my mother and had no intention of trying to help me. When he called back, I was sure he didn't have any information, but he gave me a phone number for a James Williams in Albany. He wasn't sure it was the right man, it was a somewhat common name, but it was all he could come up with. I thanked him and he wished me luck.

I called the number right away because I knew I'd lose my nerve if I waited. I held my breath as the phone rang four times, wondering what I would do if a woman answered. Would I recognize my mother's voice? An answering machine came on and a woman's voice told me that the Williamses weren't at home, but to please leave a message. The voice was unfamiliar, a friendly, musical, black woman's voice. I hung up and sighed. Then, without thinking, I called again and this time I left a message:

"Hi. This is Linda Salyers. Mr. Williams, I don't know if you're the same James who dated my mother in Auburn, New York in the late sixties. I'm trying to track her down and would appreciate any help you can give me. I'm living in Toronto, and you could call me collect." I gave him my home phone number and told him he could also call me at Sheffields.

No one called back. I guessed that even if I had phoned the correct residence, James and my mother had probably broken up a long time ago, possibly on bad terms, and he probably had no idea where she was either. I had wild ideas about going on some talk show that reunites long lost relatives, my mother and I hugging on televisions all over Canada. But maybe she wouldn't come forward, and who needs that kind of rejection twice?

I went through all the things my grandmother had left me, boxes of old photos, books, pockets of clothing. I found my old grammar school report cards tucked into a copy of *Peyton Place*. I opened each of the books I kept in a box under my bed, fanning each page so the dust flew out. From *Profiles in Courage*, two small envelopes, yellowed at the corners, fell onto the floor. I opened up the first, a flaking, brittle newspaper clipping with a headline that read: *Woman Dies in Car Crash*. The short blurb beneath the headline said: *Marie Williams is dead at 28 after having been hit Friday night on Clemson Road. The driver of the other vehicle is an underage youth whose name is being withheld. Police stated that the youth was driving under the influence of alcohol and that charges would be pressed. Mrs. Williams's husband, James Williams, also in the car at the time of the accident, sustained no serious injuries.*

I wondered why I wasn't crying. I wanted to, but my insides felt like an empty box, something stolen from it, the lid left carelessly off. I would never find her. She would never find me. She had died soon after she had left me at my grandmother's. I had spent years wondering about a woman who didn't exist anymore.

The second envelope was folded twice. I opened it flat and read the address of my grandmother's house in Auburn. The postage markings indicated that the letter had been forwarded to Aunt Selma's house in Toronto. I removed the letter and read the bold penmanship, the ink smeared in many places:

Mrs. Salyers: I hope you will reconsider having Linda come and live with me. As you well know, it was my wife's and my intention to bring Linda to Albany once we were settled here. At the very least, I want to see her and talk with her about her mother. That is not too much to ask. Mrs. Salyers, please, grant me this.

It was signed James Williams. I dropped the newspaper clipping and the letter on the floor. My mother's death came at me and hit me with the force of a car that killed her. Twenty-eight! All those years my grandmother had simply said she was dead, she really was. And she had taken my silence, my complicity, as acceptance, but she was wrong. "Wrong!" I shrieked out loud, but there was no one left for me to scream at. I suspected that in her strange way, my grandmother had held James responsible for my mother's death. If she hadn't moved to Albany with him, she wouldn't have been in that car crash. And if James had been killed in Vietnam, her son would have come home. She always had someone to blame, but I had no one.

I stayed in bed for four days. My roommates thought I was seriously ill and begged me to eat. I ignored them, nibbling on soda crackers and drinking water. I didn't want to leave my room; I didn't think it would bother me if I never had contact with another person again.

But I had to get up. That Saturday, the store was having its fall clearance sale and I had to be there. I worried that Billy Sheffield was just looking for a reason to fire me. I would be spraying probably a dozen different kinds of perfumes that would be set up on a little table right near the entrance to the store. I had to be there.

The commotion of the store helped to distract me. I sprayed so many different perfumes I started to sneeze. Women were impatient, not wanting to wait for me to spray their wrists, so they picked up the bottles themselves while I attended to other customers. Over and over I said, "On sale at counter three. But we're running out. Hurry." I don't know why, but when I sprayed Shangri La on one older woman, I repeated the words that the Ormonds perfume girl had said to me, "Would you like to visit Shangri La, land of beauty and eternal youth?" As I watched the mist fly to her wrist, I realized that all my memories of my mother were in Shangri La, that every time I remembered something about her, it would be something summoned from my childhood.

At mid-day, I was very hungry, but Billy had told me I couldn't take a break until two. The heady mix of scents was starting to make me feel light-headed, and I wondered how long I could last on my feet. The doors to the store opened and a fresh throng of customers lunged towards me. Finally, at two, I replaced the cap on every single bottle of perfume. I started to lift the little table and carry it out of sight when a tall man in a leather coat stepped forward, saying "Let me help you with that. A pretty thing like you shouldn't be lugging heavy stuff around." As I said thank you, I studied his face. He smiled expectantly and held out two hands in front of him. Before I stumbled, falling forward and knocking two perfume bottles to the floor where they shattered almost soundlessly, James said to me, "You are the *very* image of your mother."

THE MARSHALL ISLANDS

John Hammond was amused by the food. Standing on his son and daughter-in-law's patio, he surveyed the vegetable skewers cooking on the grill. The colorful wedges of red and yellow peppers flanking little pillows of tofu were worthy of a photograph in a glossy magazine. The array of salads on the outdoor table included couscous and vegetables whipped up in a mango chutney, and a bowl of scissored cabbage marinated in a blend of citrus juices.

When Steve called to invite him to the barbecue, John had recalled such gatherings when he was about his son's age. The couples in their group ate hamburgers and hot-dogs, steaks when their salaries started to go up. Debbie, his former wife, used to make a macaroni salad with tuna and black olives that everyone was mad for. There was always a messy tray of condiments: ketchup, mustard, mayonnaise, and pickle relish inevitably spilled. The highlight of the meal would be hot corn on the cob served with lots of butter and salt.

Taking in the couples in Steve's yard, John wondered how alike, how different they were from their counterparts in the late fifties and early sixties. In appearance, the men hadn't changed at all. Their pates were framed by bangs brushed back over their foreheads, the hair on the sides and back of their heads clipped short. In 1961, John was emulating President Kennedy's hair style; who was his son's crowd imitating? Their clothes made him nostalgic too, khakis and Oxford shirts, penny loafers.

The girls here tonight were dazzling. *Girls,* he'd get in trouble if he said that word aloud. Women, he reminded himself, they're women even if they're young enough to be my daughters. Every one of them was stunning in some way that reached out at him, tantalized him and ultimately depressed him. Tall and sleek and tan, they were groomed and sophisticated. Auburn-haired Katie Gleeson was especially appealing, her full lips coated with some cosmetic that made them look wet, like she'd just been kissed. John had no trouble picking out her husband, Jay, the former frat boy with a big smile plastered across his face. All the women wore shift dresses in bright colors except Katie who wore a murky indigo dress that wrapped across her ample breasts. When she stood up from her chair and walked to the grill, John noticed the way the back of her dress held the shape of her bottom for a moment, the womanly orbs gradually disappearing into the fabric.

In his day, women wore dresses that were cinched at the waist and flared out over their thighs and knees. You had no idea what a girl's derriere looked like. In the early sixties, some of them started wearing black Capri trousers, certainly form-fitting, but by then most of the women had been through a few pregnancies and preferred looser-fitting clothing. They had worn their hair flipped up or flipped under at the neck, a perky style so different from the long straight locks he saw tonight. His daughter-in-law, Ashley, was the exception with a page-boy with blunt edges that reminded him of Prince Valiant from the old comic strip.

But the biggest difference between then and now was children, the lack of them at this party. There wasn't a child too close to the grill or vomiting in the bathroom because he ate too many raw hot-dogs. The wives weren't retiring to the house to change a diaper or get more juice for a toddler.

The subject of children did surface, however, while they were eating dinner. John had decided the mango chutney was pretty tasty when Ashley asked the oldest couple there, the Holms, how things were progressing with their adoption.

"Oh, we should hear any time now," Julie answered, clasping her knees and raising her shoulders. Her husband, Tom, looked at his wife and nodded. He was clearly excited, but there was something else in his expression too—relief, relief that there was finally going to be a baby. The Holms looked about mid-thirties, old enough to have been on the infertility treadmill. The younger couples looked at them admiringly, sensing the chapter of their own lives that hadn't started yet, that might commence at any time.

"Are you both traveling?" Katie asked.

"Yes," the Holms answered in unison. Tom continued, "We've packed so much for the baby we'll need a whole plane to carry it over there."

John considered asking where they were traveling to (would it be rude?), when Steve turned to him and explained, "They're going to the Marshall Islands to bring home their baby son."

"Oh, wonderful, wonderful." John stirred his drink and asked, "Will you get to do any sightseeing?"

Julie nodded. "We're bringing a video camera so we can film as much as possible. We want Samuel to see the video when he's older." She smiled broadly, anticipating the group's approval, and said, "That's the name we've chosen. Samuel."

There were high-pitched female exclamations of delight. The men were more quietly approving. Obviously there'd been a baby shower recently because the Holms were thanking everyone again for all the gifts. Julie praised Tom's remodeling of a study in their house into a baby room. "There's this *adorable* reading nook with a window seat and big cushions. And we have an Amish rocking chair on order."

Ashley was particularly interested, asking questions about the age of the baby and how much maternity leave Julie was taking from her job at a publishing firm. When Julie told them that the baby would be six months old when they'd arrive home, Ashley asked excitedly, "What are babies doing at six months? Are they sleeping through the night? Are they eating solid food?"

Rarely had John seen his daughter-in-law so animated. She tended to be a bit of a wallflower. Glancing at her abdomen, he wondered if his first grandchild might be on the way. A grandchild. Well, wasn't life something. When his son went into the house to get more ice, John followed him.

Watching Steve fill the ice bucket, he thought, that's one thing that hasn't changed, this generation drinks as much as ours did. He wondered if he should be concerned that Steve had never appeared without a drink in his hand this evening. Were we just drinking beer at their age or were we setting up a bar in the back yard? Wistfully, John remembered how fun it was drinking cocktails with friends, at least those first few years. Then they noticed that Hal Cromby couldn't drink without getting drunk. At one party he started weeping and told everyone that he'd lost his job. The Crombys were the first in their group to divorce.

John had also noticed that no one smoked tonight. Well, that was a change. His memories of young married life were conjured through the ever-present spirals of gray-white smoke. Part of cleaning up after any party was emptying and washing the ashtrays. He and Debbie both smoked and most of their friends did too. The women practiced blowing smoke rings over their pregnant bellies, the stubs of the cigarettes kissed with festive shades of lipstick. They had all tried to quit smoking and some of them had succeeded. John managed to stop for months at a time, but always went back to it. Now he felt foolish about chewing that damn nicotine gum and his fingers ached to hold a cigarette.

He took in a raft of air and said to his son, "That's wonderful news about your friends adopting a baby."

"Yeah." Steve snapped the lid on the ice bucket and turned to leave. When he realized his father wasn't following, he turned back. "They've wanted a baby for a long time and then they found this adoption agency that has contacts in the Marshall Islands."

"That's great." John could feel a smile brimming on his lips, bubbly anticipation branching throughout his limbs. When Steve just stared blankly back at him, he finally asked, somewhat quietly, "Is there any news about a baby in your household?"

A short, guttural sound flew from Steve's throat as he set the ice bucket down on the counter. John imagined a shard of ice flying from the bucket and piercing his eye. Involuntarily, he closed it, now squinting at his son. Pulling his shoulders back, Steve challenged, "Why do you ask that?"

Wishing he hadn't brought up the subject, John stammered, then said, "Oh, I don't know. Ashley seemed very interested in the baby. I just wondered." He pretended to cough, lowering his face to cover his mouth with his hand. "Don't mean to pry. Forget I asked."

Steve spread his hands out on the kitchen Formica. He began to tap his fingers, his wedding ring clinking against the counter. "We're not in any rush. I mean, we want to do a better job than our parents did with kids."

Here it comes again, John thought wearily. And he had given Steve such an opening, an invitation for this harangue. He nodded perfunctorily, his gesture meaning: of course, of course, I understand I did the unforgivable when I divorced your mother when you were thirteen and re-married.

"You know the divorce was hell on me, Dad. Ashley had a terrible time too when her father walked out. We want a solid relationship before we start having children."

Studying the cornflower blue linoleum, John again nodded. "Good plan," he murmured. The floor was spotless. Did Ashley get down on her hands and knees and scrub it, like Debbie had, or did she have a cleaning lady?

"Dad?"

"Yes?"

Steve's eyebrows sailed upwards and his eyes pulled back. When he opened his mouth to speak, the corners of his mouth extended well beyond his teeth. "Sometimes I wonder what you parents were *thinking* in the fifties. Having all those kids. And then all the marriages busting up. Why did you have so many kids?"

We didn't have the pill! John wanted to protest, but he couldn't, not to his third of four children. He couldn't tell his son that not only did he divorce his mother, but that he and Debbie had only wanted two children. "Times were different," he said simply.

Shaking his head, Steve said, "They must have been. I mean, I'm twenty-eight. At my age you already had Katherine and Mike. I can't even imagine being a father right now and you had two kids."

John shrugged his shoulders. "So did everyone else on the block. We were all in the same boat."

"That's just what I mean!" Steve's cheeks flushed, circular pools of red rising up through his tan. "No one thought about what they were doing. They just went ahead and did it." He waved his arms to indicate the absurdity of it. "I mean, talk about irresponsible!"

John nodded and waited for his son to finish. Maybe the tirade was over. But then Steve added, "I'd never want a son of mine to feel like I did when you left Mom. *God!* It was like someone had ripped my skin off and I couldn't hold myself together."

After all these years, John still felt the pressure in his breast bone, the pressure he had first felt when telling the children that he was leaving. He looked at his watch and told Steve, "I'm glad you've thought all this through." He coughed, then added, "You and Ashley will be wonderful parents."

"You're not leaving now, are you?"

"Leaving?"

"You checked your watch." His tone was accusing.

"Oh, no. I was just wondering what time it is."

"Because another guest is coming that Ashley and I want you to meet. Our neighbor from down the street, Meredith Downing. She's stopping by for dessert. She's about your age."

Trying not to groan was difficult. John hoped his brief smile didn't look like a wince. "Setting your old man up?" He punched Steve's shoulder lightly and then realized that this sort of thing wasn't part of their father-son repartee.

Steve turned and walked across the kitchen floor. "You'll like her. She's got great legs. You're a leg man, right Dad?"

John didn't know how to respond to this, and he didn't have to since the screen door shut with a slicing sound.

Leg man. Well, yes, it was true. Trudy, his second wife, had long, shapely legs. She played tennis, and watching her dive about the court in a scant tennis dress had transfixed him. When Debbie first confronted him with her suspicion of the affair, she had said angrily, "What is it about Trudy? Those legs? Because it's not her brain, that's for damn sure!"

Debbie was smart. John had done passably well at Harvard, but she was a Phi Beta Kappa Radcliffe grad. He thought about her these days, wondered about her a lot actually. Especially since he had retired. Of all the women he had known, Debbie was probably the one who had the most interesting outlook on aging, these idle years before death. She would have talked about it with him, made it interesting instead of frightening.

Her father had been a Unitarian minister in Cambridge. John's initial discomfiture over dating a minister's daughter quickly vanished when he met Debbie's parents, politically liberal people with no belief in an afterlife. They seemed to be fearless.

But John was full of fears. During those last years of his first marriage, he feared loss of youth and what lay beyond that. Illicit sex with Trudy had rejuvenated him, his heartbeat the pulse of life again, not a reminder of mortality. He couldn't divorce Debbie fast enough, but the second marriage lasted only three years.

Everyone agreed that the divorce had seared Steve. His other children coped, but after the separation announcement Steve had wandered the house red-eyed and disbelieving. John couldn't bear to be in the same room with his younger son, his adolescent grief was so palpable. He and Debbie sent him to a therapist who advised Steve to voice his feelings. Then he began asking ghastly questions like, "Why do you love Trudy more than Mom? How can you go live with her kids when they're not even yours? Isn't our family good enough for you?" They were questions he didn't allow himself to contemplate, much less respond to. He shook his head and said, "You know how much I love you, right? This has nothing to do with you." On one occasion, Steve flung his arms forward, his clenched hands hitting John's chest, and hollered, "This has *everything* to do with me!" He fled the room sobbing.

On the patio, Ashley was piling plates and tossing used napkins into a garbage can. John walked over and stood across the picnic table from her. As she leaned forward to wipe crumbs off the table, the front of her dress folded and provided him a glimpse of her cleavage. Her delicate, very white breasts swelled just below her tan line. Her nipples, small but extended, seemed like Ashley herself, vulnerable, waiting to be noticed. John averted his eyes. "Need some help?" he offered.

"Oh, no. Just relax and enjoy yourself."

Despite her words, she sounded resentful. Across the yard, in front of the plum tree, Julie and Katie were deep in conversation, their heads tilted so it appeared their noses were touching. In the middle of the yard, Jay, the former frat boy, was demonstrating a mock golf swing to the other men. Perhaps he should join them, John thought, but walking away from Ashley, leaving her alone as the other guests had, would be awkward. He stayed although he knew his presence irked her.

Ashley stayed busy smoothing down the tablecloth. John imagined that she had probably heard a lot of bitter remarks about himself from Steve. Maybe she blamed John for the disappointments she had with her husband, surely she had some after two years of marriage. Watching as she gathered the used silverware into a Tupperware bin, John wished he could blurt, "I couldn't *breathe* in that marriage. I had to get out. Don't you see? I had to!"

Ashley lifted her head and grinned, a bizarre response to his inner thoughts. Why, she's so pretty when she smiles, he thought, and felt oddly grateful to her for her pleasant expression. Then he realized that she was looking past him. Turning, he saw a woman coming around the side of the house and into the yard.

"Meredith!" Ashley greeted her.

"It's me!" the woman called back exuberantly. At first John could only gaze at her dress, a pink and green shift. The colors were neon and assaulting and seemed to plant the woman into the green lawn and flower beds. Her head was dull in comparison with short gray hair and pale skin. But no, not entirely pale; in that face was a screaming pink crease, her lips coated to match the roses in the fabric of dress. Ashley wrapped her arms around her and the woman hugged her back. She patted Ashley on the back before she released her.

"That dress is yummy," Ashley said.

"Thanks. It's one of my favorites. So nice to be able to buy Lily Pulitzer again."

"This is Steve's father, John Hammond," Ashley told her.

The woman held out her hand and after a long moment, John said, "Oh, yes," and shook it.

"Meredith lives down the street," Ashley continued. "She's been advising me about re-decorating the living room and the study."

Hopefully the woman wasn't advocating pink and green slip covers for the furniture. "How neighborly," he said. She smelled heavily of lavender. Yardley soap, he thought, remembering Debbie always kept a bar in the bathroom.

"Oh, she doesn't need any help," Meredith insisted. "Ashley has an intuitive sense of style. I just love to look at swatches of material."

"You do a lot more than that," Ashley politely admonished, tapping the woman on the forearm. "Steve! Meredith is here," she called.

Steve was ebullient, calling out, "Mer-re-dith!" in punctuated syllables. "We were beginning to wonder where you were." He walked over and kissed the woman on the cheek. John flinched. Why did this woman deserve such filial affection? Did he greet his own mother in this manner?

Steve extended his arm to indicate John. "Did you meet my father?"

"We just met," she said buoyantly. "I hadn't gotten around to telling him that I'd heard so much about him."

John perfunctorily chuckled and pretended to be kidding when he said, "Uh-oh."

Meredith wagged a finger at him and said, "Yes, John, I know all about you, so you'd better be nice to me." Ashley and Steve laughed as if her words were original and highly amusing.

John, however, was incredulous. This woman was chastening and flirtatious at the same time. What was she expecting? Did she think, did Steve and Ashley actually think that something was going to come of this encounter? As if on cue, the younger couple joined their guests in the yard on the pretense of freshening drinks, and he was left alone with the presumptuous neighbor. Although John normally made conversation easily, he decided that he wasn't going to make an effort. This woman didn't need encouraging. After a silent moment, Meredith said, as if assessing him, "So, you're retired from estate law and now you're playing a lot of golf."

He paused, then said, "That about sums it up. And you?"

The flicker of disappointment in her eyes clued him in that she expected he already knew, that Steve and Ashley had spoken of her. Had they? Had they said something that John had forgotten?

"I used to run my own flower shop. Sold it two years ago."

Nodding, John said, "You were a florist."

"Yes, a florist and lots of other things too. Jack of all trades you might say."

"You don't say," John answered, realizing that he was simply echoing her words. Clearly she wanted to expand on her hobbies, or whatever, but he wasn't going to give her an opening. Instead he said, "Can I get you a drink?"

"Yes," she said fully, heartening.

"What would you like? They've got everything set up in the kitchen. Why don't you relax and I'll bring it out."

"No, I'll come with you," she said simply. "I'm not sure what I'd like yet."

John held the kitchen door for her and she placed her hand on his forearm as she stepped into the house. Surveying the bottles on the counter, she said, "Oh, perhaps a white wine spritzer."

He busied himself with the drink. After giving it to her, he was going to walk back outside and join the other guests. He wanted to send a clear message to his son that he didn't want to be left alone with this woman.

"Do you like the new carpet?"

"Carpet?" He slipped the rubber wine-saver into the bottle.

"Yes, in the living room. You did see it, didn't you?" Again, she was admonishing, teasing.

Slowly, appearing as if he were trying to recall, John said, "Maybe, maybe."

She motioned, her index finger curled back over and over. "Come take a peek. But we shouldn't step on it since we're wearing shoes."

They stood together at the edge of the kitchen peering into the living room. The slate blue carpet had been recently vacuumed, its pile arranged in elongated swirls.

"I think I've seen that before. They've had it a few months, haven't they?"

She laughed and tapped his chest lightly. "No, they just got it last week. The old carpet was beige, remember?"

John didn't remember the old carpet or this one either apparently. Again she tapped his chest and said, "You men! The sky could be falling, but as long as it didn't interrupt your golf game, you wouldn't notice!"

"Do you play golf?" he asked, but immediately wished he hadn't. She was probably already planning a foursome with Steve and Ashley.

Thankfully, she said, "Not well. My late husband was on the links three times a week." She stared expectantly at John and finally said, "I'm a widow." She took a small sip of her drink and said, "He was a good deal older than me. His death was expected but still sad, of course."

John nodded and mumbled, "Sorry." He was going to ask if she had children, but then the kitchen door opened and closed. John turned to see Katie, the beautiful guest, entering the house. Carrying an empty wine glass, she stopped at the counter and poured her drink. "Okay, you two," she said, "I'm supposed to come in and tell you that dessert is being served." She looked up and smacked her full lips. "Ashley's strawberry shortcake is the best. Homemade biscuits to die for. She's dishing it up now."

"Oh, it is good!" Meredith said. She looked up at John, ready to admonish him again and said, "You have had it, haven't you?" He couldn't bear another question. "Tell her I'll be right out, will you? I need to use the bathroom." She can't follow me in there, he thought.

Meredith looked crestfallen, but Katie said to her, "Ashley told me she needs your help with something."

"Oh, of course. Right away." As Meredith walked briskly across the kitchen floor, John noticed her calves. They were thin but muscular, nicely formed. But when she turned, he saw it, the bulging varicose vein snaking up one side of her leg. The vein was as dark as a black telephone cord, round and thick on her skin. He was repulsed. What had Steve meant when he said Meredith had great legs? Was it a mean joke, what? She disappeared through the door.

Katie interrupted his thoughts, whispering, "Hope I didn't intrude.

I thought you could use a rescue." She smiled conspiratorially, the center of her lips dipping mischievously.

Delighted, John whispered back, "Thank you!" He pointed outside and continued, "Did Ashley really need help?"

Smiling, Katie shrugged her shoulders. "I'm sure she'll find something for Meredith to do. Fold the napkins or slice the biscuits."

Astute girl. He asked her, "You know Meredith?"

When she rolled her eyes John saw how lovely her brown irises were, especially with her auburn hair. "She comes over and begs me to join the Newton Ladies Garden Association," Katie sneered. "Like I don't have anything better to do than trim the hedges outside the town hall. But I don't have to worry any more. She gave up on me once she saw all the weeds in my back yard."

"Lucky you."

She laughed and her sound was low, sensuous. "Yeah," she said, "you better watch out. You look like her next project."

He shook his head. "Not if I have anything to say about it," he answered, wishing he had said something wittier.

But she tossed her head and laughed. "We better get out there. She'll get jealous of me monopolizing you."

It was just talk, clearly it was just talk, but he felt the fluttering behind the zipper of his pants, his penis rising like a question mark.

The young people were seated around the picnic table. Ashley stood at one end pouring juicy crushed strawberries onto biscuits while Steve passed out plates. Meredith pronounced, "That looks positively decadent," and paused dramatically before adding, "I can't wait." Then she laughed loudly and scanned the faces of the other diners to make sure they were laughing too. As John took a seat at the other end of the table, she called out to him, pretending to be reprimanding, "I hear *you* have a sweet tooth."

"Is that so?" John glanced at Steve and wondered just what this woman didn't know about him.

She nodded as if challenging his protest and said, "I've heard all about your fondness for German chocolate cake, so don't try to fool me."

German chocolate cake, his favorite. Debbie used to make it on his birthday. When he had braved asking Trudy if she had a recipe for it, she had laughed and said, "Shouldn't have left little Betty Crocker."

Slowly, Katie turned her head towards him and, out of sight of the other diners, made her eyes comically large. He braved a quick wink at her and said breezily, "I haven't had German chocolate cake in years. These days I'm more of a strawberry shortcake man. Ashley, that looks terrific."

Scooping a dollop of whipped cream onto the dessert, Ashley almost smiled and said, "I hope it is." She turned to Steve and handed him the plate. "Pass that to your father. I made a ton so everyone have seconds."

Amid compliments about the dessert, the discussion of the adoption resumed. Meredith asked, "Which of the islands is your son on?"

"He's on Kili Island," Tom said. "We're learning about the Island from the Internet."

Arching her head down the table, Meredith asked John, "Do you know about the Marshall Islands?"

What is this, a quiz? He chewed on his biscuit and shrugged his shoulders. "Not much. Just that there was nuclear testing on Bikini Atoll after World War Two."

"I just learned that," Julie said. "To be honest, I'd never even heard of the Marshall Islands until we began the adoption process." Her husband laughed, saying, "Right, but now we could probably write a book about that part of the world." Julie nodded vigorously.

"Then you know about the horrible things that were done to the people of Bikini?" Meredith looked briefly at the Holms and then to the right to see if John was listening.

Julie faltered, "You mean the nuclear testing?"

"And the re-location." Meredith set down her fork and leaned over the table. "Because of the testing, all of the islanders were re-located from Bikini to another island. It hasn't been safe for them to go back, but they want to." She gave a lengthy sigh. "They might have to scrape the top soil off the island to get rid of the contamination. After all these years, the island is still *toxic*." As she spoke the final word, John noticed how long and narrow her teeth were, and alarmingly white. She probably was one of those people who bleached her teeth.

The table was silent although Meredith resumed eating. Julie glanced at her husband and said softly, "Samuel's island is hundreds of miles from Bikini. He's safe." Immediately Tom extended his arm around her and began rubbing her shoulder.

"Yes, but his grandparents and ancestors were native Bikinians." Meredith shook her head and looked down at the table. "I can't imagine what that would be like. Losing your home like that. Not just your home, but your whole world. Just think, those people lost their *en-ti-re* world."

"Tell me about it," Steve said, his words slurred enough to let John and everyone else know he was drunk. Ashley's complexion reddened and she hurriedly said, "Who wants seconds?"

John felt stabbed by love for his son. He wanted to stand and embrace him, apologize not just for the divorce, but for everything he'd ever done wrong in his entire life. He stared at his hands in his lap.

Julie lowered her face into her hands and suppressed a sniffle. "Sometimes I wonder if we're doing the right thing. Taking Samuel from his people and bringing him here."

Embarrassed, Tom glanced briefly at the other guests before saying quietly, "He doesn't have a family, honey. We can give him that."

The other guests squirmed nervously. John looked directly at Meredith and asked, "How do you know so much about the Marshall Islands?" Angry, he wanted to dismiss whatever credentials she had, make her realize she knew nothing.

Chirpily, Meredith answered, as if a woman wasn't crying at the table, "I traveled there with my late husband. He flew in the Pacific during the World War II and always wanted to visit there. So one year for our anniversary, we went to Ronjerik and Kili Islands. It was fascinating. The sunsets are just spectacular. I still remember—"

"Ashley, is that offer for seconds still good? I'd love some more." John held out his plate.

Meredith held her mouth open for five seconds before finally closing it. She turned her gaze away from John and pressed her lips together.

"Me too!" Katie exclaimed. "Count me in for seconds."

He felt flooded with gratitude for this gorgeous woman's approval. If he were twenty, even fifteen years younger, John would have placed his foot on hers, initiated the coy flirting that went on at barbecues in his day.

Katie's husband, Jay, belched into his hand and asked, "Hey, were bikini bathing suits invented on Bikini Island?"

Smoothing the tears off her cheeks, Julie shook her head. "No," she said, starting to laugh, her husband's face looking hopeful. "I think some French designer stole the name for his bathing suit when the nuclear testing was going on there."

"I believe the bikini is very popular in that part of the world now,"

Meredith said, her eyes resting again on John. Her voice, however, had lost its color and she spoke in a monotone. "Many of those islands are exotic resorts these days. Quite a bit of deep sea diving goes on there."

"You don't say," John said. He glanced at Steve and saw that his son was sitting with his chin cupped in his hand. His eyelids looked heavy and John wondered if he was drifting off to sleep.

John was supposed to volunteer to walk Meredith home, he knew, but he glued himself to his daughter-in-law and helped her scrape and stack the dessert plates. He raved about the meal and Ashley seemed happy, happy enough to let him assist.

The Holms departed, their arms cradling each other's waists as they left the yard. Steve walked Meredith to the end of their driveway, returning with a scowl, saying, "Way to go, Dad."

He looked up innocently. "Pardon me?"

His sons hands were determinedly in their pockets. "Do you think you could have been any ruder to Meredith?" His speech was no longer slurred. Indignation had cleared his head.

Collecting the silver ware, John placed it into a plastic tumbler before looking up and saying, "She's a very nice person, Meredith. Lovely. But I'm seeing someone and didn't want to give her the wrong impression."

He glanced at the table wishing there was something more to clean up. He felt the look exchanged between Steve and Ashley and decided to collapse some of the folding chairs on the patio.

"You don't want to give anyone the wrong impression, do you, Dad?" Steve followed him to the edge of the patio. "Hey, turn around. I'm talking to you."

Quickly, John spun on his heel, stood eye to eye with his son and said stealthily, "What do you want?"

Steve's face contorted and his breath felt hot on John's face. His son was thinking of what to say, of what words he was going to spew at John. But then his face crumpled and he whispered, exhausted, "What do I want? Why don't you ever know?" He turned and walked to the house, his steps slightly unbalanced.

John started to follow and was surprised when Ashley put a flat hand on his chest. "Don't. Let it go," she said, her voice unexpectedly forceful.

She turned from him and began to pull the tablecloth from one end. Her back sloped and she looked burdened as she wrapped the cloth into a small bundle.

As offhand as he could, John asked, "Can I help you load the dishwasher?"

"No, no," she said, formal again. Katie's already started that. Why don't you keep Jay company?

John looked and saw Jay sprawled in one of the big wooden chairs in the back of the yard. His legs were stiff in front of him, a baseball cap pulled low over his eyes. Without saying anything more to his daughter-in-law, John walked silently towards the kitchen door.

Through the screen, he saw Katie bent over the dishwasher, arranging plates and glasses so they fit snugly. He could hear her humming the tune of an old Beatles' song. He could remember twisting to that song when he was in his twenties, his knees bending in one direction, his hips in the other.

Putting his hand on the doorknob, John hesitated when he saw Steve enter the kitchen from the living room. His son wasn't quite whispering when he said, "I can't wait until we can do it on the new carpet."

Katie stood straight and murmured something John couldn't hear. She placed her finger over her lips and they started whispering. Her voice warbled and he thought he heard her say, "But he's so sweet."

"Watch out," Steve said, "he's a letch."

She spoke too clearly now, saying "Like father, like son." Steve mumbled something and Katie put her finger to her lips again. "Quiet," she whispered. She looked towards the door but John knew he was invisible in the darkness. He watched as this woman pulled his son toward her, her hand on the back of his neck, Steve's mouth meeting those full, wet lips.

CITIZEN

At the end of every academic year, when the students pack up to leave Hancock College, there's always a bunch of junior faculty members preparing to leave as well. These departures have varying impact on those who stay behind. Least affected are the oldest professors. For several years their attitude has been, "Why bother to get to know the new kids on the block when they'll be gone before you know it?" Others wince; a particular senior assistant professor may have been a rising star in a hot new specialty, might have brought huge grant money to the College. These wincing professors are sometimes jealous; they wish they were up and coming, sought after by other academic institutions.

Personally, the exodus of the junior faculty each year saddens me; I always lose a couple of good friends. We'll stay in touch for a year or two, e-mail each other, text occasionally. Last summer my boyfriend, Daniel, a European historian, moved to New York to teach at Bard. We tried to keep the romance going but long distance relationships are doomed. After a year of intermittent visits and frightening credit card statements, we called it quits. I befriend members of the new academic crop each year but know that the friendships are probably short-lived. And each year, as I head towards my own tenure decision, I become closer to becoming one of *them*, the people who are anchored here forever.

Stefan and Natasha Tetrov were a little more exotic than most new couples in town. She was hired a couple years back as a senior assistant professor in the Soviet Studies program and he was her authentic Russian husband whom, it was rumored, she had married so he could get his green card.

Natasha was just *dying* to be Russian. I laughed when I learned she was from Fort Wayne and that her real name was Nancy Schneider. She had changed it to Natasha when she studied in Kiev during graduate school. She wore an enormous fur hat in the winter along with folksy hand-knitted leg warmers under her dresses. While sipping tea at Bidwell's Cafe, she made a show of reading *Prada*, loudly creasing and re-creasing the newspaper every time she turned a page.

Stefan's specialty was translations of Lithuanian poetry into Russian, and that was far too specialized for little Hancock College. Often adjunct arrangements are made for the faculty spouses, but Stefan was on his own. After their son, Ilia, was born, people just assumed Stefan would stay home with the baby while Natasha would continue to teach full-time and add to her impressive publishing record. I considered it bad luck that we were up for tenure together this year. She was a research star in a sexy subject and I was one more woman teaching French, all but a cliché.

Secretly, I hoped Natasha would leave like so many others had. She irritated me with her Russian posturing which was escalating all the time. She began wearing her hair in braids pinned around the front and back of her head. Her long dour dresses were shapeless sacks of gray and brown, and she wore odd boots with hook and eye fastenings. Her unspoken message proclaimed, "I am a stoical, suffering Russian woman. Look at me with awe and fascination." And, of course, her power-to-the-people-Marxism meshed well with our campus climate of severe political correctness. The students considered her worldly, a role model. There was always a wait list to enroll in her classes whereas I looked out over a sea of empty desks.

I was surprised to find that she didn't turn all of the Hancock faculty off. Usually my opinion on such matters runs mainstream, but Natasha had bewitched everyone. At a particularly catty dinner party, the faculty instead sharpened their knives for Stefan: "She's such a star and he's such a disappointment," Elise Rupple announced as she refilled everyone's glass of wine. I had inwardly groaned when her husband, Simon, extended the dinner invitation to me, but he's the chair of the French department so it behooves me to show up at his soirées.

"Well," Simon said, wanting to appear a generous host, "Stefan's field *is* rather specialized. Estonian poetry. Hard to make a living out of that."

"I thought it was Armenian poetry," Ned Siddons slurred out. He was already three sheets to the wind but we were pretending not to notice.

His poor wife, Anne, was so embarrassed that she kept jumping up to help serve the food as if in compensation for her husband's inebriated state.

With a forced grin, I said, "And I thought he translated Lithuanian poetry!" We all giggled at our confusion, but I knew I was right. The chandelier over our table cast a star-pattern shadow against the white tablecloth. The two candles ensconced in heavy glass cubes in the center only had an inch left before their flames would expire. It was that comfortable time between dinner and dessert when the guests realized that they could leave in half an hour to an hour. Soon, they'd be making their excuses about having to relieve baby-sitters or having to get up early for church the next morning. We were close to the end of the evening so spirits were rising. Everyone was settling in for a good character assassination.

"I know this is shallow of me," Elizabeth Shrilly, the former Dean's wife, said, straining to sound apologetic, "but doesn't Stefan Tetrov look terribly. . .*odd*?"

Every guest, excluding myself, erupted with laughter. Elizabeth, Liz to those in her inner circle, was clearly encouraged by the mirth around the table and began to speak in more exaggerated tones. "I mean, that *pe-cuul-iar* hat with the brim that comes out to *here*," she said, holding her hands as far from her forehead as they could reach. "And those vests that—" She couldn't continue because she was choking with laughter. When Elise joined her, Elizabeth nodded her head at her and said, "Have you seen them? Don't they look like he stole them from some gypsy? They're orange and black and purple and I don't know what! When he and Natasha came for the new faculty barbecue, I told Herb to hide the good silver."

This set off several choruses of laughter and I couldn't stand it; I excused myself and went to the bathroom to smoke a cigarette. It took some jiggling to get the window open, but I wouldn't have dared smoke in an unventilated room. People have probably lost tenure over less.

At least when I came back, they were no longer dishing Stefan; instead they were praising Natasha. I couldn't believe they made fun of her husband's clothes but found her outfits "authentic" and "original." Herb Shrilley, who almost never said a word while he was Dean and even less since, stated that her analysis of *Prada*'s coverage of glasnost was about to be published in *Soviet Studies Quarterly*.

"Have you been in Natasha's office?" Sheila McClellan, a senior colleague of mine in French, asked. Not waiting for an answer, she said, too

slowly, as if unveiling a priceless painting, "She has *two* pieces of the Berlin wall that she uses for bookends."

The dinner party was awestruck. Nothing could top this, not even Ned Siddons slowly drifting under the table until only his chin held him in place.

"Really!" Simon exclaimed, "bookends! I wish I had a pair. Just think! What used to divide people is now supporting books. It's a metaphor, really, isn't it?"

Oh, *pleeez*. I wondered if the bookends really were from the Berlin Wall. I certainly wouldn't put it past Natasha to have found a pair of rocks somewhere, sprayed them with graffiti and voila! Berlin bookends.

Before standing to slice the cheesecake, Elise said, "Natasha has done so much to understand her husband's culture, and he hasn't made the slightest effort to learn English. If you ask me, that's not fair."

Was it the cheesecake that gave her some higher authority that caused everyone to agree with her? Did they think they wouldn't get a piece if they protested? I wanted to disagree, to shout out something, but I didn't. Instead I was so quiet I could hear that slight ringing noise I have in my left ear. The cheesecake, dense and slick, stopped my mouth, and I sat there feeling as if I had betrayed poor Stefan with my silence. Poor misunderstood Stefan, my lover.

The first time I realized that Stefan could speak some English was in early autumn last year. On Tuesdays and Thursdays, my first class didn't start until eleven o'clock. I liked to work at home in the mornings and then take a leisurely walk to campus. I was just about to turn the corner of my street when I saw them, Stefan and Ilia. Ilia was sitting in what looked like a sled, but it was more elaborate than that, a beautiful wooden seat with sides, arm rests, and a back, the whole thing pulled by a fat braid of coarse rope. There were blades on the bottom, just like on a traditional sled, but beneath them were mismatched wheels that caused the chair to rise up and lower itself with a smooth but rocking rhythm. "Whee!" Ilia was saying over and over.

When I reached them, I said, "How beautiful! Did you make it?" I gestured with my hands as if I were hammering so Stefan would understand.

He nodded and smiled broadly. His front teeth were perfect squares but they had an unreal quality about them because they were very off-center. "Yes, I make," he answered.

I smiled at Ilia and stooped to his level. "Hi, sweetie. Such a big boy. How old are you?"

Ilia smiled shyly and then covered his face with his hands. He looked just like Stefan with his wide-set eyes and prominent nose.

"Almost two," Stefan said eagerly, holding up splayed fingers.

Standing, I extended my hand. "I'm Susan Mondell. My office is just down the hall from your wife's."

"Ah!" He shook my hand vigorously as his eye lids pulled back, revealing a maze of tiny red veins above his gray-blue irises. "You are, what do you say, you live near each other—"

"Neighbors?" I ventured.

"Da! You are neighbors!" He laughed heartily and I forced myself to do the same. I wondered if he was homesick; it seemed as if my office's proximity to Natasha's made him regard me as almost kin.

"And you're Stefan?" I asked, but of course I knew he was. Natasha paraded him all over our little town like an exclusive accessory.

"Yes," he spoke with weight in his voice, "And this is Ilia." He gazed at the baby with such pride that I blushed and then wondered why.

"It's nice to meet you both," I said before resuming my walk. All that day, I thought about our encounter. When I found myself next to Natasha at the sink in the ladies room, I said, "Oh, I met your husband and little boy today."

She was applying lotion to her hands from a small Rubbermaid container. She rubbed every knuckle before looking at me, almost smiling, and finally said, "I'm sure Stefan will mention it to me. He hasn't met many people on his own in town." Snapping shut the container, she slipped it into her burlap satchel.

I should have just left the bathroom, but I said, "His English is very good."

She spun so quickly on her heel I almost felt a breeze. "No, it's not," she contradicted, "it's very basic. He's only learned a little from listening to National Public Radio and watching a little television."

I began brushing my hair even though it didn't need it. "I'm sure you're as good an English teacher as you are a Russian teacher." She wouldn't turn down flattery, I wagered.

"We speak only Russian at home," she said flatly.

"Oh?"

Nodding, she continued, "We consider ourselves Russians first and Americans second."

"I didn't know you were Russian," I said, pretending to be naive, but I worried, or hoped, she caught the sarcasm.

Hoisting the strap of her bag over her shoulder, she asked, genuinely surprised, "What did you think?"

"Oh, that you were American. And that you'd studied in Russia, of course."

She played with one of the braids fixed to her head with a plain metal hair clip. "Well, that's right. I was born here, but I've spent so much time in Russia and my husband and child are Russian." She paused for a brief moment and sighed, as if exasperated for having to explain something to me for the tenth time, and said, "The land and culture we identify with is Russia and that of Russia." Her last words, oddly poetic, hung in the air of the cavernous restroom.

I nodded like it made sense, but said, "Wouldn't it be easier for him in this country if he could communicate?"

She shook her head smugly. "We have so many Russian friends across the country, he's not lonely. And someday we'll return to Russia."

"Oh, you're not going to stay?"

"Not forever. We want Ilia to spend part of his childhood in Russia."

"I see."

"You'll have to come to dinner. Stefan would like to meet more Americans. They're something of a curiosity for him. I'll check our schedule and call you."

"How nice. But I don't speak any Russian. Will that be a problem?" I squelched a laugh. Would Natasha make me attend Berlitz classes before allowing me in her home?

Walking to the door, she said, "No," rather glumly. "We'll make an exception to the house rule and speak English during dinner."

House rules, the Tetrovs had many. When I first arrived, Natasha met me at the door and greeted me in Russian, or so I thought. Then she

frowned and asked me in English to remove my shoes. "No problem," I told her as I slipped off my new flats.

"Sorry," she said at my confusion, "I'll remember to speak English now." But then she turned and uttered a string of sounds with hard and abrupt edges. Stefan emerged from the kitchen, a tea towel draped over his shoulder. He smiled and shook my hand.

"Nice to see you again," I said.

"Da. Yes. I like to see you. . .again. Ilia!" He turned and called into the kitchen. "You come! You say hello!" He didn't appear so Stefan went to retrieve him. Natasha directed me to a futon covered with several crocheted afghans and we sat.

After several moments of silence, I asked, "Can I help with anything? Set the table or do something in the kitchen?"

She waved a hand in the direction of the kitchen. "Stefan's got everything under control."

I nodded. "How nice, a man who cooks."

Leaning back against the futon, she crooked her arms behind her neck. Beneath her brown dress, her legs were spread as far apart as they could be; her lap looked like a small tablecloth. "It's part of our contract."

"Contract?"

She looked at me directly for the first time since my arrival. "Yes. I earn the money and he does the housekeeping. At least for now. It'll be different when we go to Russia because it will take a while for me to get my work visa."

Appetizers sat on the low table in front of us, little wedges of pumpernickel bread smeared with what looked like cream cheese. Natasha hadn't offered, but I thought chewing and swallowing might help pass the time. She noticed my glance and said, "Oh, help yourself. Stefan made the bread himself."

That was nice, her bit of praise for her husband. I asked, "Did Stefan teach in Russia?"

Natasha picked up an appetizer. "Not really. He worked as an editor for a literary journal, but he had lots of contacts at universities."

"Yes, I've heard he translates Lithuanian poetry."

Nodding deeply, she said, "Yes, he's translated the major authors. And there are several emerging authors whom Stefan would like to translate."

"How interesting."

Stefan appeared again, this time holding Ilia. "I serve," he said handing Ilia over to his wife. "Come," he gestured to the table. "Come sit."

It wasn't the most hearty meal I ate, lentil soup with more of the pumpernickel bread. Stefan and Natasha ate several servings and I had a second helping when I realized nothing else was coming. Ilia upset his bowl, the soup flowing across the table and splashing my arms. Stefan jumped up and wiped away the mess while Natasha spoke what sounded like light admonishments to Ilia in Russian.

I tried to speak with Stefan. He was eager to speak English. Natasha didn't participate in our conversations and didn't correct Stefan when his grammar was wrong or when he groped for a word. When I asked him what he watched on television, he responded "Tel-eh-vish-shun," pointing at the TV. "I watch many times."

"Which programs do you like?" I asked.

He nodded as I spoke, deciphering each word. "Ah!" he shook his head up and down to indicate he understood my question. "News. I watch news many times."

I smiled. "You like the news."

Again heavy nodding. Then he said, with great emphasis, "Chun-nel Six." Natasha did deign to converse with me for a moment, explaining that it was a house rule that they only watched news programs on television. "We don't allow commercial American television in our home."

"On-ly news," Stefan repeated, nodding at Natasha.

We went on like this for about fifteen minutes, me asking questions and he responding. I asked him what ingredients were in the soup, what books he liked to read, about his family in Russia. His English was minimal, but I was stirred at how enthused he was to speak with me, to learn something of my world, to share something of his. He was persistent, repeating phrases until he was sure he was saying what he meant. Most of my students were only taking my classes because a foreign language was required to graduate; Stefan, however, was a student in the truest sense.

Our conversation ended when Natasha interjected, "Let's go back to the couch." It was Stefan's job to clear the table and brew the tea. Ilia, less wary of me now, joined us, squiggling up into Natasha's lap. She spoke endearments to him in Russian and he nestled into her chest.

Natasha startled me when she asked, "Are you worried about getting tenure?"

I took it as an overture that she really wanted to talk to me, that our having to jump through the hoops together to get job security would help us bond a bit. "I can't wait till it's over," I admitted. "It really is a humiliating process."

"Humiliating, why?"

So we weren't going to bond. I probably shouldn't have revealed my vulnerability about the matter. "Well," I started, "It's invasive, don't you think? All this scrutiny of our teaching, our research. I mean, it's not like we get paid a heck of a lot. . .." I hesitated. Natasha probably did make more than me since she was in a more competitive field, a woman in a sea of male Russian scholars. Still, she was supporting three people.

"The money stinks," she said. "If it weren't for all my grants, I don't know how we'd get by."

"Right," I said, as if I also had a bundle of grant money. "Are you concerned about tenure? You know, you shouldn't be. Everyone says you're a sure thing."

"I know," she said too matter-of-factly. "I just threw my dossier together at the last minute and gave it to my department chair. He told me that my recommendations were glowing and that I'll probably make full professor in two years."

I couldn't respond right away. I sat there thinking about a conversation I'd had with Simon a couple months earlier. He told me that although my department was recommending me for tenure, it was a lukewarm endorsement. He couldn't name names, but someone in the department felt my research was very weak. I'd only had three articles accepted for publication since coming to Hancock, and only two of them were actually in print. Simon hinted that another person in the department, although I suspected it was him by the way he avoided my eyes, had concerns about my performance in the classroom. Because the number of French majors was dwindling, Simon said, one of my colleagues felt that my introductory classes must not have been very good. As he spoke, I clenched my teeth. My teaching evaluations were no worse, or better, than the other members of the French department, but I was the untenured, expendable member of the group. It wasn't my fault that studying French wasn't as popular as it used to be. Simon continued, "One member of the department thinks we need to hire a native French speaker, and, obviously, we won't be able to do that if we tenure you. The whole department will be tenured up for some time, so this last

tenure decision is critical." Still, lukewarm though it was, the Department was recommending to the powers that be that I be tenured. The head honchos, however, could decide otherwise. So I couldn't help feeling jealous that day, listening to details about Natasha's markedly different situation. I asked her, "Does your department know you want to move to Russia?"

She laughed a little and I was impressed at how her features altered; her mouth, curled at the ends like that, made her look girlish, less serious. "They'd be idiots not to," she said, "but then sometimes I think they are a pack of idiots, like most of the faculty."

Wow. I hadn't expected that. "Who do you think is an idiot?" I asked, only then wondering if I was included on the list.

Resting her head against the curve of the couch, Natasha sighed. "It would be easier to say who wasn't. Hancock is so second-rate."

"You think?"

"Well, Dean Leep, Helen, is okay. I mean, she fought her way to the top, and for the most part she does a good job. When Herb Shrilley was Dean, I actually wondered if he was agoraphobic, he left the office so rarely. Probably only to go to the bathroom."

Natasha was funny! Why hadn't I known this? If only those people who idolized her knew what she thought of them. Hopeful for more dirt, I asked her, "Have you met Elizabeth Shrilley, his wife?"

"Oh, yes. Her and her crony, Elise Rupple. They tried to sign me up to serve punch at the Hancock Women's Association spring tea. As if I have time to serve punch to a bunch of Martha Stewart wannabes. I'd like to send them all to a labor camp in Siberia, let them see how the rest of the world lives."

Stefan returned with two cups of very hot tea, the steam dancing over the tops, and a plastic container of honey. Immediately Natasha began to speak to him in Russian. It took me several moments to realize that she was criticizing him for something. His expression, puzzled at first, became hurt, his eyes retreating under his unkempt brows. He remained quiet while Natasha and I chatted a little more about work. Eventually, she stood and said she was going to put Ilia to bed. Taking this as a hint, I stood and perfunctorily thanked them for a lovely evening. Stefan walked me to the door, looking back to make sure his wife was no longer in the room before he leaned down and pressed his lips hard against mine, almost biting them. The embrace was disorienting. I actually wondered at first if this was an exuberant

Russian farewell, but as his tongue entered my mouth, searching for a space between my upper and lower teeth so it could venture further, I tasted the honey in his saliva and thought, *how sweet.*

Why would I have an affair with a married man? My reasons, when I examined them, were only partly dishonorable. My department's treatment of me made me feel unwanted, like someone's poor relation. That Stefan, husband to Natasha, queen of the academic universe, was interested in me did bolster my self-esteem, and, I have to be honest, make me conclude that she wasn't as smart as she thought. Sadly, I needed that.

I guessed that Stefan's motivation was at least, in part, rebellion against a controlling wife who did her best to ensure that he remain solidly Russian. But it's also true that both Stefan and I were deeply lonely, and what brings people together more ardently than loneliness? Academic towns are brimming with desolate people who put on a brave face and go off to work each day. When you meet a kindred soul, you cling together in desperation.

Stefan's English improved with our lovemaking. I spoke to him softly as he massaged my back and stroked my inner thighs. He talked of Russia, of the black winter sky over the empty sunflower field on his father's farm. He and his friends, shivering in the night air, identified star patterns and shared a thermos of tea and, when they could get it, vodka. He had studied at a few universities. He described city life so vividly, so sensuously, that I imagined the St. Petersburg sun flashing behind my eyelids as I climaxed. It was hard not to call out my pleasure, but Ilia would be sleeping in the next room or sometimes watching a children's television program in the living room, an infringement of house rules. Our assignations were too brief; if only Natasha had a fuller teaching schedule, Stefan and I could meet more frequently. I teased him that his English would improve to the point that Natasha would become suspicious.

Stefan looked sheepish when he admitted that he married Natasha for his green card. There was no hope of a university post in Russia and he thought America was his future.

"But she, Natasha, she thinks there is love between us. I try, I try hard, but there is no love. I try to kiss her when she go to work in the morning, but she shake my hand."

"She shakes your hand?" I said, incredulous.

"Yes," he nodded. "She shake my hand because it means. . .", he fumbled. "Ah, it means we partners—we partners and we agree. . .agree to work this way. Natasha at school, me here," he finished, pointing downwards in a way that indicated he knew his place in the marriage.

I wasn't quite sure I understood their partnership, but it sounded so Natasha, more of her posturing. "Does she say that she loves you?" It embarrassed me, asking this, but I had to know.

"Sometimes. Sometimes she say that."

"Says, " I corrected, "sometimes she *says* that."

Our time together was too short to waste by talking about Natasha. I placed my hands on either side of his jaws and kissed Stefan, closing my eyes, willing us to belong to each other, I a citizen of his body, he of mine.

There was a party at Dean Leep's house for all the faculty members who got tenure that year. Our department chairs were invited to introduce each of us and speak a bit about our work. The chair of the Soviet Studies Department spoke for twenty minutes while introducing Natasha, only stopping when she stood and modestly waved her hands and said, "Enough! Enough! You're boring them to tears."

Compare that with Simon Rupple standing for less than a minute saying, "The French department is pleased to announce that Susan Mondell received tenure this year. She teaches our introductory courses and has done research on French as a second language." The demure applause said it all.

I mingled by the punch bowl for a short while, wondering how soon I could leave and not be talked about after my departure. I felt a tap on my shoulder and turned to face Natasha.

"Isn't this the most boring thing you've ever endured in your life?" she asked.

"Yes, actually, it is."

"At least I'll be out of here soon."

"OH?" The other guests heard me and stared. More quietly, I asked, "You're leaving?"

Natasha nodded. "They don't know it yet," a jerk of her head indicated the rest of the room, "but I'm resigning next week."

"Where are you going?" I hoped indeed it was "you" in the singular.

"Russia," she said simply, "back to Kiev."

Shifting feet, I said, "Did Stefan get a job?"

She refilled her cup and said, "No, I did. I got a Fulbright to go there and continue my research on their tradition of patriarchal politics."

"Are you going alone?" I asked, pretending to be casual by studying an oil painting just behind us.

"Of course not. My family is going with me. Speaking of family, I have to get home to them." She set her cup on the table and went off to say good-bye to the Dean.

My legs didn't feel strong enough to help me make my own exit, so I turned to the punch bowl again and became acutely absorbed with filling my own cup, swallowing heavily to slow the lump rising in my throat. I felt a vague pressure on my elbow and I turned to see Simon, his ear to ear grin particularly annoying at the moment.

"So, Susan, now you're one of us. I bet you're relieved."

I pretended to smile.

"How does it feel?" he asked when it became clear to him that I was not going to thank him for all he had done for me; if anything I had probably gotten tenure in spite of him.

"Oh, I'm not sure. I guess it hasn't hit me yet."

He helped himself to some punch, overfilling his cup and then stooping to sip the drink quickly. That sipping noise, small and irritating, would be what I remembered best from that day. It defined Simon and maybe the whole tenure process itself, stooping and desperate. He surprised me by asking, "Are you going to buy a house? The best ones go by word of mouth, you know. Don't bother with a realtor."

"A house?"

"Sure! Time to settle down, Susan. You can't be a bachelorette forever." Wink, wink, nudge, nudge. I thought I'd be sick. "Any eligible bachelors?"

"A house," I said, steering back to a safer subject. "I have such a nice apartment, I'd hate to give it up."

Simon spotted someone on the other side of the room. Raising his hand in a big wave, he started to walk away, but left me with these final words: "Buy a house, settle down. And, here's a tip: before the prices go up, buy a plot in Hancock cemetery. The College owns the lower meadow, you know. They'll sell you a plot for a song."

If only it had been a joke. I hadn't had tenure for five minutes, but

already I was plummeted into post-tenure depression. I thanked Dean Leep for her hospitality and told her I had another engagement.

"Congratulations, Susan," she said, a firm grip on my hand. "I've been meaning to talk to you about the women's faculty mentoring program I'm trying to launch."

I wanted to go home, order a pizza, watch some old tearjerker movie on television and have a good cry. I wanted to call Stefan and ask him why he hadn't told me of his plans to go back to Russia with Natasha. But I stood there and said, "Mentoring?" like I was engrossed.

"Yes." Dean Leep is a short, energetic woman. She sort of danced on the balls of her feet in front of me. "I'd like the senior faculty women to give some guidance to the junior faculty women. You know, help get them oriented when they arrive on campus, sit in on a few classes, coach them on lecture styles, encourage their research—"

"Gee, I wish someone would have done half of that for me." I felt too low to hide my resentment.

"I know, I know," she said quickly, "I do too. No one looked out for me either. That's why it's so important that we help each other." She looked up at me expectantly, "Can I put your name on the list?"

"Sure," I said, slipping my coat on over my shoulders. Maybe I'd make a few friends.

When I got home, I found a small note from Stefan under my door. His message, scribbled with his large hand, the same hand that stroked my brow in bed, had too much meaning: "*I must go. I do not want to be away from Ilia just like I do not want to be away from you. I have no more words to tell you.*"

I never became a senior faculty mentor, I never bought a house in Hancock, and I certainly never bought a plot in the town cemetery. Two months later I was on an airplane to Paris where I would begin my new job teaching English to secondary French students. The pay they offered was miserable, and I was going to share an apartment with two other teachers in the Latin Quarter. There was no job security, but I didn't care. If I felt unwelcome, I would leave. The best thing about my job at Hancock was getting to say good-bye to everyone, of seeing the look of surprise, perhaps even envy, on Simon's face when I broke the news.

Even before my arrival, I was seduced by Paris. I sat in the middle seat of a crowded airplane and imagined walking the curvy streets of Montmartre on a fresh morning, stopping to buy crepes and café au lait at a little shop where the owner would come to know me. Later I would climb up the many steps of Sacre-Coeur and look out over the city, its beautifully planned avenues, the pink and gray mists whispering over my cheeks. The Seine would move below my feet as I stood on an airy bridge adorned with classical sculptures painted a triumphant gold. I would walk through the city for miles and miles, until my legs ached, until I thought I'd faint with the marvel of it all. And every day I spent in Paris, I would be that much closer to becoming a native.

ONLY BEAUTIFUL

Mary Connolly

The old women sitting behind me on this bus are whispering. About me. I'm used to it. I blink slowly, lift my chin and pretend to stare out the window. I've been holding my head high, too high, all summer. Today I went shopping downtown just to forget about things for a while. No luck.

It's my stop and I stand slowly, waiting until the bus is motionless before walking down the aisle. The whispering gets louder, a hissing sound that follows me with each step. I don't even know these women. They live somewhere in the neighborhood. But they know me, or at least they've heard my story. Through the grapevine. Everyone in the neighborhood knows all about what happened to Mary Connolly. Some think I got what I deserved, some pity me. A few, just a few, feel genuinely sorry for me.

I wish I had the nerve to turn around and glare, ask them, "Don't you have anything better to do than criticize an eighteen-year-old girl? Who are you to judge me?" But I don't utter a word; I just clench the metal pole as the bus lurches to a stop. The doors swing wide open and I step down onto Abbott Road, one of the main avenues that runs north and south throughout South Buffalo. I know every inch of it, from Park Edge Groceries to the LB Smith Plaza. South Buffalo has been my home my whole life. There are no secrets here. There are endless secrets here.

Joe Gleason

When we were little, I thought Mary was a blue jay, beautiful and mean. She sat across from me in kindergarten and barely said a word. Then one day, she asked me, "What's on your chin?" She traced an invisible line on her own face. I was sensitive about the scar. I'd had it since I was two and our neighbor's dog jumped on me and sliced my skin. That day in kindergarten, when I told Mary what happened, she screwed her face up like I was too awful too look at. I don't remember her saying another word to me the whole time we were at St. Martin's School.

In junior high, she was in front of the building every morning, the other girls clustered around her, nodding as they agreed with everything she said. They knew they'd never be as beautiful as Mary, but they all vied to be one of her handmaidens, even Eileen, her best friend, who would easily have been queen bee at any other school.

I have to admit, Mary was irresistible that autumn we were in eighth grade. On the first day of school she wore a purple dress and stockings. Her long hair was the color of butter and her eyes were as turquoise as some of the marbles in my old collection. She looked like the models on the covers of magazines. I didn't gawk at her the way a lot of the boys did, but I stole a few looks. That short dress, those incredible legs. The sight of her made me ache.

Actually, a lot of the girls were knockouts that autumn. They'd come back from summer vacation with longer legs, longer hair, their make-up propelling them years forward. We boys were cowed by their make-up, by their short skirts barely covering bottoms that moved with a teasing rhythm down the halls. The best thing about Saint Martin's was that we didn't have to wear uniforms like the other Catholic schools. Sure, we were supposed to look clean and well-dressed, but the girls weren't hidden in those long ugly plaid skirts. Thank God.

These were the same girls we chased through the playground only a couple of years ago, but suddenly they were young women, leaving the boys in the dust. Their newfound beauty, so startling, was more wondrous to us than the moon landing. We could never admit this, of course, so we acted like a pack of idiots. Well, I was quiet, but most of the guys behaved like jerks. Timmy Corcoran and Mike Nelligan hooted, "36 D, DO IT TO ME!" whenever Molly Boyle walked by, her cheeks flushed, her eyes down.

Some of the girls were genuinely nice to us, like Sheila Adams. A couple others would say hello to you if you passed them on the street. But not Mary Connolly. You could be an inch from her nose and she wouldn't see you. She'd glide past me on the street and I felt like garbage.

I remember that first morning in eighth grade when I was up before my mother, stuffing my sheets into the washer, thrilled and horrified about what I'd dreamt the night before. For a few months after that, I wouldn't let myself glance in Mary's direction. I worried that if we locked eyes, she'd know. Life was embarrassing enough without a girl knowing how much power she had over you.

After a few dreams about Mary, I started doing the private hand jive under the covers before I fell asleep. My older brother had told me that that stuff about going blind was bull, and I couldn't have stopped myself anyway. Conjuring up Mary's face was easy. It was more beautiful than the stained glass Madonna at church. In my mind, her eyes met mine and her lips moved slowly over my mouth. When I came, my lust was transformed into something spiritual, something sacred. Mary was my object of worship. I knew then I'd never make it as a priest.

So, she got pregnant her senior year of high school. Turns out she was human after all.

❧

Mrs. Connolly

Why did it have to happen to Mary? Of all people, why Mary?

When she was little, people would stop us on the street and say, "Oh, what a little princess!" Later, when she grew into her beauty, everyone just stared. It's a rare thing to see such perfection, but, I tell you, my Mary had it all. We scrimped and saved so she could have the latest fashions, the cute dresses and skirts she wore to school. What we couldn't afford, I sewed or knitted. Not that she asked for it, but a girl that pretty deserves everything.

But you know how jealous people can be. The mothers of the other girls tried now and then to knock Mary off her pedestal. Mrs. Strayer thought her twin daughters were shoe-ins to crown the statue of the Blessed Virgin at the May Crowning when the girls were in first grade. When Mary and Sheila Adams were picked, Mrs. Strayer made a point of not talking to me when we ran into each other at the grocery store. Then, wouldn't you know it, we ended up sitting next to each other at the May Crowning. The only thing that woman said to me the entire night was, "Did you make Mary's dress?" I told her yes and she nodded as if to say, "I thought so." Then she comes out with, "I got my girls' dresses at Hens & Kellys." Well, good for her, she could afford to shop at Hens & Kellys. Her daughters were still just sitting in the pews with the rest of the class while my daughter got to sit on the altar.

In the sixth grade, Susie Masterson had a sleepover and invited every girl in the class but Mary. Poor thing, it cut her to the bone. "But I *like* Susie," she sobbed, "and I thought she liked *me*."

I was so mad, I called Susie's mother and said, "I hope you're happy. If you were trying to hurt my daughter, you succeeded."

Well, I knew better than to expect an apology but I was shocked when Edna Masterson shot back, "Your daughter is the star every damn day of the year. I thought Susie deserved to be the star for *once* in her life."

I swallowed and said, "I'm sorry if your Susie is so threatened by my Mary—"

"She's not!" the woman cut me off. "Susie wanted to invite her. I had to make her see that she had the right to be the center of attention on her own birthday!"

She hung up on me. I was so mad I felt sick to my stomach.

The night of Susie's sleepover, my husband and I took Mary to the movies and didn't mention the party. I was just furious every time I looked at her sad face. And what if this was just the beginning? What if everyone started giving her the cold shoulder? Why, she'd be an outcast.

You fight fire with fire. When Mary's birthday came around, we borrowed a little money and rented the roller skating rink. It was a surprise party. I mailed invitations to every student in the class, boys and girls, except Susie Masterson. It was the first boy-girl party the sixth graders had ever had. People talked about it for weeks afterwards and Mary never got left out of anything again.

Well, Edna Masterson is in her glory these days, no doubt, celebrating Mary's downfall. Not that she knows the whole story. Oh, she thinks she knows some nasty little gossip, like anyone would listen to that busybody. Only my family and son-in-law know what really happened, and we don't owe anyone an explanation. Mary is still as beautiful as ever, and no one can take that away from her. Not Edna Masterson or anyone else in this whole neighborhood.

❧

Mr. Connolly

I knew there'd be trouble. I knew it for a long time before it happened. I'd look at my wife and wonder how the two of us managed to produce such a gorgeous girl. Not that we're ugly, no, but Mary lucked out. She got my mother's enormous blue eyes and long legs. The dimple in her left cheek is from me and, if I do say so myself, so is her smile. My wife, Grace, is half Swedish and that's where Mary gets her bright blond hair. We only had one child, but that was okay. We hit the jackpot with Mary.

Grace was always entering Mary's picture in baby contests. She'd look at the label on a jar of Gerber's baby food and say, "Why, that baby can't hold a candle to Mary." There were Little Miss contests, Precious Princess contests, Miss Junior Miss contests, everyone of them a production with fluffy dresses and visits to the beauty parlor. Her picture was in the newspaper so many times, Mary was a local celebrity.

When Mary was thirteen, she put her foot down and said no more. Grace was devastated, but Mary insisted the contests were stupid, and what was she going to do with more trophies and tiaras anyway? I backed Mary up even though Grace yelled, "Al, keep out of this!" But I held firm and insisted it was Mary's choice. Well, there were no more contests, but my wife continued to display the trophies all over the house and was forever dusting them.

When she was fourteen, Mary wanted to cut her long hair off and get a shag. Jane Fonda had worn one in the movie, "Klute," and all the girls wanted to copy her. They were too young to have seen the movie, but Jane Fonda's picture was in every magazine. Grace begged Mary to keep her hair long, told her she'd regret cutting it short, but Mary went ahead and did it. When Grace first saw her with the new hairdo, she burst into tears. Mary told her to stop crying or she'd cut it shorter. A week later, most of the girls in her class had the exact same look. Mary liked blending in, but it was funny the way the other girls copied her. When the shag fad was over, Mary let her hair grow down to her waist again and the other girls followed suit.

When all her friends went through that gawky stage, Mary became even more beautiful. She never got acne. She was never gangly or chubby. Every year when she blew out the candles on her birthday, I studied her face. She was lovely at fourteen, breathtaking at fifteen. At her sweet sixteen party, I almost couldn't look at her. She was so beautiful, she broke my heart. And that was the thing; I knew that sooner or later, someone or something was going to hurt her. When she gave us the news about being pregnant a month after her eighteenth birthday, I felt calm, even relieved. It had happened. And it was only that. A baby. Well, we could handle a baby, right? Just look what a good job we did with Mary.

Mary

Books have always been my refuge. I started reading before I went to kindergarten and had read everything in the school library by the time I was in fifth grade. Mother was forever buying or making me fancy clothes, but all I ever wanted was books. My best friend, Eileen, dragged me out to the movies and the mall, but I really just wanted to stay home and read.

In sixth grade, I devoured Greek mythology. I endlessly read and re-read certain stories, Daphne transforming into a tree as she fled from Apollo, Syrinx becoming a reed along the riverbank as she fled from Pan. I understood what it was like to be chased, to feel pursued, to pray for rescue. Daphne and Syrinx simply wanted to be left alone. I did too.

But alone forever? Would I ever want to turn and face the person who desired me so much that he'd follow me no matter how fast I ran? I puzzled over this as I read Arthurian legend, the Welsh king and his knights pursuing the holy grail, something more noble than a nymph or sprite. Guenievere's betrayal of Arthur broke my heart, and I wanted to rewrite the legend with a faithful, devout queen, one who would barely glance at Lancelot. The illustrations of Arthur always showed him with dark hair and a beard. I studied his face and imagined a scar on his chin hidden beneath the beard.

My mother read Harlequin Romances. When she dusted my rooms, she'd pick up my books and squint at the titles. She'd often sigh and tell me I was going to ruin my eyes with all that reading. She worried that I'd have to get glasses as "thick as Coke bottles." When I didn't respond, she'd say in a sing song voice, "Men seldom make passes at girls who wear glasses." Good, I thought. I just wanted my mother and everybody else to leave me alone.

When I was by myself in my room, reading my books, all was well. Opening a new book was thrilling, like entering a secret world where no one knew or cared about Mary Connolly. Relaxing with an old book one was like spending time with a close friend. So, no, I wasn't lonely when I was reading. It was when I was out in the world, seated in a classroom with forty other students, that I felt so alone I listened for the sound of my own heartbeat.

✻

Mr. Harrigan

I've been a pharmacist in South Buffalo for almost thirty years now. It's a beautiful place to live; I would never move. We have more parks than any other section of the city, vast acres of green and trees planned out by Frederick Law Olmstead. I've never been to England, but our Botanical Gardens are modeled on the Crystal Palace and the Kew Gardens Palm House. The Gardens are housed in beautiful, Victorian glass structures that look like the Taj Mahal. It's world class architecture and it's right here in South Buffalo.

If there's a lovelier street than McKinley Parkway, I've never seen it. Of course, the Dutch Elm disease of the fifties killed the trees that used to be so tall and dense. Everyone misses the trees and talks about the days when they formed an emerald tunnel. But the houses that line both sides of the avenue are stately Georgian and Victorian-style homes, beautifully maintained. There's great civic pride here. The north and south ends of the Parkway are marked with huge circles planted with a rainbow of flowers in the spring and summer. In December, huge evergreens are put up and decorated for Christmas. The circles keep the drivers from going too fast. The cars arch gracefully around them; traffic on the Parkway is respectful and leisurely, no one is in a hurry.

There are good schools here in South Buffalo, public and Catholic, no end of stores, and a beautiful rink where the kids skate in the winter. There's a YMCA where everybody learns to swim, and a beautiful outdoor pool in Cazenovia Park. The fireworks here on the fourth of July are the best in the city. No one ever said the Irish were great cooks, but if you like good, solid tavern fare, we've got it in spades. And every Friday, the topic of conversation is which restaurant has the best fish fry. I love it here. There's no need to leave this section of the city for anything. South Buffalo has it all.

My wife, Marie, and I were lucky to grow up here. Our parents were immigrants who lived in the old First Ward, struggling to save every dime so they could move further south to this beautiful area. It was paradise to them when they first arrived, and it's still paradise to us. Our sons, Michael, John and David, were born in Mercy Hospital on Abbott Road. David is the only one still at home, but his older brothers still live in South Buffalo. Hopefully we'll have grandchildren in the near future, children we'll get to see every day of the week. Family is everything here. No one moves away unless they absolutely have to.

I pretty much know everybody in South Buffalo. I know more than I'd like to about some people's medical conditions, their emotional problems, but there you have it. Comes with the job. I never filled a prescription for Mary Connolly, but I think I was one of the few people who understood her. Most people saw her beauty and couldn't get past that. If you gave her a chance, you'd see that she was shy, very shy. When she was just an itty bitty thing, her mother would bring her into the pharmacy to buy Goody barrettes and pink nail polish. Grace Connolly talked a mile a minute and kept urging Mary to talk to me. "Tell Mr. Harrigan hello," she'd prompt her over and over again. Mary would glance at me bashfully and then stare down at her patent leather maryjanes. Mrs. Connolly would sigh, exasperated, and say, "Honestly, Mary, if you don't say something, people are going to think you don't know how to talk!"

I admired the girl's reserve. From the time the poor thing could walk, her mother paraded her around town like she was the next Shirley Temple. People stared at Mary, couldn't take their eyes off of her. Of course she was shy. Who wouldn't be with people gawking like that?

They'd leave the store and when they were safely outside, her mother searching in her purse for something, Mary would look through the window and give me a little smile. I'd smile back and think, that's right, Mary, live life on your own terms.

When she got older, she knew how to make small talk, hold her end of a conversation, but she never revealed too much about herself. She didn't brag or talk loudly to call attention to herself like a lot of the girls who came in the store did. She didn't have to; all eyes were on her wherever she went.

I don't have a daughter. My wife and I hoped for a fourth child, a little girl, but it didn't happen. I'm not complaining. We're lucky to have three healthy sons. But I felt a fatherly protection towards Mary and I think she sensed it. I wish more people had been looking out for her. If they had, things might have turned out differently.

Eileen Sullivan

On the first day of kindergarten, I wore a green dress with a daisy flower on the front. The center of the flower was a large yellow button. That's why I wanted the dress, because of the pretty button. The dress came in red too, but my mother insisted on the green. "The green matches your eyes," she told me.

My mother rarely complimented me, so I immediately decided that the green dress was prettier.

"We both have green eyes, right Mommy?"

"Mm hmm," she'd said absently, taking the dress to the cashier's counter. We were also buying a brown plaid dress with smocking across the bodice and a navy blue sailor dress. Three new dresses for kindergarten! More than the excitement of wearing the clothes and finally going to school, I relished the sugary feeling in my chest that my mother loved me.

The shopping outing helped steady the jumpy feeling in my stomach that had been there since last week, since the Friday night Mrs. Boyer, our next door neighbor, came to baby sit. I was in bed but still awake when my parents got home. They had gone out for a fish fry and then to play cards with the O'Briens, their friends who lived a few streets over.

After Mrs. Boyer left, my mother started talking loudly, something about Mrs. O'Brien cheating at pinochle. My father's voice was quiet, I could only hear his murmurs from the kitchen. And then Mother shouted, "Oh, shut up! I only had two glasses of wine."

Automatically, I squeezed my eyes shut and pushed my index fingers into my ears. I pretended I was under water, unable to hear anything other than quiet waves. After a minute, I loosened my fingers. My parents were both speaking at once, each voice rising. Then Mother's voice grew louder, finally hollering, "Who cares if she wakes up! I'll tell her that I never wanted her! If Jimmy hadn't died, she wouldn't even be here! IF JIMMY HADN'T DIED—"

And then the sound of breaking glass. All the way from the bedroom, I knew it broke hard, that it had been thrown into the porcelain sink. But who threw it? Then Mother's voice, quieter now but scarier, "Goddamn you! You clean up that mess!"

In the dark, I imagined Daddy picking up the shards of glass from the sink. I worried that the tips of his fingers would bleed, that when I saw him in the morning, his hands would be covered with band-aids. Then Mother spoke, but her voice sounded muffled. I heard the refrigerator door open and close and knew Mother had taken out the wine bottle. There was always at least one bottle in the refrigerator, tall and skinny and filled with a liquid the same color as pee. The label was beautiful though, a colorful bouquet of flowers tied with a red ribbon. I imagined the bottle in Mother's hands now and wondered if Daddy would grab it from her. I closed my eyes and started to sing softly, *I'm swimming under water, I'm swimming under water, I'm swimming under water and I can't hear a thing.* I'd hummed this song to the tune of "The Farmer in the Dell" lots of nights. *And I can't hear a thing.* But I did, I heard Daddy's voice, angry but broken: "MARGARET, I AM SICK. . . AND TIRED. . . OF THESE SCENES. I LOST A SON TOO, GOD DAMN IT! YOU'RE NOT THE ONLY ONE AROUND HERE. . . SUFFERING!" I heard him walk into the bathroom, slam the door and lock the bolt.

Now the house was as quiet as if I really were under water. And so dark, but still I saw his face peering at me from a corner in my mind, the baby boy who had died in his crib when he was three months old. His picture was tucked in the mirror of Mother's vanity. Once I reached out to run my finger along the edge of the photo and Mother slapped my hand. "Don't you touch that! Don't you ever touch that!" My lips started to quiver and I ran into my room.

But a week after Daddy broke that glass, my mother took me shopping. She wore her navy suit with white piping and matching shoes, a small navy clutch purse tucked under her arm. Like always, I watched people watching my mother. They thought she was pretty, like Jackie Kennedy, but she made them nervous. The saleswoman tried to converse with her, some friendly banter, but Mother made a small, tight smile and averted her eyes. Then the saleswoman counted out the wrong change, apologized, and appeared timid as she laid the bills and coins into Mother's palm.

Still, as we walked out of the store, I was carrying a bag with three new dresses folded in crisp tissue paper. The weight of the bag eased the weight in my heart. I half-skipped and said, looking up, "I'm glad we both have green eyes, Mommy."

Kevin Walsh

Mary lived down the street from me. She was my first friend. Our mothers used to sit in one of our kitchens and drink coffee together while Mary and I sat on the floor and tried to eat Play-dough. There are the home movies of the two of us dressed up in Halloween outfits, in swimsuits in a dinky blow-up pool, in our First Communion outfits, a bunch of events caught on camera. When I was little, I didn't see what the big deal about Mary Connolly was; she was just my friend.

We had a swing set in my backyard. Mary and I liked to swing spider, you know, where I would sit forward and Mary would climb on me and sit backwards. That way we both got to pump and we got twice as high twice as fast. Every other kid in the neighborhood was afraid to swing spider, but Mary and I loved it. We pushed and pulled against each other, making the swing climb so high that one of the metal poles of the swing set used to jump out of the ground.

Then in second grade my mother said, "You and Mary are too old to swing like that any more." I pretended I didn't know what she was talking about, but I did. I liked the pressure of her bottom on my lap when we swung, and I wouldn't have liked it if she did spider with any of the other boys. My older brother, Jerry, used to tease me with that song, "Kevin and Mary sitting in a tree, K-I-S-S-I-N-G. . ." I'd try to punch his arm, but he'd get me in a neck lock and hold me until I started crying. Then he'd call me a crybaby and I'd cry even harder.

In fifth or sixth grade, the girls stopped being our buddies. They became, well, they became girls. That was the long and short of it. And we were boys and proud to be boys. I never went through that stage where I hated girls, thought they had cooties and all that, but I figured out it was definitely not safe to act like I cared about them. In a couple years it would be okay, but not when you're nine and ten. So Mary and I drifted apart. We didn't go over to each other's houses any more. We might say hi to each other at school, but that was it. She lived down the street, but she may as well have lived in a different country. I'd see her sitting on her front steps, her nose in a book, and just walk quietly past her house.

But junior high and high school were like old times. We kidded around and usually ate lunch at the same table in the cafeteria. Mary dated a lot of guys, but no one for very long. When I asked her why, she said that her parents thought she was too young to get serious with anyone. I didn't want to blow my chances, so I was content to wait until we got older and be the one she'd fall in love with. And in the meantime, there were plenty of pretty girls at St. Martin's. I was funny, not bad-looking; most girls liked me. It was fun being popular, but I was just biding my time, waiting for Mary.

Joe

I've been running for as long as I can remember. When I was little, we didn't own a car. My mother would realize we were out of milk and ask me to run to the deli around the corner and be quick about it. Or she'd send me to the library to return her books. When I was in sixth grade, Mom bought a used Volkswagon, but by that time I was so used to running, I still did all of the errands. Jogging all over the neighborhood like that, it wasn't any wonder I went out for track.

As long as I was running, nothing bothered me. I didn't think about school or my weekend job at the A&P or even girls. The only thing that mattered then was the instinctual motion of my legs bending to propel me forward, the rush of air against my face, the feeling of weightlessness that always came to me after about ten minutes, a feeling I would hold onto until my last step. Running made me feel so free of everything and everyone. All of my obligations were on hold and my body flooded with relief, with a kind of ecstasy.

Running was predictable. You ran a mile, you ended up a mile away. You turned around and ran a mile and you were back where you started. Nothing made more sense. I'd always felt that nothing bad could happen to me while I was moving. Standing still, that was when life could sneak up and deal you a low blow.

I was three when my father died. He was a fireman at Engine 30, right across from South Park High School. His ladder took the call when an old bank building around the corner caught on fire. The men were on top of the building checking for hot spots when my father went right through the roof, falling into hell itself.

I was sitting on our living room floor playing with blocks when Uncle Jim came to the door to break the news to Mom. He was the Captain of Engine 30, not really my uncle but all the firemen treated each others' kids like their own.

For years, I thought about seeing Mom and Uncle Jim at the door, his quiet voice, her scream, his catching her so she didn't fall to the floor. I yell at the memory, telling myself to get up off the floor and go help Mom. I should have run to her, comforted her. It makes no sense, but sometimes I think if I didn't just sit there, the news might have been different. So I'm vigilant. I'll never let anything bad sneak up that way again. I study hard, I go to my job, I run track. When I leave South Buffalo, it will be because I earned it, because I know what my next step will be and where it will take me.

Eileen

The first day of kindergarten, I was only four years old and small for my age. When we stepped inside the school, the corridor was bustling with mothers who blocked my view of the doors to the classrooms. Other children were there, holding onto their mother's hands, looking as bewildered as I felt. The mothers were chatting and laughing, their voices fusing into a single ringing sound. I was scared and covered my ears with my hands.

Right then, a little girl peeked out from around her mother and smiled. She pointed to her dress and I saw that she had on the same dress as me, but hers was red. We both touched the yellow buttons in the center of the daisies on our chests and started to laugh. And although I was so young and so little, I knew this girl would be my best friend. She didn't look at anybody else, only me. Her curly blonde pigtails bobbed on either side of her face, a face as sweet as a kitten's, that button nose and eyes like big blue plates.

"How sweet! They have the same dress!" The girl's mother was talking to Mother. Glancing down at the two of us now standing side by side, Mother said, "Oh, yes." The girl's mother talked rapidly, smiling as she said she didn't know how she was going to get through the morning, that she would miss Mary so much. *Mary*, I thought, her name is Mary. Mother didn't speak, but Mary's mother didn't seem to notice. Mrs. Connolly babbled on about embroidering Mary's initials on her sneaker bag and naptime rug. Mother nodded and at least appeared attentive. When it was time for the parents to go, the children lined up in twos. Mary and I stood side by side, holding hands as we entered a classroom for the very first time. By the time we'd finally leave school thirteen years later, the little girl in the red dress would be pregnant, and I'd be as happy as anyone on earth had a right to be.

Father Louis Gibbon

I had my eye on Mary for years. I knew she was someone to watch over, to pray for. I knew it back in 1964 when she made her First Communion. I was standing in front of the altar when the little girls came walking down the aisle in their immaculate white dresses. If only they could have stayed that innocent, the heartbreak that could be avoided.

Being one of the taller girls, Mary was toward the back of the line. Her dress wasn't as fancy as some, but she was the girl who stood out that day. It wasn't just her beauty, though that was often remarked upon, no, it was her soul. Her soul was the purest I've ever encountered; it made her glow from the inside out. She had an inner light. As she knelt at the altar railing that morning to receive communion for the very first time, the sun cut through a stained glass window of the Madonna, and Mary's eyes, those enormous, innocent blue eyes, reflected the light. I watched her irises flash until they gleamed with heavenly love. My fingers trembled as I held the communion wafer in front of her face and uttered, "Body of Christ."

She whispered "Amen" and accepted Christ into her body. As she bowed her head, I promised God that I would always protect her. Evil seeks the most innocent amongst us, and Satan delights in corrupting those most precious to God. I knew then that Mary would be tempted and tempted again. More than any other child at the altar rail that day, she needed the protection of our Lord Savior. As a priest, I am God's channel of grace, and he was calling upon me now with a divine assignment. I would deliver this blessed child from evil.

Mary

Joe Gleason was different from everybody else, right from the start. When he started kindergarten with us, I noticed the vertical scar on his chin, a jagged white line that started below his lower lip and wrapped beneath his face. He told me about his neighbor's German shepherd and I wanted to kill that dog for hurting Joe. I know a lot of people thought that the scar marred him, kept him from being good-looking. To me, it only made him more handsome. The rugged scar was such a contrast to his pale green eyes that turned amber when they caught the light, eyes that spanned wide under dark, heavy brows. During junior high, Eileen once told me that there was something about Joe that frightened her, that she thought he was somehow dangerous.

"What makes him dangerous?" I asked her.

She bit her lip for a second and said, "I don't know. He's so separate from everything. It's like he doesn't need anyone or anything."

Did that make someone dangerous? Maybe Eileen was right. Could you ever be with someone who didn't need you? Dangerous. I decided Joe was. Why else did my heart race when I passed him in the hall, almost dropping my books because my limbs went numb? That kind of love, the kind that encapsulates your very being, that makes you see the world through the thick haze of your emotions, was dangerous. And it was my most cherished secret. My love for Joe kept a steady pulse with my blood. I felt like it was the very thing that kept me alive.

Joe didn't play baseball or basketball like the other popular boys, no, he ran track, broke every school record. During senior year, he placed third in the sectionals for the 3200 meter run and second in the state. None of my friends went to track meets and I couldn't have suggested it. I would have died if word got back to him that I liked him. But in my mind, I thought endlessly of Joe running far ahead of the other athletes, so out front that he was essentially alone on the track, his long kick carrying him farther and farther away.

During track season when we were in high school, Joe ran every morning before school. Like clockwork, he'd pass our house at 7:20. For years I stood at my window, the curtains only slightly parted, and waited for him to sprint by. Our house was towards the end of his route; his face was clouded with red patches and his breath came hard as he ran down the block. He was visible for all of fifteen seconds and then he vanished. I'd let the curtain fall and sigh, knowing it would be twenty-four hours before I'd glimpse him running again. It was hard to be patient. Like Emily Dickinson wrote, "Patience—is the Smile's exertion through the quivering—" I understood that well. Fifteen seconds a day was enough sustenance because that was all I was allowed.

Joe was running away from me, running away from all of us. Anyone could see that he was just biding his time, that he knew what the rest of us didn't, that there was a world outside of South Buffalo, a world where no one knew you, no one knew your story. I liked to pretend that when Joe left, he'd take me with him. I imagined standing in front of my house, Joe stopping his run when he saw me. I wouldn't say anything. I had never said anything to him. Whenever he was near me, I froze, my stomach lurching, my tongue swelling in my mouth. I used to worry that I might faint when we crossed each other's path around the neighborhood. But I fantasized that when Joe saw me standing in front of my house, he would know, he would simply *know* that I was alone too, that I was waiting for him to take me away. I would feel the heat of his run as he put his arm around my shoulders. He would say softly, "Come with me." Down the street we'd walk, one foot in front of the other until we were so far away from here we'd never be able to find our way back.

Kevin Walsh

When I was twelve, I got a pair of speed skates for Christmas. The boots were jet black and the long silver blades gleamed. All the boys wanted speed skates that year. We couldn't wait to meet at the rink and race. I still remember leaning out over the skates, my arms swinging to keep pace with my feet, the cold air rushing against my face. The first time I slept with a girl, I thought about how familiar the pace and rhythm seemed, that last thrust of exertion I always felt skating up to the finish line.

The girls wore those bright white figure skates. They moved more slowly, stopping in little clusters to chat on the ice. You could always spot Eileen Sullivan. She dressed in pale pink and blue skating outfits, big fluffy sweaters with matching hats and mittens. Mary wasn't as dressed up but, like me, she wore a long, colorful stocking cap with a tassel on the end. I'd skate up behind her and pull it off her head, skating away as fast as I could. I'd hear the girls all yelling, "KEVIN! GIVE IT BACK! GIVE IT BACK!" Sheila Adams would look for a rink guard to tattle on me, but on my next turn around the ice, I'd toss the hat back at Mary. She'd roll her eyes but curl her lips in a tiny smile. She didn't mind the attention. I might pull her hat off five times in an afternoon. I'd skate off with it whistling to "Georgie Girl," a song they played over the speakers a lot. One time, I put Mary's hat on my head and tossed my own at her. The pack of girls started yelling at me, but Mary just put the hat on. She started after me, surprisingly fast in those figure skates, and when she was close enough, yanked her hat off of me and skated off with both of them. The girls cheered her as she re-joined them, but she tossed my cap back at me when I skated by. I gave her a wink and felt a thrill in my chest.

As I walked home from the rink with the other boys, we'd talk about the girls. Mike Nelligan was the biggest bragger. He claimed that he kissed Sheila Adams once behind the Dairy Queen and that he could do it again any time he liked. If Eileen Sullivan had any idea the way Timmy Corcoran stared at her breasts in those sweaters, she would have died. When Mary's name came up, I took some ribbing.

"What's so special about you, Kevin?" Timmy asked. "You're the only one she gives the time of day to."

"Yeah," Mike chimed in, "what's your secret? You doing her homework for her?"

I'd just laugh and say, "No secret. I guess she just likes me. She can't help it since I'm so good-looking." The guys would hoot and shove me a little, but I just kept smiling.

But I did have a secret. I knew that Mary liked that I wasn't afraid of her, that I'd treat her like anybody else. That information made me feel like I'd been dealt a winning hand, and I played those cards very close to my chest.

In junior high, when I'd see her with her friends outside the school, I'd whistle as I walked past and sing out, "Looking *gooood*, Connolly, very, very *gooood*." Mary would shake her head at me, but there was that little smile. Eileen would yell, "Hey, Kevin, don't be so fresh!" but I kept on like I didn't even hear her. I didn't feel even one-tenth of the bravado I was showing off, but that didn't matter as long as Mary bought my act.

Joe

When I started school, Mom got a job at Treadwell Furniture Store on Abbott Road. I went to the firehouse every day after school and did my homework, all of my uncles slipping me quarters and feeding me sandwiches until Mom picked me up a little after five o'clock. She was always tired, from the job and from the grief she still carried with her. Mom didn't complain, but she made it clear that I was going to have a different kind of life, one that was never in her reach.

My older brother Pat worked at the Bethlehem Steel Plant in Lackawanna, just south of here. He was smart, but he didn't get a scholarship to any of the colleges he applied to. He had flat feet so he didn't have to go to Vietnam. His plan was to work at the plant a year or two at most, save his money and go to the University of Buffalo. But then he met Katie O'Neil and got married. He stopped talking about college. He and Katie had two babies in two years and then Katie got pregnant with twins. Mom loved being a grandmother, but she was always quiet around Katie. She wasn't mean to her or anything like that, but I knew Mom held it against her that Pat never went to college.

I remember one Sunday after mass as we were getting ready to pull out of the parking lot, Mary Connolly walked past with her parents. Immediately, I glanced down so Mom wouldn't catch me staring at Mary. I was embarrassed, worried that the blood I felt thumping through me was making my face bright red, that Mom would recognize my hunger for Mary in an instant.

Mom made a small sucking noise with her tongue. "That girl is going to be no end of trouble."

"What girl?"

She looked at me and smiled tightly as she lifted her eyebrows. "The one you're trying not to look at." She raised her voice a bit and said, as if she were pronouncing a verdict, "Mary Connolly."

I looked up but the Connollys had passed. I hoped I sounded genuinely confused when I said, "Why is she going to cause trouble?"

Mom inhaled and exhaled deeply. "That kind always does. Mark my words, she's nothing but trouble. Stay away from her."

I tried to joke, "Well, that'll be easy since I barely know her."

"Keep it that way." Her words sounded bitten at the edges. That was the only time we ever talked about Mary. Not that I'd ever have had a chance with Miss Stuck-up, but even if I did, I wouldn't have upset my mother by asking her out.

Eileen

When we were in junior high, it was clear that Kevin had a huge crush on Mary. Luckily, all the other boys did too and Kevin was lost in the crowd. But it bothered me that Mary, usually so shy, could laugh and joke with Kevin. I knew they'd been friends when they were little and that's probably why Mary was comfortable around him, but I also saw the way Kevin watched her when he thought no one else was looking. Sure, he clowned around in front of her if there was an audience, but he also looked out from under his long bangs and stared at her in class as often as he could get away with it.

Of course I liked Kevin. He was so funny. Do you think anyone ever laughed in my house? Ever since we were little kids, Kevin was telling jokes and pulling pranks. But nothing about him was ever mean-spirited. He was happy and he wanted everyone around him to be happy too. Even the nuns liked him. A sister would be reprimanding Kevin to get his pencils out of his ears, but she'd be fighting a smile.

So, when I'd catch him secretly looking at Mary, I'd feel a rage that surprised me. I should have been mad at Kevin for not liking me, but I pinpointed my anger at Mary. One day in eighth grade, when Kevin stared openly at Mary when it was her turn to recite a poem in front of the class, I left the classroom and went to the girls' restroom. In one of the stalls, I wrote with purple marker in large letters, "MARY CONNOLLY IS A SLUT!" I trembled as I stared at the words. Before leaving the restroom, I threw the marker in the trash.

Back at my desk, I wondered how many people would see what I wrote. How long would it take for word to get back to Kevin that the girl he worshipped was, was what? What did slut mean, exactly? Something very bad, very bad in a sex way. A slut was a girl who let a boy do whatever he wanted to her. It was the worst thing that could be said about a girl.

Looking over two aisles, I saw Mary copying down notes from the board. Her blonde head dipped as her pen traveled over her notebook. She was so studious, a model student all the teachers said. I closed my eyes in shame. A few minutes later, I went back to the restroom and wiped away the words with wet toilet paper. Little rivers of purple-stained water ran down the wood door. Another girl entered the restroom and I ran out.

Back in the classroom, I was a million miles away when the teacher was asking for examples of literary metaphors. My body seemed seized by a hundred different emotions that I couldn't sort out. How could you be so envious of your best friend? How could someone who was supposed to mean the world to you make you so angry? It didn't make sense. I looked at Kevin. He was tossing a small eraser in the air and catching it. Be mad at him, I thought. But then he threw the eraser high into the air and he jumped out of his seat to catch it, tumbling onto Sheila Adams desk in the process.

"Kevin!" Sister Mary Charles bellowed as he caught the eraser and quickly slid back into his own seat.

He clasped his hands, sat up straight and said, "Yes, Sister. What can

I do for you?"

The class burst out laughing and Sister reluctantly laughed. "How about paying attention?" she asked.

Kevin raised his hand to his forehead, saluted and said, "Aye, aye, Sister."

Well, it was no use. There was no way I could be mad at Kevin. No way at all.

Mary

When my name comes up at class reunions, I wonder if people will bother to remember that I was smart. Not the smartest in our class, that was Joe Gleason, but I was always in the top five.

Every Halloween through sixth grade, I brought cupcakes to school frosted with bright orange icing, a jack-o-lantern face made out of Indian corn. My mother and I made them together, making the icing ourselves with food coloring. Maybe someone would remember that? Or that I went to the state spelling championships in seventh and eighth grade? During the summers in high school, I worked at the Dairy Queen on Abbott Road, giving extra ice cream to the neighborhood kids whenever I could get away with it. Maybe a few people remember that?

My biggest hope is that someone remembers that I sang with The Buffalo Belles, our high school choir. Actually, I was one of the founding members. A group of us girls were sitting at lunch one day freshman year talking about old songs we liked, songs like "Cherish" and "Leaving on a Jet Plane." We started humming, then singing a few lyrics, and I said, "Maybe we should start a choir?"

Sheila Adams clapped her hands and said, "Yes, just for girls!" A couple of people wanted to include boys, but most people thought it was a good idea to keep it to just girls. I wrote up the flyers and posted them around the school, and in three weeks time twenty-two of us were practicing together. A few of the girls didn't have the greatest voices, but they figured it out on their own and dropped out. And, to be honest, Eileen couldn't sing in tune, but she sang very softly with the other altos and managed to camouflage her voice. Among the remaining girls, we had a nice blend of voices. I was one of three true sopranos along with Kelly Sheridan and Colleen Catalano.

We started out singing in hospitals and nursing homes. On St. Patrick's Day, we sang at the Irish Center, a lot of the audience teary-eyed when we sang "Danny Boy" and "Molly Malone." Then a local reporter did a story on us for the *Buffalo Evening News* newspaper and the bookings started to come in. We sang at a lot of weddings, mostly that Carpenters' song, "We've Only Just Begun," or "The Wedding Song." We started to earn money, and Sister Lucia Marie, our advisor, opened a bank account for us.

We became pretty well known in South Buffalo and even had some performances in other parts of the city. Lots of girls wanted to join the choir. Each year during September, we held auditions. Parents car-pooled us to our performances, so proud of our growing fame.

Being in the choir was the best part of high school. Whenever I sang, I didn't feel like Mary Connolly. I was one of the Buffalo Belles, a member of a special little community with a simple purpose, to sing. I didn't stand out in any way, I was just like all the other girls.

Then, junior year, a poster with my picture on it was used to advertise the annual Buffalo Arts Festival. It had been clipped from one of our group shots and enlarged by one of the festival planners. My picture was plastered all over South Buffalo, on bulletin boards at the library, the laundromat, on storefronts. Anyone who saw the poster would conclude that I was the star of the choir. My mother, naturally, was in seventh heaven, but a bunch of the girls in the choir were angry. I didn't blame them. Eileen was the only one to say, "It's not Mary's fault! She had nothing to do with it." But I caught the eye rolls, the exchanged glances.

Eileen helped me take down the posters. We rode our bikes around the neighborhood and took down every single one. But there were still some sore feelings. Nancy Myers didn't talk to me for a couple of weeks and Kelly Sheridan dropped out of the choir altogether. I tried talking to her, but she told me she was babysitting a lot and didn't have the time to sing any more. A few days later, Eileen told me that Kelly had admitted that her mother was making her drop the choir because it had turned into "The Mary Connolly Show." I wanted to die. Eileen said, "Don't sweat it. Your voice is ten times better than hers. We're better off without Kelly." I knew that no one else in the choir saw it that way.

I made sure I was never singled out again. Periodically, we'd buy new matching t-shirts with our logo, a tiny buffalo on top of a bell, with our earnings. I convinced the other girls that we should spend some of the money for a professional photo. Afterwards, that was the only photo allowed for advertising. I think that did smooth some ruffled feathers. No other girls dropped out, and we recruited another soprano to replace Kelly.

During my senior year, the Buffalo Belles recorded a tape that was sold in some of the local stores. I wonder how many of those tapes are floating around the neighborhood, if anyone still listens to it. If so, maybe someone remembers me as one of the sopranos. That would be nice, but it's probably too much to hope for. When something like getting pregnant happens, your whole life gets reduced to only that.

It's not fair, but I'm used to it. People have always reduced me. Before the pregnancy, I was only beautiful. The things I like to remember about myself don't matter to any one else. And when that's all you are, beautiful, everyone's waiting for you to take a big fall. Well, I guess I didn't let them down.

🐝

Mr. Harrigan

There's a bit of fun and a bit of embarrassment to being a pharmacist. During their high school years, a few boys always tried to buy condoms. They came in the store and wandered around for way too long. I knew they were trying to get up the nerve to approach the cash register, to try and nonchalantly purchase a pack of Trojans.

Sometimes I'd approach a boy as he walked about, say something like, "Say, you're so and so's son. Tell him I said hello. Now, is there anything I can help you with?" The boy would turn scarlet, mumble "No thanks," beneath his breath and leave the store. Sometimes, to save face, he'd buy gum or a candy bar.

Every now and then, I'd see a boy open the door, catch a glimpse of my wife at the register, and not even bother coming in. I had to chuckle. Poor kids, they're just trying to figure out life and it's damn scary when you're sixteen, seventeen. I wouldn't go back to that age if you paid me.

Of course, a lot of high school boys had older brothers who helped them out, bought beer and condoms for them. I knew that, but what could I do? Kevin Walsh's older brother was a steady customer as was Mike Nelligan's. They could have been supplying an army of high school boys, but that was none of my business. If a person is of age and has the money, he's entitled to buy whatever we stock in the store.

My wife once said that she worried that one of the priests would come in and see that we sold condoms and then what? When I just smiled and shrugged, she said, "We could be excommunicated!"

I threw back my head and laughed. "Look, Marie, if you want me to stop selling them, we're going to lose business. People buy an armload of stuff so they don't have to come to the counter with just a box of condoms."

She shook her head. "I don't know. . .we're Catholics."

"But not all of our customers are. We can't discriminate," I said briskly, "wouldn't be right."

When she still didn't relent, I said, "Well, if you want to try not selling them for a year, we can give it a try. But if we lose money, we'll have to give up our summer vacation."

That did it. Marie stopped grousing, and I continued watching the anguish of teenage boys. Sometimes I wanted to just say to them, "Don't be in such a rush!" But they'd only laugh at me, and, heck, I wouldn't blame them. You know, people talk about the times changing, but kids are still kids. They have to go through the same things we did. They think we don't understand them, but it wasn't that long ago we were in their shoes.

❧

Eileen Sullivan

A few days a week, I'd go to Mary's house after school. There was always a tin of cookies on the kitchen table and Mrs. Connolly would pour big glasses of milk for us. She was eager to hear everything about our day. Mary and I would chew cookies and answer her between swallows. When we were in elementary school, conversations would go like this:

"Mary, did anyone compliment you on your new scarf?" It was a red and blue one that Mrs. Connolly had knitted herself. Mary would shake her head no, but I'd answer, "Yes, Kathy and Karen Strayer did." They complimented Mary on everything; chances were they had admired her scarf.

Mrs. Connolly would nod and say, "Did anything else happen?"

One day we both burst out laughing in response to her question. "What? What?" Mrs. Connolly asked eagerly. Mary and I both tried to answer, but we kept breaking into giggles. Finally, I blurted, "Kevin Walsh brought a kitten to school. He saw it in front of Murphy's store and thought it needed a good home."

Mary nodded. Wiping the crumbs from her mouth, she said, "And Sister Kathleen Anne thought the kitten was cute, so she took it from Kevin and it peed all over her habit!" That set us off again laughing, and we could barely finish the story, gasping for breath while we explained how the cat escaped from the classroom and was somewhere in the school.

Mrs. Connolly also laughed. "What else happened today?" She studied Mary's face. She wanted to know everything that happened to Mary when they were apart. Unless something major like a cat coming to school had occurred, Mary was pretty quiet. I think that's why I was always welcome at the Connolly's. Mrs. Connolly knew she could learn a lot about her daughter's life from me. And I didn't let her down. I would recite minute details about who gave what dumb answer in science class and how David O'Shea had to go see the school nurse after lunch because he had a stomach ache from eating so many Hostess Ho-hos. They were just silly tidbits, but Mrs. Connolly couldn't get enough. Mary spent most of her time at home reading and I was Mrs. Connolly's window into her daughter's school life.

She was even more curious when we were in high school, eager to know who was dating whom, asking Mary if anyone had a crush on her. She'd smile broadly when I'd answer, "EVERYONE has a crush on Mary." Mary would deny it over and over, but I would insist that every boy I knew had a thing for Mary. Mrs. Connolly would pour us more milk and pump me for details.

It wasn't that way at my house. In the afternoons, my mother was in her room resting, the shades pulled down. I was supposed to do my homework quietly. I'd tiptoe around the kitchen getting a snack and then opened my books. Afterwards, I'd turn on the television with the sound so low, I had to sit right in front of the set to hear it. At six o'clock, the alarm on my mother's bedside clock would go off and she'd get up so my father wouldn't find her asleep when he came home at half past six. Mother's dinner preparations generally consisted of her heating soup and making sandwiches. Sometimes Dad would cook hamburgers or sausages, but Mother only ate a bite or two.

We barely spoke when we ate dinner. Dad and I would steal glances at Mother to try and figure out how much she had drunk that afternoon. After dinner, she would say she was going to read in bed, but she was usually fast asleep by the time I was done with the dishes. In the morning, she'd be at her best, making coffee and pouring juice for me. She talked about her plans to shop, asking me if I needed a new blue skirt or if any of my knee socks were getting worn in the heel. Dad and I would almost smile at one another. But we knew that after Mother's shopping excursion, she'd drink in the afternoon and we'd have to endure another slight meal pretending that she wasn't hung over.

Mary and I stayed over at each other's houses often. Dad was always nice, taking us out to dinner and then to a movie or a Sabres game. He'd make apologies for Mother, saying she didn't feel well. In the morning at breakfast, Mother would be so polite to Mary it was embarrassing. She'd say things like, "Mary, you're getting more beautiful every time I see you. That sweater is darling, just darling. It brings out the blue in your eyes. Did your mother make it? She must be so clever. No wonder you're so smart." I could have died of embarrassment. As I watched Mary grow more and more uncomfortable, my brain screamed, "Shut up, Mother!" But she'd prattle on and on and not notice that Mary was barely answering her.

All the years we'd been friends, and Mary never said a word to me about my mother. It was clear Mother was an alcoholic, that she was strange, but Mary never questioned me about her, not once. She also never said a thing about Mother to anyone else. Any other girl in our class would have blabbed to everyone that Eileen Sullivan's mother was a real nut case, but Mary was so kind and loyal. I was more than grateful to be her best friend. I was desperate to be her best friend.

I was with Mary whenever possible. I didn't sing well, but I managed to get into the Buffalo Belles choir with her. We walked to and from school together every day, sat next to each other at lunch. And I was vigilant; I didn't let anyone else get too close to Mary. When the Strayer twins invited her on a weekend camping trip, I told Mary that they talked about her behind her back, said she was conceited and stuck up. Mary looked shocked, but she didn't go on the camping trip. Another time I told her, "Molly Boyle calls you

'The Jolly Green Giant,' because you're so tall." That was really cruel because I knew Mary was sensitive about her height. And I told her, "Sheila Adams thinks you're in love with yourself." Lies, all lies, but my fear of losing Mary was greater than my guilt. She was my best friend and I was hers. I made sure of it.

Father Louis Gibbon

As she was growing up, I encouraged Mrs. Connolly to send Mary to confession every Saturday so her soul would gleam like the chalice on Sunday mornings when she took communion. "Send her to me," I'd say to Mrs. Connolly, "Father Wright tends to scare the children."

All those Saturday afternoons she came to my confessional. Now and then I wondered if she made up her minor misdeeds just to have something to confess. Her mother assured me that Mary was an obedient child, somewhat quiet, but always polite and respectful.

Most of the children and their parents called me Father Lou. You know, it was the late sixties and we were all trying to get to know each other. The nuns were bringing guitars into church for the folk masses and it was all very friendly. Mary, though, always called me Father Gibbon. She was more reserved than the other children. She had an old-fashioned respect for authority.

She stopped coming to confession when she was thirteen. Of course, many of the children stop about that age. They think they know what the world's all about, that adults are old fogies. When I mentioned Mary's absence to Mrs. Connolly, she wrung her hands and set her mouth in a firm line. "Father, I've tried and tried. She tells me she hasn't anything to confess."

Well, maybe that was true. But I had to stay in her life. I had made a promise to God to protect the child. So, I began a required class for confirmation students on Saturday mornings. Mary sat quietly at the back of the classroom while I lectured about what it meant to be an adult in the eyes of the church, that the students were now truly accountable for their sins because they were old enough to know the difference between right and wrong.

During the last class before the children were to make the sacrament, I asked the students what confirmation names they had chosen. Michael, James, Thomas, Patrick. The boys' names were pretty run of the mill. A lot of the girls were taking the names Mary, Marie and Anne. A few of them had convinced their parents to allow them to take less common names like Nicole and Michelle. I stopped in front of Mary's desk and asked, "And what name are you taking?"

A blush crept up her throat and onto her cheeks. Softly, Mary answered, "Louise." Louise! Well, that was hardly a popular name at the time. The female form of Louis, my own name. Perhaps her mother had suggested it? But no, a mother who couldn't make her daughter attend confession wouldn't have been able to make her take a name she didn't care for. No, this was something else. Mary was trying to tell me something. I could feel it. She was acknowledging my role in her life. This was her way of saying thank you. I felt pleasantly startled, but of course had to appear composed. I nodded at her and went on to the next student.

After Mary was confirmed, I suggested to Mrs. Connolly that she host a weekly Bible study group for women at her home. I was there every Wednesday morning instructing the wives of the parish. Inside the Connolly's house, I could look for any sign that Mary was straying from God's path.

It was a comfortable home, not fancy, but clean and tidy. Mrs. Connolly always made sure there was plenty of coffee and the women brought all kinds of things to eat. I sensed that some of them were jealous that it was always Mrs. Connolly who hosted; a few of them were always offering to have the group at their homes. I thanked everyone but noted that the Connolly home was ideal because it was centrally located in the parish. That made Mrs. Connolly beam. I suspect my weekly visits helped her social status.

So, we met from ten until noon on Wednesday mornings. We started with selected readings in the Old Testament, reading passages and discussing their meaning. I listened carefully to the women, but I glanced about noticing the photos of Mary everywhere, the trophies and rhinestone tiaras that were so out of place with the crucifixes and the Infant of Prague statue.

One day when Mary was a sophomore in high school, I excused myself from the group to use the restroom upstairs. Before rejoining the women, I stepped quietly into Mary's room. It was a beautiful day in April and a shaft of light stretched from the window across the bed. It was a room like most girls, I suppose, with homemade floral curtains that matched the bedspread, the walls painted a robin's egg blue. I imagined Mr. Connolly picked the color because it matched his daughter's eyes. I glanced at all the little items on the dresser, hair barrettes, a jewelry box, a small porcelain statue of a little girl holding a balloon. Coiled into the doily was a child's rosary made of pink plastic beads.

There were stacks of books everywhere, on the makeshift shelves next to the bed, in piles on the floor, on top of the dresser. I scanned the titles; there was nothing questionable although I wasn't familiar with some of the books. It would have been comforting to come across a Bible amongst all these volumes, but perhaps Mary read her mother's.

On the door to her closet were several colorful posters and pictures cut from magazines. I recognized Robert Redford although the caption of the photo read, "The Sundance Kid." There was a poster from the movie, "Love Story," the words, "Love means never having to say you're sorry," scribbled across it. Absurd. Why love is all *about* forgiveness. I hadn't seen the film, but I knew it wasn't appropriate for a girl Mary's age. Somehow, I'd have to broach the subject with her mother. But the most disturbing image was that of the Beatles, those four English musicians who caused such hysteria. I didn't know which of them was John Lennon, they all looked alike, but I knew that he had make a remark some years ago about the Beatles being more popular than Jesus Christ. Heresy in our times. Beatles music should have been banned from the radio. And here, in Mary's bedroom of all places, this poster was up on her door like some kind of shrine.

God knows, I almost wept. I needed to do something to interrupt Mary's journey down the wrong path, give a sermon or two on the corruptive influence of popular music. I'd encourage parents to read the lyrics of the songs their children were listening to, to not allow WKBW, the rock station, to be played in their homes. Would it amount to anything? All I could do was pray.

The light shifted and the room became suddenly dark. I sensed something ominous; a faint shiver traveled up my spine. From my shirt pocket, I removed the tiny bottle of holy water I always carried. Removing the cap, I sprinkled its contents onto Mary's bed. "Dear Jesus," I prayed, "Let me do all in my power to save Mary Connolly from the forces of darkness. Let me guide her to your divine love." I made the sign of the cross over the bed and left the room.

Downstairs the women bustled about to refill my cup and serve up more coffeecake. I looked at Mrs. Connolly as she set more napkins on the table. She was well-intentioned, but not very smart, I'm afraid. Her daughter was being corrupted before her very eyes and she didn't have a clue.

Joe

Ever since I could remember, Mom drilled it into me that I was capable of winning a scholarship to a good school and becoming a doctor. Every now and then I'd say something like, "Why a doctor? How about a teacher or a bike shop owner?" I made different occupations up. Shaking her head, Mom would raise her hand and pretend she was going to slap my head. "Don't joke about your future," she always said, "be the best you can be and nothing less."

Lucky for me, I *was* interested in medicine. Mom made more novenas for me than I could count. She checked my homework every night and drilled me before every test. I appreciated her help, but I didn't need it. School was always easy for me. I liked all the subjects, but especially math and science. Why not be a doctor? I kidded around with her, told her I'd make her call me "Doctor Gleason" once I graduated from medical school.

Still, Mom was always worried that I'd ditch her plan. When I dated Cheryl Byrne sophomore and junior years, she fretted that I was going to fall in love, get married, and end up just like Pat. I think every time I took Cheryl out, Mom sat at home saying the rosary, praying to God that I would still go to college. I tried to joke, saying, "Mom, you want me to be a doctor, right? Not a priest. Of course I'm going to go out with girls." She'd shake her head at me and then make the sign of the cross.

She stood over me while I filled out my college applications, reading and re-reading the forms until she was all but cross-eyed. The guidance counselor, Father Stephen, encouraged me to apply to Catholic universities. All Mom's prayers paid off when I was offered a full track scholarship to Fordham University in New York.

Mom cried the day the letter came, and then she immediately got ready to go to church and give thanks to God. I laughed and said, "Mom, I had *something* to do with it, you know! Who do you think got those grades? Who do you think won all those races?"

She shook her small tight fist, but then she kissed my forehead and said, "You be grateful to God, young man."

Actually, I was grateful to her. I had studied hard and ran track, but she had raised me without a father and worked all those years when every other mom in the neighborhood stayed home. I knew it would be years and years before I was a doctor, that this was just the beginning, the easy part. It would be years before she could say, "My son, the doctor." A lifetime of novenas away.

I celebrated the scholarship the only way I knew how. I put on my running shoes and stepped outside. The fresh air filled my lungs and every slap of the pavement beneath my feet pounded with victory. I ran the length of McKinley Parkway, past all the fancy houses, and back. I stopped at the firehouse to share the good news with my uncles. They hooped and hollered until the alarm sounded and they had to jump on the truck and be off. I ran out of the house with the bell sounding in my ears, adrenaline chugged through me, making me feel like Superman. I ran and ran, feeling more euphoric with each block. I didn't want to stop; I felt like I could run forever. I thought about what it would be like to run in New York and wondered if there would be guys there faster than me. I ran harder, feeling my body want to take flight. I was going so fast it felt like the sidewalk was pushing me ahead. Maybe I had too much oxygen in my brain, I don't know, but there was a moment when I lifted my arms and thought the air might lift me. I tripped and came close to landing head first on the pavement, but then I caught my balance and kept on running. When I stopped, I was standing in my driveway, exactly where I'd started out from. I had a glorious sweat, perspiration running down my head, my arms, my legs. I thought, if I died now, I'd die happy.

Sheila Adams

I genuinely liked Mary. Anyone who really got to know her would. There was nothing phony about her. She didn't talk about people behind their backs or brag about all those beauty contests she'd won. Everyone assumed she'd be head cheerleader in high school, but she didn't even try out for the squad. It killed Eileen, because she was dying to cheer, but she followed suit and sat in the bleachers with Mary. Ironically, I got to be head cheerleader and became popular. Not that it really mattered to me, just like it didn't seem to matter to Mary. I think she and I would have gotten along, but Eileen surrounded her like a fortress. She never left me alone with Mary long enough to have a real conversation. I would have liked talking about classes with her, studying for tests together, shopping, going to the movies. Mary was a big reader and it would have been fun chatting about books together. But Eileen was almost always there, standing next to her like a bodyguard. And Eileen never shut up. She dominated every conversation and Mary, like the rest of us, barely got a word in edgewise.

So, we went through school together, Mary and I, friendly but not close. The gossip that's flying around now is so mean, so awfully cruel. People only talk about Mary, they don't mention the guy's role in this whole mess. This would be the time to offer friendship to Mary, but I can't. I mean, I look at Mary and think, God, that could have been me. Well no, it could never have been me and that was my whole problem.

Mary

I hated dating. It was so awkward and embarrassing. I felt guilty about the boy spending money on me when, emotionally, I felt nothing for him. I went out to movies and out for pizza more times than I could count. I saw "The Sting" with three different boys because I felt too shy to mumble more than, "Okay," when someone asked me out. Sitting in a dark movie was all right because I didn't have to talk. Afterwards, at Jacobi's Pizzeria, there would be the really awful ten minutes or so when we talked about the movie and I had to actually make conversation. Then, without fail, the guy started talking about himself and all I had to do was listen for the rest of the night. Or pretend to listen. I found that if I propped my chin in my hand and nodded occasionally, the boy never even realized I was a million miles away. Once in a blue moon, I'd realize my date was as shy as me, and that was agony, the two of us chewing our food so slowly and taking long sips of Coke to fill the time. I did date one guy, Mark Schiffer, who seemed to read as much as me, but he was a science fiction fan and spent the whole night talking about his favorite Star Trek episodes. Boring, but at least I didn't have to do any talking.

Of course, saying goodnight was the worst part of all. As soon as we drove up to my house, I opened the car door immediately so my date would realize that I wasn't going to neck in the car. Boys were usually shyer on my doorstep, probably nervous that my parents were spying from a window. I was as tall as most of them so usually they just leaned in quickly and brushed their lips against mine. Some guys would reach around my waist and hold me to them for a longer kiss, their tongues trying to penetrate my mouth. That always made me feel like a prisoner and I learned to jerk my head down and step sideways out of an embrace if it went on too long.

In the house, my mother always pressed me for details. I said things like, "He was nice," and "We had a good time." Mother always wanted to know more, asking what we talked about, did he hold my hand during the movie, blah, blah, blah. Thankfully, my father would interrupt and tell her to stop bugging me.

I dated very few guys more than a couple of times. I had a standard line: "My parents think I'm too young to date any one person seriously." They'd never said that, but it seemed like a reasonable stance to take. I tried to be nice, especially since some of the guys were clearly a nervous wreck about going out with me. I never wanted to hurt anyone's feelings, and the truth was, by high school standards, I was a lousy date. I didn't make conversation easily and my romantic experience didn't go beyond kissing. Probably I should have just said no when boys called on the phone, but I knew it must have taken a lot of courage to call. I'd never called a boy in my life and couldn't imagine how awful it would be to have to make the first move. I felt sorry for the boys and I didn't want to hurt their feelings. So I went out with anyone who called for at least one date. Every Friday night I had a date. Luckily, Eileen and I had been staying over at each other's houses on Saturday nights since we were little kids. Otherwise, I would have had two dates every weekend.

As ridiculous as it sounds, when I was on a date, I felt like I was being unfaithful to Joe. Clearly, he didn't know I was alive, but still I felt disloyal going out with other boys. But how long was I supposed to wait for someone who obviously couldn't care less about me?

Once, while I was at Jacobi's with a date, Joe and Cheryl Byrne came in and were seated just a couple of tables away. As hard as it was seeing Joe with Cheryl, I felt worse about Joe seeing *me* with another guy. Can you beat that? He totally ignored me but I felt like I was betraying my love for him by dating someone else.

Later that night, while I was in bed, I imagined Joe saying good-night to Cheryl. Did they kiss for a long time? Did they do anything else? I had sketchy notions of them making love, but that didn't bother me nearly as much as the thought of Cheryl looking directly into Joe's eyes for as long as she wanted to, or her sliding her hand into his. The thought of someone else being affectionate in that way with Joe killed me. Sex, in my mind, could never equal the intimacy of Joe simply holding my hand. Sometimes I dreamed that we were walking down Abbott Road together, our fingers interlaced. When I woke, I could still feel the weight and warmth of his hand on mine. I would whisper softly, "Don't leave without me, Joe. Hold my hand and take me with you." I kept my eyes closed to block the light creeping into my room from beneath the blinds. The pressure of his ghost hand on mine would fade and I would sadly open my eyes to a day no different than yesterday.

❧

Sheila Adams

I was sixteen and I still didn't have my period. It was humiliating. At sleepovers, when girls talked about how gross they thought the whole business was, I made faces and pretended I was a member of the club. When the topic of whether virgins could wear tampons came up, I nodded my head with other girls who proclaimed that the thought of putting something *"up and inside me"* was positively sickening.

But before long, I had something up and inside me and it wasn't a tampon. It was Kevin's penis, hard and hot, hitting my cervix with such force I felt as if my entire body was hiccupping. Looking back, I'm grateful that I didn't get labeled a slut, that ugly word that got tossed around. I told Kevin that if he told anyone, and I meant *anyone,* that I'd never sleep with him again. Well, he was quick to promise every time and, as far as I know, he kept his end of the bargain.

The sex helped. It calmed that buzzing in my head, the constant thought that I was some kind of freak. Mother's younger sister, my Aunt Maureen, got her period late and when it finally came, it hardly came. She might menstruate twice a year and then go another year with nothing. She wasn't married; she still lived at home with her parents, sleeping in the same room she'd slept in her entire life. Aunt Maureen worked as a salesclerk at Kresge's, scooping goldfish out of the fish tank and into little plastic bags for kids to take home. She folded and re-folded the clothes on the sales table and measured fabric for customers. Each night, she ate her dinner alone at Crean's Soda Fountain, the restaurant right across the street from Kresge's. Sometimes I would walk past and see her sitting all alone in a big booth. I wondered why she didn't eat at home with her parents, but maybe she liked being able to afford her own meals.

She had a serious boyfriend once. I remember when I was a little girl that Aunt Maureen brought him to some holiday dinners. When he stopped coming, I asked my mother what happened. She said, "Shh, don't talk about it. And never, *NEVER* say anything to Aunt Maureen about him. Do you understand?" I nodded even though I didn't. A few years later, my older sister

told me that Aunt Maureen's boyfriend left her when she confessed that she'd probably be unable to have children.

So, I would likely end up just like her, living at home with my parents while all my friends got married and started families of their own. The idea of spinsterhood terrified me.

That's when I came up with my plan, my hope to lead a normal life. Maybe if I was really, *really* nice to the boys, then maybe one of them would marry me. He'd think I was enough for him. No need for children. We'd both work and have a lot of money to travel, maybe go to Florida for a couple weeks every winter. I would be tan all year long and people would envy me instead of feeling sorry for me.

I'd always liked Kevin. Everyone did. He was cute and funny, always smiling with that chipped front tooth he got skating when we were kids. One night senior year, after a basketball game, he offered me a ride home. He had his older brother's beat up car. I only lived four blocks from school and usually walked home with a bunch of other kids in the neighborhood, but I said, "Sure."

As he turned the key in the ignition, I thought, "If he knew I was a freak, he wouldn't even talk to me." That buzzing in my head started and I began to perspire. When Kevin drove to park behind the Botanical Gardens, I assumed he just wanted to neck. Lots of kids made out there after the games and would talk the following day about whose cars were there. And maybe necking was all Kevin wanted, but the look of happiness, of sheer *thanks*, he gave me when I pulled my sweater over my head stopped the buzzing in my head completely. *He likes me*, I thought, my heart pumping with a hopeful rhythm. At least for now, right this second, he likes me. I gave him my ultimatum, he gave me his promise. He didn't have a rubber; he wasn't expecting to get lucky. It was over in a few minutes. Part of me wondered if it actually happened. I had only felt a dull pressure, a pinch that wasn't as bad as a shot of novacaine at the dentist, and then some squirming around. This was the big deal? This is what meant so much to the boys? As we were fumbling to get dressed, Kevin shyly murmured, "Do you think you got pregnant?"

In the dark, he didn't see the way my face fell. Now it felt like there were butterflies between my temples, a soft flapping of tiny wings that gradually grew louder until that buzzing sensation returned. I had already slept with Kevin. What else could I do so he would like me? Now he'd know

I was a freak, damaged like Aunt Maureen. My lips started to quiver, but I managed to say, "I can't get pregnant. The doctor says it would take a miracle." I waited a long moment and asked fearfully, "Do you mind?"

"Are you kidding? I don't mind!"

Well, if I knew more then about the sex drive of a sixteen-year-old boy, I would never have asked such a ridiculous question. I laugh now, but then, as crazy as it sounds, all I thought then was, "He doesn't think I'm a freak!" I exhaled a huge breath and said, "You'd better take me home now. My parents will worry if I'm too late."

There were plenty of nights at the Botanical Gardens. A lot of girls liked Kevin and asked me what we were doing after the games. I'd smile and say, "Just necking." They smiled and nodded. Of course that's all we were doing. No girl from Saint Martin's would be doing anything more. Well, if they only knew.

Kevin was nice to me. He took me ice skating and to the movies. When his friends were around, he didn't pay too much attention to me, but, always, by the end of the night, we'd be in the car together heading to the Botanical Gardens. I lived for the feel of Kevin's touch, and wished he didn't get down to the main event so soon. We didn't spend a lot of time kissing beforehand or cuddling afterwards. It was all about him being inside me, his fevered rush extinguishing itself in a matter of moments. For me, it wasn't pleasurable, at least not in a physical way. But emotionally, I savored that all too brief time when Kevin was inside of me. Then he was all mine; I wasn't sharing him with his family or his buddies or anyone else. For that little time, I was the center of his universe. I was sliding into love with Kevin the way he slid into bases when I watched him play baseball, fast and with some pain. My fingers were crossed that he was falling in love with me, and that I wasn't just an easy lay. Was that silly to hope for? I had to believe it, to feel it. And maybe someday we'd get married and we'd love each other so much that we wouldn't miss the babies that would never come.

Eileen

Kevin was always confident, but mid-way through senior year he developed a swagger. At school he sauntered down the halls like he owned the place, grinning from ear to ear. He'd call out loudly to his friends or just start singing at the top of his lungs, "GONNA HEAR SOME FUNKY DIXIELAND, PRETTY MOMMA COME AND TAKE ME BY THE HAND." There was no doubt about it, he was having sex.

At lunch, he sat next to Sheila Adams, so that's how I knew she was the one sleeping with Kevin.

Sheila Adams. The girl had everything; why did she have to take Kevin too?

Sheila's family lived in a cute house on Eden Street. There were two spruce trees on the front lawn; she told me once that her parents had planted each of them to celebrate her and her sister's births. Imagine that, being so wanted that someone would plant a tree for you! Her parents ran a dry cleaning business on Ridge Road, and her older sister was in nursing school. During the summer, the family spent weekends at their cottage in Crystal Beach, just over the border from Buffalo in Canada.

In late August of every year, Sheila would invite a bunch of us girls for a day at the cottage. We'd swim and lay in the sun, a transistor radio blaring, and work on our tans. That evening, Sheila's mom would make a huge bowl of potato salad, and her dad would grill hamburgers and hot dogs. Nothing was fancy, but it was nice, really nice. Mrs. Adams called all of us "sweetie" or "honey" like we were all her daughters. She probably couldn't remember all of our names, but I liked someone calling me something other than Eileen. Sheila's dad called her "Dumpling." She pretended to be mortified, grimacing when he said it, but I was jealous. I'd never had a nickname.

When it was dark, we made a bonfire on the beach and toasted S'mores. I was always sad when it was time to go. At home, I'd tiptoe through our dark house and slip quietly into my bed. I'd think of Sheila at the cottage with her parents, her mom casually putting an arm around her shoulder, dropping a kiss on her forehead, and feel even more alone.

And then, on top of everything, Sheila got Kevin too. All those years, I worried that Mary, my best friend, would end up with him, but I was wrong. It was Sheila who had the perfect life.

❧

Father Louis Gibbon

High School is fraught with temptations. These older boys and girls look almost like young men and women, but, emotionally, they're still children. They still act on impulse, have no sense of patience. What matters is only what's immediately in front of them; they don't see the big picture. They have no idea that one wrong decision can impact their entire lives.

And girls and boys are so different. When it comes to the opposite sex, the girls have romantic ideas about love and marriage. They're not ready for any of it, but that's the way they think. And the boys. Well, the boys are at an age when they're not thinking clearly at all. They're full of curiosity and eager to experiment, but they're too immature to understand that the girls don't have the same desires they do. Yes, it's a very difficult time of life for young people, and television and the movies make it worse, much worse. The boys and girls are pummeled with images of inappropriate intimacy that they think they should copy.

When Mary and her classmates were in high school, I was observant. I'd see young couples walking around the neighborhood holding hands, and I'd think, well, that's nice, as long as it ends there. But, of course, there are always students who want to push the envelope. It's inevitable that there will always be a few who stray from the path. I saw that I had a duty to keep the children on the straight and narrow.

Father Wright, my senior colleague in the parish, saw no reason to talk about intimacy with the students. "No sense getting them all fired up about things they don't need to know until they're married," he said. It made no sense to tell him that it was a new world, that birth control was out there, that our young people would be tempted more than ever to experience physical love. In the end, he didn't support my idea to hold half-day retreats on the subject, but he didn't stop me.

The morning retreat, held on a Saturday in the school's auditorium, was for the parents. I was disappointed with the turnout; only seventeen attended, mostly mothers but a few fathers too. Mrs. Connolly and the other women in our bible study group were there, even Mrs. Hansen who didn't have children. That struck me as odd, but perhaps she had nieces and nephews she was concerned about.

I spoke to the parents about the Catholic Church's stance on pre-marital sex and what made the times we lived in so dangerous. I was startled when one of the father's raised his hand and asked how birth control pills work. Without the slightest hesitation, he asked, "How does the pill keep a woman from getting pregnant? I mean, an aspirin takes a headache away. There's actually a pill that takes a baby away?" He ended with a slight chuckle, like it was a comical matter. Some of the women turned pink in the face and others looked down at the floor. Clearing my throat, I said, "It really doesn't matter how they work because the Pope condemns their usage. Preventing life is an egregious sin in the eyes of God. We have to make sure that our young people understand this."

Mrs. Hansen timidly raised her hand. "Father, is preventing life as great a sin as taking life away? I mean," she stammered, "is using birth control the same as committing murder?" She slowly raised her eyes to meet mine and I saw the fear in her face. I was encouraged to see that someone was grasping the seriousness of the subject. "YES," I answered as loudly as I could, "in a sense, birth control is legalized murder." There were audible gasps in the audience, and I noticed Mrs. Hansen was blinking her eyes rapidly, as if to contain tears. I had underestimated her. She was one of the quieter women at bible study, but today I realized that she was filled with compassion, grieving for the children of God who would never be born.

I concluded with encouraging the parents to have discrete discussions with their children about the importance of waiting until after marriage to engage in sexual relations. "Make them understand that sex has one purpose and one purpose only: procreation." As I finished speaking, I noticed that Mrs. Connolly was nodding in agreement with me.

Fifty-seven students attended the afternoon session, more than three times the number of parents I had in the morning. There wasn't assigned seating, but I noticed the girls were up front while the boys took the back seats. I started the class by saying loudly, "So, you think you know everything there is to know about sex, do you?" There was some embarrassed laughter and several of the boys hollered, "Yeah!" I laughed heartily and said,

"Well, good, because I have a quiz for you to take." Ha! Several seconds of complete silence. "Just kidding," I said, and there were audible signs of relief. I continued, "But how many of you think you would pass?"

I walked up and down the center aisle, my eyes scanning each row. "If you came here today thinking I was going to talk about the actual sex act, you'll be disappointed. I'm not." That remark elicited several loud groans. I reached the back of the room and turned around, walking slowly as I examined each and every face. "But I am going to talk about something much more important than that. I'm going to talk about *why* procreation is a sacred gift from God and *why* you must treat that gift with utmost respect." I reached the front of the room again. I turned around and looked at the auditorium filled with curious boys and girls. If they listened to me today as the parents had, if they took my words to heart, they'd approach marriage and reproduction as God intended. I was about to teach them one of the most important of lessons to be learned, one they'd think back on over and over again throughout their lives. Looking out over the seats, I scanned the audience one more time hoping I might have missed her, but I hadn't. Mary Connolly wasn't there.

Here I'd gone to all this trouble and she was absent. Of course the other children would benefit from my words, but Mary had been my motivation for the retreats. I knew God was testing me, commanding me to help her keep her soul pure. But how could I if she didn't allow me to guide her?

Perhaps Mary was ill and couldn't attend. No, her mother would have mentioned that to me this morning. Thinking of Mrs. Connolly, I shook my head. She was a devout Catholic, but she wasn't looking after her own daughter properly. It made my job that much more difficult.

Then I looked at the girls seated in the first rows and I realized that it was a gregarious group. The Strayer twins, their faces bearing too much make-up, were there along with the rest of the cheerleaders. And Pamela O'Malley, a trouble-maker since the lower grades. It dawned on me that the subject of my talk had drawn the loud, over-bearing faction of the students. Why, of course Mary had stayed home! She was much too shy to attend the lecture. She hadn't been insolent, no, the poor thing was too embarrassed to attend. No need for worry after all. I felt grateful reassurance. Mary was innocent, and with God's grace and my guidance, she would stay that way.

Mary

The school made a big deal about Joe's scholarship. His senior class photo was put in the glass display case outside the principal's office. Someone made large letters out of construction paper, blue and gold, the school's colors, that said, "CONGRATULATIONS, JOE GLEASON, ON WINNING A SCHOLARSHIP TO FORDHAM UNIVERSITY." An old pair of his running shoes were in the case along with a bunch of newspaper clippings from all of his high school track meets.

I thought of what that first morning would be like, the one where I would stand at my window waiting for Joe to run by, only he'd never come. I'd be left staring out at the empty street. Of course, Joe had been running away from everyone and everything for years. I thought of the myth of Atlanta, the fleet-footed woman who tried to outrun Melanion, but she lost time by picking up the golden apples he threw to her. Golden apples so beautiful she couldn't resist picking them up, but they caused her to lose the race. And what could you do with golden apples? You couldn't eat them, they couldn't nourish you. Beautiful, yes, but they were useless. Of course, Atlanta married Melanion after losing the race, but I never even got to run beside Joe.

I wouldn't be going to college. No one in my family ever had and it wasn't discussed. Even if I had begged to go, my parents couldn't have afforded it. They had a mortgage that would take years to pay off and we never had a new car. We were no worse off than lots of families we knew, with the exception of the Sullivans, and I certainly never felt bad about not having more. But now money was separating my classmates into those who were going on to college and those who weren't. Some girls were going to secretarial school, and a couple were already engaged. I had no idea what I'd do after graduation. Get a job, I suppose, and read books during my off hours.

I moped around the house. Mother noticed me reading the job ads in the newspaper. "Girls don't need to go to college," she kept telling me. "You just have to marry a boy who went to college and you'll make out just fine." Who did she think I was going to marry? I didn't ask her for fear she'd get out a notebook and start jotting down names. If she had her way, mother would probably have raffled me off to the highest bidder. Now and then I let myself pretend that Joe would come back after he graduated from medical school. We'd run into each other on the street and end up getting married. No chance. He'd marry some smart classmate, a woman doctor, and they'd set up a medical practice together in New York.

How many times a day did I pass that display case at school? The smile on Joe's face laughing at me, telling the whole school, "I'm out of here, losers!" The thought of walking around South Buffalo without even the hope of seeing Joe depressed me. In the library, I looked up Fordham University. I had heard it was in New York City, but I didn't know that it was in the Bronx or even that the Bronx was north of Manhattan. It was a Catholic school, a Jesuit school just like our high school.

A few days later, I was getting a study hall pass in the office when I overheard Father Dennis say to another priest, "Who knows? Maybe Joe will become a priest. Maybe he'll come back here and teach with us some day."

Joe, a priest? For a solid day I thought about how I'd feel if Joe couldn't be with any girl in the whole world. Would that make it easier that he wasn't with me? I glanced at him in English class a few times one day and imagined going into a dark confessional to tell him my misdeeds: *"Bless me, Father, for I have sinned. It has been ages since my last confession."* Then what would I say? The words of one of my old favorite songs came to mind: *"You don't know how many times I wish that I had told you, you don't know how many times I wish that I had showed you. . ."* Yes, my sin, Father, is that I cherish you. And what would he give me for confession? Would three Hail Marys forgive an illicit love for a priest? And was it really so illicit if I started loving him before he took his vows?

"MARY!"

I jerked my face forward and found Father Anthony at the side of my desk.

"Yes, Father."

He shook his head gravely. "Pay attention, dear. Graduation is just around the corner. Pretty girls are a dime a dozen in the real world. You're not going to get through life on your looks."

Some boy at the back of the class muttered, "Wanna bet?" and the whole class laughed. I bit my lip and looked down at my book.

"Silence!" Father Anthony yelled. "Mary, read question number seven and give the answer."

That was the day I decided I was getting out too. When I went home after school, I counted all my money from years of babysitting and working at the Dairy Queen. I had a few hundred dollars. At dinner, I told my parents I wanted to try modeling, that I already had the name of a downtown photographer to do my portfolio. Of course, my mother was thrilled. She had no doubt that my photo would be plastered on magazine covers everywhere. "Have the photographer take your picture with one of your tiaras on. Let him know you won thirteen contests. No, wait! Fourteen if you count that one in Batavia." I didn't waste time arguing with her. Dad was worried about the cost of the portfolio. He wanted me to use my savings to get a car so I could apply for jobs at the West Seneca Mall. "You could work at Walden Books," he said, "you'd like that, Mary." Actually, a couple of weeks ago, I had thought of the same thing, but now I wanted out of Buffalo. It was my own money, so Dad couldn't stop me.

That evening, Mother and I went to the drugstore to pick up the latest issue of *Seventeen*. Then she bought sewing patterns and got to work. When I had the photo shoot a couple of weeks later, I had an entirely new wardrobe. Del, the photographer, also had me wear some outfits he had on hand, and there were a couple of shots where I wasn't wearing much more than a large scarf. Mother almost swallowed her tongue when she saw those photos, but I insisted, "It's not pornography, it's art."

"Well, no one in South Buffalo should ever see you in a magazine dressed like that. It's positively shameful!"

Shame? What did I care about shame? All my life people treated me a certain way because of the way I looked. The way I figured it, it was time for payback.

Del knew several girls who were already working in New York, and he thought my chances were good. He had ideas about which agencies to submit photos to and urged me to make a trip to New York right after graduation. "When they see you in person," he said, "they'll sign you. You've got the right look, and you're tall and thin. You've got a really good shot at this."

I was excited, not only at the prospect of a career, but also about living in New York. I'd be in the same place at Joe. I daydreamed about doing a photo shoot at Fordham, posing on some grassy lawn while he caught sight of me as he crossed campus. He'd notice me outside of South Buffalo. He'd realize I was like him, eager to be out in the world. After he graduated from college, we'd get married and stay together in New York. We'd never have to come back here again.

Mrs. Connolly

After her wedding, the prom is the most important event in a girl's life. It's her moment to shine, to let the world see her at the height of her beauty. Two months before Mary's prom I went to Joanne Fabrics and put the most gorgeous material on layaway, a satiny royal blue worthy of her eyes. I asked Mary to pick out a pattern, but she said she didn't care. Once she said she might not even go to the prom. I was horrified and said, "Mary! You have to! You can't stay home like you're some kind of wallflower. People would talk!" That did seem to get through to her, at least she didn't mention not wanting to go again. I imagined she was just nervous, nervous about who would ask her and how she'd look. I didn't give it a second thought. I knew every boy in the class would want to be her date, that she'd have offers galore. And there was no question that she'd be the prettiest girl there by far. She just needed the right dress to showcase her beauty.

Halter-style dresses were popular and that was a good thing. Mary's bust was perfect, not too big, not too small. And the empire waist would emphasize her sleek figure. Being tall, Mary never wore heels. No boy likes to feel short next to his date. I found some ballet slip-ons and had them dyed to match the color of the dress.

The tricky part of the outfit would be the shawl that Mary would wear on the way to and from the dance. Most mothers were crocheting their daughters shawls to match their dresses, but I wanted something different for Mary. Something special that would make her stand out. I scoured through my sewing things and found a sweet old pattern for a short cape that I could make in the same fabric as the dress. If I made it right, it would fall to just below Mary's elbows and tie simply at her neck. Then I got the idea to sew tiny rhinestone buttons all over the fabric. That way the cape would sparkle in the dark with all its little stars. I wanted Mary to feel as special as Cinderella at her prom, and the dress was part of the magic. And who would be her lucky prince? I couldn't wait to find out.

Father Louis Gibbon

Mary's class was about to graduate. Mary had turned eighteen at the beginning of May. Legally, she was an adult now, eligible to vote, get married, raise a family. Of course, she was still just a child, most of life's experience beyond her grasp. But I had gotten her this far; eighteen years, and she was the same beautiful child of God as she was on her communion day.

At one of the Bible study sessions, the women were excitedly talking about the upcoming prom. Mrs. Walsh, a sly smile on her face, asked, "Father, did you ever go to dances with girls?"

Chuckling, I nodded and said, "Oh, yes. That was before I went to seminary."

This information seemed to startle the women, make them curious. They asked me about my dates, what they wore, the music at the dance, all kinds of things I could barely remember. I laughed. "Ladies, it was so long ago! I honestly can't recall."

Mrs. Connolly asked, "Wasn't your graduation dance one of the most important days of your life?"

At first I thought she was joking but I noticed all the women nodding as if they agreed. I cleared my throat and said, "For a priest, your ordination is the most important day of your life."

They readily agreed with this, Mrs. Walsh saying, "Of course," loudly. But they chattered on about the prom. One of the women asked Mrs. Connolly about Mary's dress, but her mother smiled tightly and shook her head. "It's a secret. I've told Mary not to say a word about it. When we know who her date is, we'll let him know what color flowers he should get."

This struck me as absurd. Keeping the details of a dress secret? And yet the other women seemed to understand. Mrs. Kenney asked, "Mary doesn't have a date yet?" She sounded incredulous.

Laughing, Mrs. Connolly sang, "Not *yet*. But I'm not worried."

A few of the women laughed but I noticed a quick, disapproving glance between two of them. I was curious about that, but my thoughts were interrupted by Mrs. Walsh who jumped off the sofa and proclaimed, "MARY

AND KEVIN SHOULD GO TOGETHER!"

Mrs. Connolly looked up. She appeared puzzled. She blinked her eyes and said, "But I thought Kevin and Sheila Adams were going together."

Shaking her head vehemently, Mrs. Walsh said, "Grace, Sheila's in the hospital with mono! She's going to be off her feet for weeks!"

How odd. Mrs. Walsh seemed happy by this turn of events. A poor girl was in the hospital and she could only think of prom dates. Mrs. Connolly leapt up and clasped Mrs. Walsh's arm. "Oh, that would be so sweet! Kevin and Mary together again. Just like old times." The women giggled, sounding like teenagers themselves.

They began reminiscing about Kevin and Mary as children, the hours and hours they'd played together, on and on with anecdotes. I did listen, of course. I hadn't realized that Kevin and Mary had such a history and it was important that I know as much about Mary as possible. At one point, Mrs. Connolly looked at me and said, "Oh, Father. You have to see this." She took down a box from a bookcase shelf and began rummaging through it. "Ah, here it is!" she said, and came towards me with what appeared to be a black and white photo.

Handing it to me, she asked, a tease in her voice, "Do you recognize these two little munchkins?"

I looked down at the photo, at the boy and girl in their First Communion finery. Of course it was Mary Connolly, and the boy was apparently Kevin Walsh. The children stood stiffly side by side, almost frightened expressions on their faces. The formality of the occasion had probably made them nervous. Kevin could have been any boy in a white suit, his hair freshly cut, his face scrubbed clean. But there was only one Mary Connolly. Even in that black and white photo, her eyes were luminous and her skin was as white as her dress. There was an unusual illumination in the background of the photo, a gathering of light that hovered above Mary. I tilted the photo a bit to see it more clearly. A halo! Yes, it was certainly a halo of natural light. It had been all but visible to me when she came to the altar that day to receive the communion.

The women were still chattering, and I finally interrupted and said we needed to get back to our study of the Psalms. The two mothers looked pleasantly guilty as they murmured apologies to me and went back to their seats. I was about to return to our lesson when Mrs. Walsh called out to Mrs. Connolly, "I'll put a bug in Kevin's ear. He'll call Mary tonight."

I returned to the rectory puzzled that day. Clearly I had underestimated the importance of the prom. The women had made it sound like a social rite of passage for the young people, an event that they would look back upon over and over. And why? It wasn't a sacrament, a moment of transcendence. All the prom amounted to were fancy clothes and a spin around the dance floor. What was special about that?

Kevin Walsh. I shook my head. He wasn't the boy I would have chosen for Mary. He had always struck me as the class clown, a jokester with no sense of the seriousness of life. He was a poor match for a smart, sensitive girl like Mary. No, he wasn't worthy of her. Her mother should have realized that. But then again, Mrs. Connolly had never impressed me with her judgment.

Eileen

I toyed with the idea of asking Kevin to go to the prom with me. Oh, sure, he'd tell me that Sheila had already asked him, but it would be a way for me to let him know I liked him.

But then there was a windfall, or so I thought at the time. Sheila got mono and had to be hospitalized for two weeks. She would be out by the time of the prom, but she couldn't leave her house for a couple more weeks. So, one morning on the way to school, I stood outside Kevin's house and waited for him to come out. I had rehearsed everything I would say: *I'm so sorry that Sheila's in the hospital. But, if it's okay with her, would you like to go to the prom with me?* If he said yes, I'd be thrilled. If he said no, I would try to sound funny with, "Oh, well, can't blame a girl for trying."

The morning air was cold. By noon, it would be nice, the heat of the May sun warming the pavement, but at that moment, I shivered.

"Eileen! Eileen!" I turned and saw Mary running up the street to me. She was no doubt wondering why I didn't stop to pick her up as I always did. I didn't want to tell anyone about asking Kevin to the prom until I had his answer. Now what could I do? Tell her my plan and ask that she walk on to school without me? No, I couldn't bring myself to tell her. It might jinx everything. I sighed and decided to postpone asking Kevin until the next morning. But what if someone else asked him before me?

As Mary reached me, I heard the front door of Kevin's house open. He grinned at us and I felt my stomach jump. Kevin called out buoyantly, "*Mornnn-ing*, ladies. And to what do I owe the honor of having two beautiful girls outside my door?" He was so confident, at ease. He walked towards us and I had to turn my head so I didn't stare at him.

"Did you explain the plan to Eileen?" he asked Mary.

Mary smiled, "I didn't have a chance. You called so late last night."

What were they talking about? Plan? I tried to smile at Mary, marveling again at how relaxed she always was around Kevin when she hardly spoke to other boys. Well, she'd known him all her life and she didn't have a crush on him like I did.

"We're going to double-date for the prom!" Mary said, so excited. "Eileen, who are you going to ask?"

If it weren't for the cool air, I wondered if I would have become dizzy and fallen to the ground. I didn't know if I could make my tongue work, but finally I said, "Oh, you two are going together?" My voice sounded far away, like it was traveling back to my ears from blocks away.

Kevin and Mary looked at each other and I could see there was this horrible bond between the two of them, a friendliness that slapped my face.

"Are you *absolutely* sure it's okay with Sheila?" Mary asked Kevin.

"For the millionth time, it's *fine*," Kevin insisted, rolling his eyes like he'd die if she made him say it one more time.

Mary looked at me and said, "We're going as friends."

Sliding his arm around Mary's shoulder, Kevin laid his head on hers and joked, "*Really, really good friends.*"

"Oh, you!" Breaking out of his embrace, Mary asked again, "Have you decided who you're going to ask?"

I looked down at my feet, my new navy blue clogs smudged with dirt at the toes. Slowly, I said, "Um, I'm not sure I'm going."

"What!" they yelled together. Then Mary said, "You *have* to go." She looked at Kevin and said, "I'm not going unless Eileen goes. Fix her up."

She was so animated. I'd never seen Mary this happy; it made me feel even more strange.

His hands in his athletic jacket, Kevin bounced on the tips of his feet, looking so adorable and boyish, and said, "I know! Joe Gleason doesn't have a date yet. I'll see him first period in Calculus. I'll set the whole thing up."

Joe Gleason. The runner, not to mention our soon-to-be class valedictorian. His locker wasn't too far from mine, and we chatted now and then. He was nice, a little shy, but nice. Lots of girls would be happy to go out with him. Not that I was interested in dating him or anybody else except Kevin.

The three of us walked to school together, Kevin talking the whole time. My stomach quivered and I kept swallowing in case the cereal I ate for breakfast was creeping up my throat. We were all the way to school before I realized that Mary was as quiet as I was.

Mary

When Kevin asked me to the prom, I was relieved. We'd known each other for so long, and he had a girlfriend. There'd be no pressure. Instead of worrying about the goodnight kiss, I'd only have to worry about how hard Kevin was going to punch my shoulder. My mother was thrilled Kevin and I were going together, his mother was thrilled, everyone was happy. And then the news that we'd be double-dating with Eileen and Joe.

Joe! Mentally, I had itemized a list of everything wrong with this situation: I wouldn't be able to talk around Joe. In fact, I might faint. I'd blush scarlet and look as if I had a fever. He was going to be at the prom with my best friend. *My best friend!* If he had to be there, why couldn't he be there with someone I didn't know that well? Some girl from another school whom I'd never laid eyes on before. It was torture when Joe and Cheryl were together for a couple years. I'd see them taking walks together, his arm around her shoulder while she leaned her head into his chest. When they broke up, I cried with relief. But as bad as that was, Cheryl wasn't my friend, and certainly not my best friend.

Eileen! Why had I never confided in her?! Why was it that everything about Joe was sacred to me? It was like he was my religion. I believed in him with a rock solid faith. And to talk to anyone about him would have been somehow wrong, a desecration. Yes, he was going away to college and didn't have a clue how I felt, but maybe I would end up in New York modeling and he would see my picture in a magazine. It was a ridiculous fantasy, but I was desperate.

Now he would fall in love with my best friend. I knew it in my bones. Eileen was so pretty and so chatty. She wasn't afraid to talk to boys. She knew how to compliment them and flirt with them; she made the boys feel good about themselves. And she was so petite. Five foot two and small boned. Every guy felt big and strong around her. Sophomore year when she dated Michael Cantellini, he used to carry her home from basketball games on his back.

It was torturous, but I thought of Eileen and Joe together, a couple. She had dark hair like Joe's, and they both even had green eyes, although different shades. The thought of watching them dance together at the prom threw me into despair. I stopped eating. I laid in bed for hours. Maybe, I thought, I could make myself really sick and just stay home. Like Sheila, lucky Sheila.

My mother drove me nuts those weeks before the dance. She kept measuring and re-measuring me for the dress she was making. She kept saying, "You don't seem very excited, Mary. Aren't you looking forward to the prom?"

"I don't feel well," I always answered, but my mother would brush that aside and make me a milkshake, sitting at the table with me to make sure I drank the whole thing. "It's just the excitement, honey," she said, "You'll be fine."

Well, the dress was done and my mother had stayed up late every night for a week sewing this ridiculous little cape with sparkles all over it. I had shoes the same shade of blue as the dress. My mother had dug out a small clutch purse from her closet that must have been twenty years old. She wanted me to have my hair styled, but I insisted on just washing it and blowing it dry the way I always did. I did let her help me with my make-up. I sat there while she rubbed blush into my cheeks and applied eye make-up. Just let this night be over, I thought.

At seven o'clock, the doorbell rang and Dad opened the door. I remember Kevin smiling wide as he slipped the rose corsage onto my wrist. Mom kept saying, "Oh, aren't you the cutest couple," embarrassing me to death, but Kevin knew how to handle her.

"If Mary's not a good dancer, I'll bring her back and take you to the prom Mrs. Connolly."

"Oh, Kevin! You're still so funny. Well, look at the two of you. And to think you used to play in the sandbox together."

"Mother, please. Not that again."

Laughing, Kevin said, "Yeah, and see if you can find those movies of us taking a bath together. Mar was saying just the other day how she'd like to see those again."

My parents thought he was so funny. I pinched his arm to make him stop clowning around. Dad took too many pictures of us, and then Kevin said, "Well, we should be going. We have to pick up Joe and Eileen, and we're going to stop at a pre-prom party."

Then I became numb with fear, oblivious to my mother wrapping the cape around me. Kevin guided me down the porch steps and held the door while I slipped into the front seat of his father's Buick. It was still light out, but the sun was bleak that night. I briefly turned around when Joe and Eileen got into the back seat, the lilac scent of Eileen's perfume filling the car. I know I told Eileen how pretty she looked, and the boys joked about their ruffled tuxedo shirts. I didn't dare look directly at Joe. We stopped at a party, but I can't remember anything about it. I guess I drank some punch, I don't know. I was just going through the motions. By the time we reached the school, the sun was behind thick clouds and everything was in shadow.

Joe

Mary was an ice princess on prom night. She barely said hello and ignored me the rest of the night. Some things never change.

At first Eileen seemed nervous and that surprised me. At school, she was friendly, and I was happy to go to the prom with her. But that night she'd start to say something, then stop mid-sentence. I didn't know her well, so I didn't know what to talk about. But Kevin talks as much as five people put together so he made it less awkward.

Like always, I faked my way through the fast dances. Dancing was all about picking up one foot and setting it down next to the other, sort of like running. And slow dancing wasn't really dancing at all, just a girl and a guy sandwiched together and stepping slowly in a circle.

The band played a lot of slow dances and it was nice holding Eileen like that, her head laying sideways on my chest. She was wearing really big heels, but she was still pretty little. Most of the couples were necking, so I kissed her as well, moving my lips against hers until her mouth parted and let my tongue enter. She tasted like apples, filling my mouth with a sweet, cool juice, and we found a rhythm to slowly push and pull our lips together. She became more and more relaxed as we turned. I felt her fingers playing with the hair on my neck and everything in that moment felt just right. For the first time, I understood what my mother was so worried about. I could see that you could fall for a girl in a heartbeat and nothing else in your life would matter.

The song ended and we broke apart to clap. Eileen looked a little flushed, so I asked her if she wanted some punch. When we got to our table, Mary and Kevin were already there. I remember Mary was laughing at something Kevin said, but when she saw me, she got quiet and stared down at the table. Christ, she was pissing me off. Would it have been too much for her to smile a little, to say something like, *Are you having a nice time, Joe?* I didn't know why I was letting her get under my skin like that, especially when I was having such a nice time with Eileen. So maybe Mary Connolly didn't think I was good enough for her, not worthy to even sit at the same table with her. So what? I looked at Eileen, at those green eyes, eyes as dark as a Christmas tree. She was every bit as pretty as Mary. More if you liked brunettes and I did. I reached across the table and put my hand on Eileen's. She looked surprised, but then she smiled and met my eyes.

We sat for about ten minutes, Eileen and Mary talking about all the dresses the girls were wearing, which ones they liked and which ones they didn't. Then the band started playing "Stairway to Heaven" and Kevin jumped up and said, "Okay, back to dancing. Mar stepped on my foot good last time so let's switch partners."

"I did not step on your foot!" Mary looked outraged, like we'd really believe she was a bad dancer. The four of us walked on to the floor, Kevin pulling Eileen deep into the crowd. I kind of turned and put my arms out and waited for Mary to move against me.

Our arms were wrapped around the tops of each others' bodies, but we didn't let our bodies touch. Clearly, she felt as awkward as I did. Mary is taller than Eileen, though, able to rest her head on my shoulder. Or maybe she put it there so she wouldn't have to look at me. We started to turn in a circle. My cheek was touching her hair and it felt as soft as flannel against my skin. When I inhaled, I could smell whatever shampoo she used, something lemony, and I got this heady feeling, like I was slightly high. There was something familiar about it all, like this had happened before, maybe in a dream? It was nice feeling, but a little scary too.

We moved slowly around and around. I tried to step a little closer towards Mary and she responded, moving towards me until our chests were touching. For a moment, I asked myself if I'd been wrong about her all these years. She never spoke to me but, to my surprise, she was clinging to me now. The band was playing a long version of the song, repeating verses. . . .*When she gets there she knows if the stores are all closed, with a word she can get what she came for.* . . We were holding each other tightly now, and then it happened. I felt myself get hard, my penis pressing against her stomach, rising so fast like it was trying to bury itself in her. Oh, shit! This hadn't happened when I was dancing with Eileen. I was embarrassed all to hell and broke away from her. I walked off the dance floor and out the door. In the front of the school, a number of couples were sitting on benches and smoking cigarettes. I walked to an empty spot on the sidewalk and wished I smoked so it would look like I had a reason to be there.

The erection vanished but I didn't know how to walk back in. I could never face Mary Connolly again. I could feel the heat of my shame, as if she knew about all those times under the covers. Would she say something to Eileen? Shit! Why had I agreed to dance with Mary? Eileen was my date; I should have said no.

Kevin came out and said, "Hey, Joe, what's up?"

I turned so he couldn't see me directly. "Nothing. It just got so hot in there, I needed some air." I loosened my tie.

"Yeah, it is hot in there. The girls are in the can fixing their make-up."

He sounded relaxed so maybe Mary hadn't said anything. Kevin put a hand on my arm and led me away a few feet so we could talk privately. "So," he said in a low voice, "you think we can take them to the Botanical Gardens?"

Even in the dark, I could see the determination on Kevin's face. "Wait a minute," I said, "what about Sheila? I thought you and Mary were just going out tonight as friends."

He chuckled. "Well, there's friends and then there's *friends*."

I slapped him on the back like I admired his thinking, but I felt bad for Sheila. She probably really liked Kevin and here he was planning to cheat on her.

Kevin said, "Well, don't say anything. When we all get in the car, I'll just drive to the Gardens. If one of them gets in a snit, we'll just head over to Timmy Corcoran's party."

I didn't want to go. This was the first time I was out with Eileen and I didn't want her to think I expected anything. We'd had a nice time. I wanted to ask her out again, just the two of us. I wanted to date her and never think about Mary Connolly again. How was that going to happen if we went to the Botanical Gardens? But I was a coward. I didn't want Kevin to think I wasn't hoping for some necking, some petting, for whatever I could get. I was eighteen, after all. If an opportunity came along, I wasn't supposed to say no.

Eileen

The nerve of Kevin, driving us straight to the Botanical Gardens from the prom. Mary and I had talked beforehand and thought it would be fun to go to Timmy's party or maybe for a drive to the lake. Lots of couples would be there and they'd make bonfires and open bottles of champagne. But Kevin just headed over to South Park Avenue and parked behind the glass pavilions like it had all been arranged in advance. When he took the keys from the ignition, Mary glanced at me over her shoulder. I looked back at her. We couldn't really see each other in the dark car, but I knew we were each waiting for the other to speak, to object.

Then softly, so only I could hear, Joe leaned over and said, "Is this okay with you?" His breath was soft on my ear. I could barely see the outline of his face, but I heard the shyness in his voice. *Is this okay with you?* I couldn't remember the last time someone cared enough about my feelings to ask. Kevin didn't care a lick about me, that couldn't be more clear. Joe whispered again, "We don't have to stay here if you don't want to. Whatever you want to do is okay with me." Again, the sweetness and concern in his voice. I leaned against him and slowly put my mouth on his. We kissed like we had at the dance, with that slow, rocking rhythm. Joe stroked my cheek with his hand. He gently pushed back the tendrils of hair that had come undone from my chignon. Where had he learned this gentleness? I laid my hand on his chest and felt the quickened beat of his heart. Had *I* done that? Had *I* caused his pulse to race? Me, who had never felt in control of even a moment of my life? When Joe laid his hand nervously on my breast, I felt his fingers tremble and he whispered, "Eileen, you are so beautiful. I'll always remember this."

And then my heart opened up to him and all the cold years I'd endured in my house melted away. The vacant look on my mother's face. Dad's apologetic expression. The pain, the rejection, it evaporated with Joe's words. We kissed more deeply. He unzipped the top of my dress and laid his face on my breasts, his breath becoming louder and halted. He took his time, kissing them, cradling them. There was something worshipful in his touch. I might even have gone all the way, it felt so natural, but Joe didn't seem to expect that and I didn't want to shock him. My nipples hardened with the swirl of his tongue, a luscious ache that would still be there when I went to sleep later. And maybe my parents argued that night and maybe they didn't. It didn't matter because I couldn't have cared less. For the first time ever, I decided I was worth something. Joe did all that for me in a single night. Of course I started to love him.

Mary

How many people have lost their virginity on prom night? It's so cliche it's ridiculous. Still, if you had told me only a few minutes before it happened that it was *going* to happen, I would have said you were crazy. In fact, I would have laughed. I always thought of Kevin as a brother, actually a little brother because he was such a prankster. Yes, he was annoying at times, but I knew I'd miss him next year when he went to the community college and I would be sitting around hoping to model. It would be nice to stay friends, but I didn't plan on dating him let alone sleeping with him.

When he kissed me in the car, I wanted to laugh. I was about to say, "Kevin, you've got to be kidding." But Joe was in the back seat. *Joe.* And he was with Eileen. I glanced back at her, trying to make out her expression.

But then I saw Joe whisper something to her and she turned to him. I heard the soft movements of their clothes, the silhouettes of their faces coming together.

It was so dark I hoped it was all a terrible dream. The corners of my eyes stung with tears, and to keep Kevin unaware, I leaned forward and kissed him back. I prayed, *Dear Jesus, let this night be over. Please let me go home and fall into the deepest sleep ever.* How long did we kiss? Moments, minutes? *Dear Jesus, take me home.* And then the sound of the zipper on Eileen's dress like a razor cutting fast and deep into my flesh. Joe! Joe and Eileen! Now their names belonged together. It would never be Joe and Mary. I thought of singing "Cherish" with the Buffalo Belles: *I am not going to be the one to share your dree-ams, and I am not going to be the one to share your schee-mes. . .*

I couldn't control my tears; they leaked onto my cheeks and fell over my lips, the salt biting my tongue. I turned from Kevin and whisked the tears from my face with my fingers. Immediately, Kevin's hands were on my dress, the fabric falling away from me as he unzipped me to the waist. Maybe he thought my turning my back to him was permission to unzip me. I reached around and tried to gather up my dress, but Kevin was kissing my back, wet blotchy kisses that felt cold and gave me a nasty shiver. *Dear Jesus, save me. Get me out of this car, out of this night.* If I could just open the door, step outside, and then Joe's whisper floated from behind, "Eileen, you are so beautiful. . ." I collapsed onto the seat.

Kevin knew how to hold my breasts, no hesitation at all, and I realized it couldn't have been his first time. Sheila flashed through my mind. Sheila! Why wasn't she in this car instead of me? Why wasn't her dress lifted to her waist, her underwear slid down and off her legs with humiliating clumsiness? Why wasn't she witnessing Kevin fumbling with the condom. Sheila knew what it was like to have a boy enter you. She wouldn't have been shocked by the pressure, the pain, the mortification of bleeding on the car seat. Did she also flinch when Kevin came, his throaty howl announcing to Joe that he had spilt himself inside of me? I felt like a toilet, like a disgusting receptacle of the ugly part of Kevin. But as much as I loathed him at that moment, I hated myself more. I hated myself for lying there like a zombie and not kicking his teeth out. And maybe I wouldn't have had to do that, maybe all I needed to do was shout, "No!" Did I think so little of myself that that one tiny syllable escaped me? Was I so afraid of making a scene in front of Joe that I couldn't speak up for myself? And now I felt such shame I thought it would choke me. It was like poison leaking from the center of my chest, spreading out into my arm and legs, reaching the very tips of my fingers and toes. I wanted to run away from myself but I was trapped in my own skin.

On the way home, I sat as close to the door as I could. Kevin tried to make conversation a few times but stopped when he realized I wasn't speaking. Eileen and Joe kissed the whole way home.

I didn't know what time it was when I got in. Mother was waiting up for me, but she had fallen asleep on the sofa. I tiptoed past her and hurried upstairs. I threw the prom dress over the back of a chair in my room and got in the shower. The hot water pounded down my back and made my skin look sunburned. With a washcloth, I scrubbed every inch of my body as hard as I could. But then I held the cloth between my legs and was frightened of the soreness *there*, at the white cloth turning pink from the dried blood. How long did I cry? Somehow, I got out of the shower and made it to bed. I shut my eyes so tightly that my forehead was creased, but still I couldn't keep out images of me and Kevin in the car. Then I started rubbing my eyes with softly clenched fists, remembering how I used to do that when I was little because I liked the colors and shapes it created behind my eyelids. I started to fall asleep and Kevin faded from my thoughts. Instead, I remembered Joe's arms around me, that most secret part of him pressed to me, the music fading out, . . .*and she's buying the sta-iirr-way to hea-ah-venn.*

Eileen

I used to weave elaborate daydreams before I fell asleep each night. There was never enough time to think about all the things I wanted to happen in my life before my eyelids grew heavy. A common daydream was that my brother Jimmy had never died, that I had a big brother who cared about me and was proud of me. My mother didn't drink. She and Dad were happy and Mother smiled when people told her I looked just like her. For a few months in the past year, the daydream was Kevin, thinking about him calling me on the phone, our going to the prom together, him telling me that he couldn't keep it a secret any more, he just had to tell me that he loved me.

Joe changed all of that. My life became better than any dream possibly could be. At night in bed, I didn't want to imagine anything because nothing was more wonderful than my real life. I just wanted to think of Joe's face, mentally repeating everything he'd said to me that day and the day before that. And most miraculous of all, I knew he was doing the same thing. I made him happy, so incredibly happy, and I was proud of myself for that. When you fall in love with another person, you fall in love with yourself too.

Every day, every moment of every day, was bliss. Joe and I ate lunch together in the cafeteria. We took walks in the evening, always ending up in Morgan Park, that cute little park between Hancock Avenue and McKinley Parkway. Sometimes I would sit on one of the benches and ask Joe to run. I loved to see him in motion, his brown hair blown back, the slight tilt of his face. One night, he wanted me to run with him and I laughed, "I can't even run a block."

"You just have to pace yourself." We held hands and did a slow trot around the park. "Good," Joe said, "you've got the idea. Just give yourself a chance to warm up." We started running like that, holding hands, every night. If anyone saw us, we didn't care. Joe wasn't afraid to hug me in front of his friends. When Timmy Corcoran hooted at us and yelled, "Hey, Joe, Give her a kiss for me!" Joe just flipped him off and said, "Get lost." The girls said things like, "He treats you so nice," and "You two make such a cute couple." It's true; we did.

I told Joe about my parents, about my brother's death and Mother's alcoholism. He held me close, told me that it would be okay, that now we were together nothing could hurt us. He understood that I didn't want him to pick me up at our house, that I wanted to meet him at the corner. I was terrified that my mother would taint my happiness in some way. That she'd say something nasty to me about Joe's family not having money, or, just as bad, insist on meeting him so she could be so polite that she'd embarrass him. But Dad understood. And he admired Joe, the way he got good grades and got a track scholarship to Fordham. "The boy's got a future," he said.

I didn't know how I'd live when Joe left for New York at the end of August, but he promised me he'd be home as often as he could afford it. And I could afford to go to New York now and then. Dad was going to hire me as an assistant secretary at his firm, so I'd even be earning my own money. Joe and I talked about walking together in Central Park, about staying together in a hotel. The thought of getting to spend a whole night in Joe's arms made me delirious with joy.

We never went all the way. We did everything but, but not that. I knew how much pressure there was on Joe to go to school and become a doctor. If I got pregnant, his dream would be over. And as much as I longed to hold him inside me, we were in no rush. Everything would happen in time, and as long as I could stare into his bright green eyes, run my fingers lovingly over her face, and kiss his mouth, life was all that it could be.

Kevin

Geez, we made love at the Botanical Gardens and then Mary didn't even let me walk her to her front door. No, she jumped out of the car before I'd even turned off the engine. "Well, goodnight to you too," I said as she ran up her porch stops.

I'd already dropped Joe and Eileen off. I had hoped Joe and I would have a chance to compare notes, but after kissing Eileen at her door for ages, he came back to the car and said he wanted to sprint home. Then he took off running, forgetting that the jacket to his tux was in the back seat.

I'm not an idiot. I knew something was wrong. A girl doesn't give you the cold shoulder for nothing. But come on, it wasn't like I forced her. She never put the brakes on. She wasn't like Sheila, that's for sure; Sheila enjoyed sex, she was part of it. Mary was stiff, but I figured lots of girls were probably like that the first time. I mean, since they were little, they had the nuns warning them not to even think about sex, so of course the first time was going to be tough. Maybe it really hurt, I thought, maybe that's why she wasn't talking in the car. Sheila and I didn't use rubbers, didn't have to, and maybe the rubber made things worse for Mary. I wanted to apologize if it hurt, but she didn't give me a chance jumping out of the car like that.

Mary didn't talk to me at school and she didn't talk to me the day of the senior class picnic. On graduation day, I watched as she walked across the stage to get her diploma. Even in the silly robe and hat, she was beautiful. She stopped at the end of the stage so her father could take her picture, smiling so she almost looked happy. I ached to be inside her again even though it had been so awkward. Time would change that, I thought, and soon we wouldn't be able to keep our hands off each other. I stopped calling Sheila and took walks past Mary's house. I went around and around the block waiting for her to appear, to talk to me, to tell me that she wasn't mad at me. I knew she was inside reading her books. I wondered if I should buy her a book, wrap it and leave it on her doorstep with a note. What book? Was there anything she hadn't read? Or maybe I should just leave a note telling her I missed her and needed to talk to her. I didn't know my next move. With most girls, I didn't have to try to hard. They liked me, they wanted to be with me. Why didn't Mary? Why did I have to want the one girl who didn't want me?

Mary

I got my first period when I was twelve. I was sitting in a stall in the girl's restroom at school when I noticed the blood on my underwear. Not a lot but gross enough. My mother had always told me that if it happened at school to go to the school nurse and ask for a sanitary pad. As if that wasn't humiliating enough, Nurse Kelly made me show her that I'd put the silly belt on right before letting me go back to class. I sat at my desk, my knees pressed together but the tops of my thighs held apart by the lumpy pad. Later, at recess, I sat on a bench in the playground and watched the seventh grade boys play basketball. They were leaping into the air as they made their shots. Their faces were as red as a fire engine, and sweat marks stained their shirts. My veins felt clogged with trapped energy. I was dying to move but I felt so cumbersome wearing that pad that I just sat on the bench and thought how my life had changed in a single morning.

Girls got the wrong end of the deal for sure. At all those sleepovers when the topic of periods came up, girls would say things like, "I can't wait to see what it feels like to be a woman." Well, it felt like gross. I wanted to turn the clock back, to be young enough to play freeze tag or jump rope. Anything to be able to move freely. The boys had it made.

Some girls had irregular periods, but not me. Every twenty-eight or twenty-nine days there'd be a red circle on my panties. I should have been prepared and worn a pad as protection, but I refused to wear that stupid belt until I absolutely had to. Mother made too much of a fuss, insisting I drink chamomile tea for the cramps and sleep with a hot water bottle on my stomach. When I finally stopped bleeding, I would get on my bike and pedal until my legs were ready to drop off, until I was so winded I couldn't catch my breath. But it felt so good to move, to feel like my body was my own again.

My mother bought boxes of Kotex every month and put them in the linen closet. Three weeks after the prom she asked me, "Is your period late? I noticed the box is still full."

I'd been eating breakfast, taking small bites of toast and chewing very slowly to delay leaving for a dentist's appointment. The toast was dry; my mother's words made it scrape the soft part of my throat. I shook my head. "I have it now," I lied. "I woke up with it."

Mother just nodded and refilled my orange juice. My heart separated into tiny islands that flowed into my arms and legs, my whole body throbbing with multiple beats. "I left my purse upstairs," I said, and fled to my room.

On the back of my door was a full-length mirror. I stood sideways and stared at my abdomen. Nothing stuck out. My jeans weren't tight. I walked closer to the glass and stared at my face. My skin was so white. I'd tried to get a tan before the prom but it had rained a lot. I stared at my eyes. Was I different? Would I be able to tell if I was pregnant? Blinking, I looked at myself as hard as I could. Nothing was different. At least on the outside.

I went to the linen closet and took out a few pads and put them in my purse. Knowing Mother, she'd be checking the box. While walking to the dentist's office, I felt that I could stave off the panic. As long as I didn't allow myself to get scared, none of this was real. Probably just the stress of the prom, the shock of Eileen and Joe becoming a couple. And was it true that you couldn't get pregnant the first time, that it was almost impossible? Some girls said that although I never felt you should rely on it. Now I was praying it was a scientific fact.

I sat in the big chair in the dentist's office, my eyes closed so I didn't have to stare into the big light overhead. While the dental hygienist took X-rays of my back teeth, a vague thought about safety for the baby floated in my mind, but I pushed it away and concentrated on the music piped into the office.

Afterwards, I walked to church. A few people were there praying silently. On one side of the church was a statue of Saint Theresa of the little Flower with devotional candles in red glass cups. My middle name, Theresa, is in honor of her. When I was very young, my parents gave me a dime every

Sunday, and after mass and I would drop it into the contribution box and light a candle. I wasn't praying for anything in particular, although Mother always told me to pray for a clean soul. I liked picking up the long thin stick to light the candle and then plunging the stick into the small tin containing sand. As the flame extinguished, it made a noisy *hussshhh* sound that gave me a small shiver.

Today I lit five candles and knelt on the small vinyl cushion in front of the shrine. I only knew a few things about Saint Theresa, that she had entered a Carmelite convent when she was just fifteen and that she had died of tuberculosis when she was twenty-four. It occurred to me now that she was a virgin when she died, that no man had ever done to her what Kevin did to me. I made the sign of the cross and bowed my head. Silently, I prayed, *Dear Saint Theresa, Please don't let me be pregnant. I'm so frightened. I'm too young to have a baby. My parents will be so upset. Please don't let me be pregnant. Please, Saint Theresa, I would rather die than be pregnant. I wouldn't mind dying young, like you, but I can't be pregnant. Please, please, please, Saint Theresa, let my period come right away. Amen.*

I made the sign of the cross and left the church. My mother had made tuna fish sandwiches for lunch but the smell made me want to retch. I went to my room and looked at some old fashion magazines and dozed off. Then, suddenly, I was sitting up in bed wondering how I'd woken up. I was gasping for air because my lungs had stopped working. I was breathing hard yet somehow the air wasn't getting into my chest. I felt as if someone was squirting me with a hose, pin pricks up and down my arms and legs. Somehow, instinctively, I knew to lean over and rest my head on my knees. Slowly, the panic lessened. My breathing became normal, I inhaled and exhaled deeply, and I faced what I couldn't deny a second longer: I was pregnant.

Kevin

So, after ignoring me for weeks, Mary called and said she needed to talk to me. It was good to hear her voice on the phone. She sounded a little strange, but there was bound to be some awkwardness. I mean, we went from being buddies to lovers in a single night. Switching gears that fast wasn't easy for everyone.

"Lady Sings the Blues" was playing at the Towne Theater. I told Mary I'd pick her up at seven. At first she said, "No, we don't need to go to the movies, I just need to talk to you." I laughed and said, "We can talk during the previews."

She was stiff as a board while we sat side by side watching the movie. I had my arm around the back of her chair, but I didn't try anything. She stared straight ahead, crying almost all the way through. Yeah, it was a sad movie, but I didn't think she'd keep the waterworks going all night. She kept sniffling into tissues and blowing her nose.

Then on the way home she told me she was late. "Nah," I said, "I told your mom I'd have you home by eleven. We got time."

"No, Kevin, I'm *late*."

I stopped walking. We were under a lamplight and I remember Mary took two steps backwards into the dark. She wouldn't meet my eyes.

"Late," I repeated.

She nodded. Then she whispered, "I'm a month pregnant." Her eyes, her nose, her mouth, her whole face seemed to crumple in the center like one of my mother's fallen cakes. I reached for her and she collapsed onto me, her arms around my neck, the sobs seeming to go backwards, inside of her. She was making muffled, choking sounds. I was in shock for a while, but I kept holding her. She relaxed her body and settled against me. I started to rock her gently. I smoothed her hair and said softly, "Don't cry. It's okay, don't cry."

Mary needed me. That was almost as much of a revelation as her telling me she was pregnant. I loved feeling that, loved knowing that I was holding her world in my hand. Her entire future depended on me and what I'd say to her, what I'd do. I never hesitated. I told her everything would be all right. With her head against my chest, I smoothed her hair and told her no problem. I already loved her, I'd love our baby.

We stood like that for a long time, our arms wrapped around each other. Funny, I felt closer to her like that, just holding her, than I did when we had sex. It really was the happiest moment of my life. A lot of guys would have been scared or mad as hell finding out they were going to be a father. Not me; heck, I was grateful. I felt like I'd been waiting for this my whole life. Mary Connolly was finally mine.

Eileen

I had just gotten in from an evening walk with Joe when my father told me Mary was on the telephone. Mary. I felt guilty. Since Joe and I had been going out, I almost never saw her. When we were together, I knew I was boring her to death by talking about how wonderful Joe was. She'd have a tight smile on her face and I knew she was bored silly, just trying to be polite for my sake.

So when she called, I figured she wanted to arrange a time to go shopping or to the movies. When she told me she had some serious news, I wondered if she'd heard from a modeling agency. But then she said she was pregnant and getting married. She said it just like that. She and Kevin were getting married on July 1st and could I be the maid of honor? She sounded apologetic that it was a small wedding and hoped I'd understand that I couldn't bring a date. She just went on and on and finally I blurted, "Wait, you're *really* getting married?"

I heard her sigh. "That's what I said," she answered matter-of-factly. "Mother has forbidden me to tell anyone that I'm pregnant, but nobody's going to be stupid enough to believe anything else."

And then she did ask me to go shopping. "I don't want my mother with me when I pick out a dress. And you can pick out any dress you want. Dad took out a loan and he's paying for everything."

When I hung up, I looked at my own father. I broke into tears and said, "Mary's pregnant. She's getting married."

He looked shocked, the wrinkles around his eyes becoming more deeply creased. He sat down at the kitchen table and breathed in and out heavily. Looking at me, he said, "Eileen, don't let that happen to you. You kids know a lot more than we did when we were your age. If you need to see a doctor about how not to get pregnant, do it. Just make the appointment and don't tell your mother. Have them send the bill to me at my office."

Well, the night was full of surprises. I never expected Mary to tell me she was getting married and I certainly never expected my father to be so blunt with me about birth control. I sat next to him and put my hand on his arm. "Dad, Joe and I aren't doing anything. We won't take any chances."

He looked at me as if he was going to say something, but he didn't. I moved my hand softly up and down his arm. I knew he was as lonely as I was in this house. We should have comforted each other more often, but we had been playing the same roles for so long. Then he blurted, "I learned the hard way that birth control doesn't always work." He swallowed and looked down at the table. "Eileen, I don't want that to happen to you."

I saw the embarrassment in his eyes and the sadness too. Something hard lodged in my throat. I swallowed, but it wouldn't go away. Jimmy, my ghost brother. I never knew him and yet he had shaped my life more than anyone until Joe. I asked, "You and Mother had to get married?"

He nodded and took in a long, slow breath. "Your Mother thinks that's why Jimmy died. Because we sinned." His eyes were moist.

"Oh, Dad," I immediately said, "you know that's not why. A lot of babies die from crib death."

Slipping a hand into his pocket, he pulled out a handkerchief and quickly dried his eyes. "I know that. But your mother. . .well, it's not just grief that makes her drink. It's guilt too."

It was hard to hear. After so many years of feeling like my mother's invisible daughter, it was easier to be angry at her than feel sorry for her. It would take time before I'd let myself consider the enormity of her pain. But a small sprout of sympathy planted itself in my chest and I knew that it would grow even if I tried to stop it.

"You don't have to worry, Dad," I said. "Joe and I aren't doing anything and we won't until after we're married."

Maybe that assured him. He patted my hand. "Honey, you're so happy now. And you're young. Most of your life you'll be a grown-up and there's no going back. You can't turn back time. Just enjoy being young while you can."

I stood and kissed his cheek. "Don't worry, Dad. I won't get pregnant

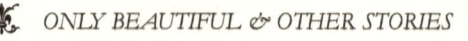

until I'm Mrs. Gleason. I promise."

That night I laid in bed and thought about Mary. She hadn't sounded upset, but she hadn't sounded like herself either. I guessed she was just accepting her fate. Well, a girl could do worse than Kevin Walsh, that's for sure. And she and Kevin had always been such good friends. I hadn't even asked her, "Do you love Kevin?" I guess I was just too distracted because I was in love with Joe and living in this perfect little bubble that just floated along.

I should have been a better friend to Mary. I should have insisted that we get together and talk about the baby, the marriage. But even that night, with news of her pregnancy so fresh, it was hard not to just think about Joe and the things he'd said to me that night while we were walking through the woods on Lockey's Hill. Joe had picked a deep green leaf from a lilac bush and held it next to my eyes. "Your eyes are even greener than this," he'd said, pulling me to him and kissing each eyelid. Then he plucked several sprays of lavender lilacs together and wove them together in a crown, placing them on my head.

"You look so beautiful," he told me.

Hugging his middle, I said, "You make me feel beautiful." I didn't say it out loud, but I was thinking that when Joe and I had a baby, it would undoubtedly have green eyes. But would they be bright like Joe's or dark like mine? When we walked down from the hill, I took the lilac crown off, but Joe said no, leave it on. So I kept it on, wore it all the way home. I planned to weave a ribbon through it so the flowers would stay together. I knew the flowers would lose their color and dry out, but I also believed that one day I'd show the crown to our baby and say, "See what Daddy made for me."

So is it any wonder that in the midst of all that I almost forgot about Mary? I was too intoxicated with Joe to let anything bring me down. I brought my arms to my chest and rocked back and forth slightly against the mattress. I fell asleep inhaling the promising scent of the lilacs.

Mary

Before Kevin and I got married, my mother made me go see Father Gibbon, like that smug priest knew anything about life. He stared at my legs the whole time and told me that I was adding to Jesus's suffering. *Really?* I thought, *and you're adding to mine.*

"Are you sorry for your sin, Mary Louise? Truly sorry?"

I looked up. "Mary Louise?"

He fumbled with his words, "Yes, yes, now I think. . .I think I recall that your confirmation name is Louise?"

"Oh, yes. Mother made me take my grandmother's name." My words seemed to unnerve him further. He continued to stutter, "Yes, yes, your grandmother, her name, my name, well, Mary, the point is ARE YOU SORRY FOR THIS TERRIBLE SIN?" He finished in a loud voice, staring at me like I was a criminal in court.

My mother pressed her lips together and looked at me hopefully. I nodded slightly, avoiding his eyes as he prayed over me. When we walked out of the church, my mother told me, "Now you're safe from hell, but every day, every *single* day, Mary, you have to pray to God to forgive you. Do you understand?"

Forgive me? I thought I was the one who deserved an apology.

The memory of that night with Kevin stirred in my mind. It was a memory I couldn't push down, like a beach ball on the surface of deep water. I could still feel the latex of the defective condom pushing and pulling against my insides, Kevin looking ridiculous above me, like I was a mat he was doing push-ups on. I could almost laugh. Sex is a sin? Sex is too ludicrous to be a sin. The real sin was that I let it happen.

I never liked being an only child. I always wanted a sister, someone to confide in. Or a big brother, someone who wouldn't allow anyone else to hurt me. When you're an only child, you don't really have a family, just parents. If I'd had siblings, my mother wouldn't have been obsessing over just me. The Merrills, who lived on the same block as us, had six kids. They didn't need anyone else to play hide and seek; they were a whole team. I bet not one of them was ever lonely. Their parents didn't believe in owning a television, but the kids didn't care because they always had each other to play with. Every summer while we were growing up, they wrote and put on a play. The whole neighborhood came and watched. When I was really little, I used to imagine that they'd invite me to be part of their family. I would have fit right in the middle with three older siblings and three younger.

When I found out I was pregnant, I agonized about breaking the news to my parents and Kevin. But after that was over, I realized it wouldn't be just me any more. I was going to have a baby. A *baby*, a whole other *person*. I would never be alone again. At night, I warmed my stomach with my hands and sang softly to my baby, *Twinkle, twinkle, little star, how I wonder what you are*. There really are no words more beautiful if you sing them very slowly. During those crazy days before the wedding when my mother was booking the church, the hall, flowers, all that stuff, I slipped away whenever I could and laid on my bed. I thought about girls' names and boys' names and I sang twinkle, twinkle over and over again. My baby would be here in seven months. I couldn't wait.

Kevin

I went through with the marriage, played the smiling groom, the whole bit. Except for one thing. I didn't kiss the mother of the bride.

Mary called me the night before the wedding and told me she'd lost the baby a few hours earlier. She admitted that her mother had told her to keep quiet about the miscarriage until after the ceremony, but Mary told me straight out, "Kevin, we don't have to get married." Her voice sounded flat, numb. I couldn't tell what she was feeling. But I knew what I was feeling: panic. I was desperate to marry her. It would be my only chance.

My mother had been crying for weeks, shrieking about how my life was over. She called Mary a whore, said she trapped me. Dad had enough sense to laugh at that one. As if Mary Connolly needed to trap anyone. No, she'd been caught.

"Well, I think we should still go through with it," I said. Mary was quiet on the other end. That's when I realized she was hoping I'd pull out.

She didn't want me.

"You think we should go through with it?" she finally responded.

I scratched the back of my neck. "Yeah, I do."

"Oh." Her breathing got louder. "Why?"

"Why?" I had a million reasons. The church was booked, people were coming, we'd spent a bundle on the clothes and the deposit for the VFW hall. We'd already caused one scandal that summer. Calling the thing off would cause another. I said, "Because I love you. I always have. I want to be your husband."

"Oh, Kevin." I heard her start to cry. "Why would you want me?"

"Are you kidding? I've always wanted you."

I heard muffled sounds through the receiver. "Wait," she said, "I need a tissue." She blew her nose and I could hear her breath pushing against my ear, pushing like it was trying to push me away.

"Marry me," I blurted, my voice loud, "we can make this work, I know it." She didn't say anything and her breathing stopped altogether. "Mar, you there?"

"I'm here," she whispered.

"Marry me. I'll take care of you. I know we can make it work." I hoped it didn't sound like I was begging. I wanted to sound like I was in charge, that I could take care of her. I said again, "I KNOW we can make it work."

"You do?"

"Promise me you'll show up tomorrow. Don't leave me waiting at the end of the aisle. You know I don't like to get stood up."

"Kevin," her voice was as soft as I'd ever heard it. She was starting to give in.

"If you don't show up, I'll come over and get you. I'm not kidding."

She laughed then and the panic I felt started to lift. I told her to get some sleep and meet me at the church in the morning.

Mr. Connolly

The morning of the wedding, Grace was in a tizzy. She had the sewing machine out and was taking Mary's dress in at the waist even though Mary insisted there was no reason to. When Mary put it on, she looked like a picture. Grace kept sliding her hand over Mary's flat stomach. "Well, this dress will put the rumors to rest," she said.

"Rumors? Mother, they weren't rumors."

Adjusting Mary's veil, Grace said firmly, "Nasty rumors, nothing more."

"Mother—"

"Ah, ah," Grace waved her finger, "this is a case of young love, nothing more."

Smoothing Mary's hair back, she continued, "When everyone sees how thin you are, when you *stay* so thin, they'll realize that those pregnancy rumors were just gossip. Just nasty gossip."

Mary sighed and looked at me for help. I had no idea how to rescue her.

"You and Kevin are in love and that's all there is to it," Grace continued. "Now promise me, look at me Mary, promise me you'll never tell *anyone* about the miscarriage. No one has to know. I wish you hadn't told Kevin, but what's done is done. Just tell that boy to keep his mouth shut!"

Mary raised her arms and let them flop to her side. "Not tell Kevin! Gee, Mother, don't you think he might have suspected something if a baby never came?"

Grace put her finger to her lips and said, "Now, hush! I meant I wish you hadn't told him about the miscarriage until later."

Mary sat on the couch and held her face in her hands. I hated to see her cry. I sat next to her and put my arm around her. "Don't cry, honey. It's bad luck."

Angrily, she rubbed the tears into her cheeks. "It's bad enough without all this lying." She lifted her face and glared at Grace. "Mother, aren't you forgetting about Kevin's parents?"

Grace flew across the room. "Do they know about the miscarriage?" Her face filled with blood and I knew she was furious.

Mary put her head on my shoulder and whispered, "Kevin said he wasn't going to tell them."

"Thank God!" Grace clasped her hands like she was praying. "Maybe that boy has some sense after all."

I knew it was the worst day of my daughter's life. She was the most beautiful bride ever, but she looked like she was going to her own funeral. Before we started down the aisle of the church, Mary's chin was on her chest. I told her, "Honey, hold your head high. You're better than anyone sitting in this church. You have nothing to be ashamed of. You're Mary Connolly and don't you forget it."

Father Gibbon

I'd failed. I'd failed miserably. As Mary came down the aisle on her father's arm, I could scarcely notice how lovely she looked. A vision in white, as they say. Perhaps the most beautiful woman to put on a bridal dress.

I stood in front of the altar, just as I'd done at her First Communion, that day so full of promise eleven years ago, and blamed myself. Mary had been defiled, shamed before God and her community.

Forgive me, God, I prayed. I didn't do enough. The hours I spent thinking of ways to guide her, to be a part of her life, clearly they weren't enough. But what more could I have done? It was a question I would ask myself the rest of my life.

Mary's sin showed on her face. Yes, she was beautiful, but there was an arrogance to her beauty now. She didn't bow her head demurely, even when the Lord's name was spoken, no she lifted her head and locked eyes with me. There was something of an accusation in her icy blue stare. The devil's look of triumph.

And what of her child? In a few years, would there be another blond angel at my altar receiving communion? And would that child have a chance or was it already destined to be corrupted by his parents' sin? My parishioners have no idea of how I suffer for them. I don't complain; it's my lot as a priest.

But I wished they all could know and take warning: if Mary Connolly, with all my tutelage and guidance, could fall from grace, so could any of you.

❦

Mr. Harrigan

My wife didn't want me to hire Mary Connolly, said she didn't project the right image for our pharmacy. Nonsense, I said. A pretty girl at the cash register is always good for business. Yes, I heard all the gossip, but Mary wasn't the first girl to find herself in the family way before marriage and she won't be the last.

And there was something else. Despite her beauty, there was a look of heartbreak in Mary's face that was too adult for an eighteen-year-old girl. The poor thing, she'd been through too much. A pregnancy, a wedding, and obviously, since she stayed as thin as ever, a miscarriage. What more could the poor girl go through? When she saw my help wanted sign in the window and came in to apply, I had to hire her.

Now Mary's here five days a week, always eager for more hours. I couldn't ask for a better employee. When she's stocking shelves, she's always mindful of the bell, and when a customer walks in, she heads immediately for the cash register. She always gives the correct change and politely thanks every customer.

Marie just works in the mornings. At first she tried to talk to Mary, asking her about how she liked being married, what meals she was cooking for her husband. Mary would politely murmur a brief response and then get busy with sorting greeting cards or spraying the glass cases that held our jewelry.

"Well, it's a good thing she's a good worker," Marie says, "because she sure isn't sociable."

"I don't pay her to be sociable. She catches on quick and works fast, that's what counts," I say.

I pay Mary every other Friday. After the first month, I gave her a raise, ten cents an hour. I didn't tell her, just let her figure it out when she got the check. She didn't say anything to me, but a couple of days later I found a note tucked into my inventory notebook: *Dear Mr. Harrigan, Thank you very much for the raise. I appreciate your confidence in me. Sincerely, Mary.*

Sometimes Kevin stops in to see her. When you see them standing side by side, you have to think what a good-looking couple they are. Both of them blond and blue-eyed. They could pass for brother and sister. Mary smiles when he walks in, but she's not eager to see him like a young wife should be. They've both been through too much. I know Kevin wasn't ready to be a father, but I can see that Mary has the natural instincts of a mother. She's hurting and Kevin, poor kid, is too young to know what to do. He's always got this hopeful look on his face when he comes in the door, but when he leaves I can tell he's deflated. It just takes time. When you're that age, you don't realize how much time helps everything.

Kevin

My parents will pay my college tuition, but Mary and I don't have enough dough for our own apartment yet. I paint houses in the summer, but it's not steady work. We moved in with my parents, taking over the third floor of their big old Victorian. We have our own bathroom and kitchenette, so it's not that bad. Still, my mother is always snooping around, asking me all the time why Mary looks so glum.

"She had a miscarriage," I remind her. "Give her a chance to get over it." Yeah, my mother thinks Mary miscarried a week after the wedding. Probably that's what most people think because who would get married at eighteen if they didn't have to? They don't get that if you have a shot with Mary Connolly, you don't waste it. But my mother's right. Mary looks glum.

I don't know how to make her happy. She pulls away from me more each day. Sometimes she surprises me, reaching for me during the night. She doesn't say anything when we make love, and she barely kisses me. She says that condoms hurt too much and to not put one on. She wants a baby I think, and I get excited, but then in the morning she's quiet, looking out the window as she sips her orange juice. A few days ago, I snuck up behind her and wrapped my arms around her shoulders. Leaning over, I kissed her cheek and whispered, "You're looking beautiful today, Mrs. Walsh," in her ear.

She spun around so fast, she almost knocked me over. "NO,

KEVIN!" she yelled at me. "NO, NO, NOOOOO!" She pushed against my chest with her fists. "Don't you EVER sneak up on me like that again! I don't want you to do that! DO YOU UNDERSTAND? DO YOU!" Then she locked herself in the bathroom for over an hour.

A guy can only take so much of this. I'm just eighteen, but I know how lonely marriage can make you feel. It's weird how you can be all by yourself and feel fine, but when you're in a room with someone who doesn't care about you, you're really alone.

But maybe things will change. Sometimes while I'm painting, I think about when we were kids riding on that swing. I imagine what it would be like to be with Mary on that swing now, her legs wrapped around the back of me, our bodies pushing and pulling against each other. It was so easy then. Why couldn't it be like that again?

Joe

All the firemen are happy for me. Every time I stop by, they tease me about Eileen, but they also say she's a great girl, so pretty, so nice. They stuff money into the back pocket of my jeans and tell me to take Eileen out to dinner. One day towards the end of summer, my Uncle Jim takes me to the back of the firehouse and asks me if I know how to keep Eileen from getting pregnant. It's hard not to laugh, he looks so serious, but then he puts his hand on my shoulder and says, "Hey, pay attention. You got any questions about any of that?" Fifteen minutes later I'm still assuring him that I know all about sex and that I'm not planning on getting Eileen pregnant. "Don't end your future before you have a chance to live it. You can call me," he says, "call me collect from college if you have any questions, any problems. You know that, Joe."

I do know that. Every one of my uncles would do anything for me. Before walking out of the firehouse, I take a long look around and think about just how damn lucky I was to grow up here. How many times did I slide down the pole or sit in the driver's seat of the truck? My uncles let me run the siren on my birthdays when I was a little kid. Nothing topped that. As I walk out of the house, I silently pray, *Dear God, please keep every one of them safe.*

 This has been the best summer of my life. Every day I mow lawns at Cazenovia Park for a good buck, and every night I see Eileen. We usually don't do anything special, just take a walk, spend time together. We talk, we listen to each other. I could tell her anything. I have too, all about missing my father, being worried about my mother, things I've never told anyone, not even my brother. Eileen had so much bottled up inside of her. All these years we were in school together, I had no idea what she was going through. Eileen is so strong, way stronger than she gives herself credit for. Her life hasn't been easy, but she never let anybody know it. In that way, she's as tough as my mother.

 Love has a rhythm to it, just like running, just like breathing. After dinner, I run over to Eileen's. I can't wait to see her standing on the corner of her street. There's that moment when she first sees me, and I know that all this running all these years comes down to her. I've been running to her my whole life.

 If all goes well, I'll be a doctor eight years from now. Eileen and I will be married. Maybe we'll be starting a family. I don't know why kids my age are always saying that the future is so scary. I know exactly what I'm going to do. The only hard part is how long it's going to take.

Mary

 If it weren't for this job, I'd lose my mind. The pharmacy is my refuge. At Kevin's house, I watch the clock, willing the hands to move faster so I can escape and come to work. I love the soft tinkling of the bells as I push open the pharmacy door, Mr. Harrigan's quick smile, his simple greeting, "Good morning, Mary." The little cleaning and inventory jobs keep my mind busy. Keep me from thinking about my own life.

 I never clean at Kevin's house, but I sweep the aisles of the pharmacy continually. Stock can get dusty just sitting on the shelves, so I rub the bottles of vitamins, shampoo and deodorants with old dish towels Mrs. Harrigan brings in. Every day I inspect the front windows and the glass cases for smudges and fingerprints. Once a week, I carry the little porcelain figurines into the back room and rinse them off. We have a set of tiny angels painted in pastel colors to match birthstones. Each little angel wears a tiny wreath on her head with a little crystal meant to be a birthstone. I'm especially careful with the February angel, the little angel wearing a lavender dress to go with the pretend amethyst. If I hadn't lost my baby, she would have been born in February. I would have bought the angel to put in her room. I know in my bones my baby was a girl. Every time I pass the angel, I smile at her.

My steadiest customer is Mrs. Sullivan. She comes in every morning and buys only one thing at a time, a box of scented soaps, a nail file or some other grooming item. It takes her a while to pick out what she wants and I feel her eyes on me the whole time. One morning while she's at the register paying for a hairbrush, her hand jolts out and catches mine. She squeezes it tight. "Mary," she whispers, "I'm so sorry for your loss."

I am stunned. She is the first person outside of Kevin's and my families to say something so directly about the baby. Everyone else is simply pretending that I was never pregnant. I'm surprised to feel such gratitude that someone cares enough to offer sympathy. Lifting my eyes from the register to Mrs. Sullivan's face, I see that she hasn't entirely lost her beauty. There are spider veins on her cheeks and nose that she's tried to cover up with powder, but her eyes are still remarkably green, as green as Eileen's, and her lips are expertly lined and coated with some expensive cosmetic. I blink and slowly say, "Thank you."

She gathers up her purchase and nods. "I've wanted to tell you that for some time." She walks out and I wonder if she'll ever come back.

I'm supposed to leave the store every day at five, but I always offer to stay later. There are times when Mr. Harrigan gives me an extra project, changing the display in the front window or delivering a prescription to a customer in the neighborhood. Finally, though, he says, "Call, it a day, Mary. Good job."

Kevin's mother ambushes me as soon as I enter the house. I still call her Mrs. Walsh and she hasn't asked me to call her anything else.

"How was work?" she automatically asks, but it's not a real question, just a prelude to pouncing on me. Her next question is always, "What are you fixing my son for dinner?" In the beginning, I'd mumble, "A chef salad," and she'd frown. "Kevin's used to a good hot meal every night. If you're not going to cook, send him downstairs. He's still a growing boy you know."

But during these last weeks, Kevin isn't home at dinner time. As I walk through his parents living room to the stairs that lead up to the third floor, Mrs. Walsh looks up from her knitting and purses her lips. "Maybe if you'd cook once in a while, your husband would come home."

I don't answer. I walk hurriedly up the steps, eager to turn on the television, to keep my mind occupied until I can sleep. Kevin comes home late, usually after midnight. He whispers, "Mar?" and I don't stir. I get up very quietly in the morning, drink orange juice and watch the clock. At 8:45, I escape to the pharmacy and it all begins again.

Mrs. Connolly

Well, all's well that ends well, that's what I say. Mary has a nice job at the pharmacy and Kevin is headed towards community college. They're doing as well as any young couple. Yes, I hoped Mary would have a modeling career in New York, but who knows? Maybe she'll be able to do that right here in Buffalo. She won't make as much money, but she'll be near her family and that's what counts.

Al is worried about her, but that's just how he is. He thinks that when the kids come over for dinner on the weekends, Mary looks sad. "She's just tired," I tell him. "She's got a new job and her own place to clean." But he shakes his head and says for the millionth time, "She's got a good mind. Maybe she should get out of that marriage and go to college."

I could scream when he says that. We don't have that kind of money and I don't want Al selling the car and taking the bus to work. Yes, Mary's smart, but I know she wants to be a wife and mother, just like me. I often tell her to wait to have children until Kevin's out of school, when they have a little saved up. One time she looked at me and sassed back, "I'm going to get pregnant as soon as possible!"

That shocked me. That whole terrible business ended as soon as it started and now Mary has a fresh lease on life. Why does she want to go through that again so soon? I held my tongue, but I asked her, "Does Kevin know? Does he want a baby right away?"

She didn't answer. Now, Kevin is a lucky boy to have my Mary, but I hope my daughter realizes that marriage is a two-way street. There's give and there's take. She shouldn't do anything without discussing it with her husband. But that Kevin, he's so smitten with her, I know he'll go along with whatever she wants. So maybe I will be a grandmother sooner than later. Well, it won't be easy for them money-wise, but it will be fine with me. And if the baby is a girl, it will be so much fun taking her to the beauty pageants just like I did with Mary. Kevin is handsome, but it would be a shame if the baby didn't look just like Mary. Oh, that would be wonderful, having a little Mary to fuss over and dress up. Walking all over the neighborhood again with a little princess. It would be just like old times.

Mary

It's been weeks since I thought of Joe. When I was carrying my baby, I didn't need to think about him. But now, feeling so empty inside, I look for Joe around the neighborhood. Eileen told me he's not leaving for Fordham until the end of August. I pray I'll see him at least one more time.

At night, I think about how he held me at the prom. If he hadn't run out that night, how different would everything be now? I curse myself for not running after him. I should have followed him outside, wrapped my arms around him, whispered, "It's okay," in his ear.

Oh, I'm such a fool for never having told him that I love him, that I've always loved him. I was so afraid of feeling embarrassed. How stupid. Embarrassment is the reason I'm so miserable now. Yes, I know, he's madly in love with Eileen; I don't expect him to drop her and come to my side. I know I lost my chance. But if I see him, I'll say hello and wish him well, congratulate him on his scholarship and tell him I'm so happy for him and Eileen. Then I'll say good-bye, turn around and walk away.

I hope Joe doesn't feel sorry for me. I can stand everyone's pity but his. The gossipers think I'm mourning the loss of my life as I knew it, but they're dead wrong. No, my grief is for the stain on the bedroom floor. I mourn for that part of me that I lost too soon. I want to kneel before the blood, sweep it together magically with my hands and press it back up into myself. I ache for the child who would not desire me as a friend or a girlfriend, the child who would look at me and see only one thing: a mother.

Kevin

The day I find the note on the kitchen table, it's a relief. Terrible and sad, but a relief. I collapse onto a chair and pick up the paper:

Dear Kevin,

I don't know how to say I'm sorry, but I am. I will never ask you to forgive me because I cannot forgive myself for making you play this charade with me. It's gone on too long. Please know that the brief time I carried our baby was the happiest time of my life.

I'm going to my parents, but please don't call me there. Come to the pharmacy and we can figure out how to end this. I'm sorry. I will be sorry forever.

Mary

Not even "Love, Mary." It's for the best, I know, but I still feel as if I've been shot, that there's a hole in my chest so big that the slightest wind could knock me over. It's a struggle to pull my wedding ring off my finger. When the ring finally slides over the knuckle, it comes off so fast I hit my chin with my hand. It doesn't hurt, but I start blubbering anyway. It's always been easy for me to cry, too easy, since I was a kid. I fold the note and put it with the ring in a drawer.

I look around the apartment and it's like she was never here. If it weren't for the note, I could almost convince myself that the last two months had never happened. I was never the smart kid in school, but I know a few things, like even when I'm an old man, in my seventies or eighties, I'm still going to be thinking about Mary Connolly.

Father Gibbon

These misguided young people. They come to the rectory with their mothers and ask about an annulment. What are they thinking! A baby conceived out of wedlock and they think they have grounds for an annulment?

"You've made your bed and now you must lie in it," I tell Kevin and Mary. "Yes, it's hard now, but down the road you'll see that staying together is the right thing to do. It's God's will."

Mary's mother nods her head over and over. "I agree with you completely, Father, completely."

But Mrs. Walsh is of another mind. "Father," she asks, "I want to know the worst thing that can happen to Kevin if he gets a divorce. Remember, he's not the one who got pregnant. Yes, he fell to temptation, but—"

"Mom!" Kevin stands and shouts at his mother. The skin around his eyes is red and swollen; clearly the young man has been crying for hours. "Stop it! Mar and I were in this together at the start and we're in it together at the end. If one of us sinned, both of us sinned." He falls back onto his chair and crosses his arms over his chest. Well, he is stepping up to the plate, as they say, taking responsibility for his actions. It's more than I expected of him.

Throughout all of this, Mary remains curiously quiet. Her head is lowered, her face filled with shame. Perhaps all of this has taught her a badly needed lesson. A fall from grace can be an opportunity for redemption. Perhaps my work with her is not over yet. I need to meet with her alone, without Kevin and the mothers. We need to talk, really talk about what has happened and how she will make her amends to God.

Mrs. Walsh is pursing her lips and staring angrily at the ceiling. "Father, I just want to know what's the worst that can happen to my son if he gets a divorce? Is it a venial sin or something worse? Surely, it can't be mortal—"

"No, no, no," I interrupt, raising my hands and waving them in front of her. "I'll hear no talk of divorce. Divorce would mean excommunication from the Church and all that follows."

"Shit," Mrs. Walsh says before whisking her hand to her mouth. She looks at Mary and says, "Well, I hope you're happy, Missy. If you get divorced you'll be going to hell in a hand basket and you'll be dragging my son with you!"

"Agnes, don't talk like that to my daughter! For heaven's sakes, we're old friends!" Mrs. Connolly dabs at her eyes with a handkerchief. Sniffling, she adds, "Mary and Kevin are not getting divorced. They'll stay married and go to heaven." She puts her hand on Mary's shoulder and rubs it vigorously. She leans in towards her daughter and says, "Right, Mary?"

Slowly Mary uncrosses her legs. She smoothes the front of her skirt with her hands and takes her time standing up. Looking at her mother, she says calmly, "No, that's not right, Mom. Kevin and I are getting divorced, and if the church wants to kick us out, fine. Good riddance."

"Mary!" her mother gasps. "You don't mean that! Don't talk like that in front of Father Gibbon."

So, I was quite wrong about the girl's feeling shame. No, she was averting her eyes because clearly she feels she's above us all, that we have nothing to say to her. She adds the sins of pride and arrogance to her growing list. The girl is beyond redemption. Despite all my efforts and prayers on her behalf, she is shunning the Church, myself, and her family. She's an ingrate as well as a sinner.

Mrs. Walsh swings her head so that it's an inch from her son's. Slapping his shoulder, she says, "Fine girl you picked out. Of all the nice girls at St. Martin's, you had to bring her home."

"I'm not listening to this." Kevin stands also and reaches to take Mary's hand. Avoiding his clasp, she nevertheless walks with him to the door.

"Mary!" Mrs. Connolly wails, "Mary! Come back, honey! We can work this out! Mary!"

The heavy church door swings shut and I know with certainty that I will never lay eyes on Mary Connolly again. This chapter of my life, one that spanned many years of ardent dedication and determination, is over. I make the sign of the cross. Thank goodness their child did not survive, a child who had no chance of salvation and eternal life. That death was evidence of God's mercy.

Mr. Harrigan

Now my wife is after me to fire Mary because the girl is getting divorced. "A divorcee working right in our own store," she says over and over again. I stand firm and tell her, "It's 1975. A divorce isn't that shocking any more."

"Maybe not to you," Marie snaps, "but the Catholic Church has plenty to say about it."

I try not to chuckle out loud. "That excommunication stuff is a lot of baloney. The way things are going, the priests should be happy when anyone shows up for mass." She purses her lips and shakes her head. "God forbid Father Gibbon should catch you talking like that."

"Let Father Gibbon run his church and let me run my pharmacy." She starts to speak, but I say, "Those are my final words on the subject. Mary stays."

Why would I fire her? Mary does a great job day in and day out. I sense that these days are tough for her. A bunch of the kids she graduated with are going off to college, and Mary's probably smarter than any of them. Well, there's time if she wants to go. Maybe she's saving for tuition. I only hope she'll go to a local college so she can keep her job here.

Today is Wednesday, normally a slow today, but I hear the bell over and over, the door opening and shutting. Mary's ringing up a sale at the cash register when the phone rings. I pick it up and it's her mother. I can't understand what she's saying, but she's excited, shrieking something. "Just a second, just a second, I'll get Mary for you."

The news is good, I can tell by the expression on Mary's face. There's a glow in her face and she's grinning ear to ear. "Yes, I'm excited, Mom. Yes! Okay, I have to tell Mr. Harrigan. No. I'll be home at my usual time."

"Good news?" I ask when she hangs up.

At first she's too flustered to speak. I offer her a chair, but she shakes her head. "No, I'm fine. I'm better than fine." She clasps her hands under her chin and sings in a high-pitched voice, *"I'm going to be a model!"*

Mary has never displayed such a lack of reserve and it takes me a moment to respond, "A model! That's wonderful!"

I start to pat her on her shoulder, but she surprises me by throwing her arms around me and giving me a hug. "When do you start?" I ask.

She teeters on the back of her heels and then I insist that she sit. I slide the chair over to her and she drops onto it, still smiling ear to ear.

"Um, the Ford Agency in New York City is sending me a ticket for this weekend. They want to interview me before I actually sign with them, but the woman told my mother that based on the photos I'm a shoe-in." She looks up at me, shocked. "A shoe-in! Can you believe it?"

"Of course I believe it. So, you leave this weekend?"

Oh," she covers her mouth, "I'm so sorry, Mr. Harrigan, I can't give you two weeks notice. I'm awfully—"

"Don't you worry about it. Don't give it a second's thought."

"I hate to leave you without help."

"We'll be fine. My wife mentioned something about wanting to work more hours. You don't give it a second thought."

During the afternoon, I take a couple of pictures of Mary with an old camera I keep in the back room. "When you're famous, I'm going to put these in the front window." Mary laughs and poses by the cash register, by our Kiwanis gumball machine, and by a little collection of porcelain angels that she likes. I promise to send her copies of the pictures in New York.

"Thank you! I'll frame them and keep them in my room. I'm going to share a room at the Barbizon Hotel with a few other girls. I'll get you the address before I leave."

"Good. I'll send them there."

She nods. "Yeah, I guess it will be a like a dorm room." Laughing, she continues, "So maybe I'll get a taste of college life after all."

I head back behind the pharmacy counter, lifting my head from time to time just to look at Mary. It's such a pleasure to finally see her happy. About mid-afternoon a woman and her little boy come to the pharmacy counter. The little boy has asthma and is wheezing terribly while I'm filling his prescription for an inhaler. His mother is anxious. "He wasn't this bad at the doctor's office. We just left and came straight over here." It's not often something like this happens at the pharmacy. People are ill, but I don't recall seeing anybody in such respiratory distress. The mother tries to take the inhaler out of the box, but she's too nervous and she fumbles. "Could you help me?" she asks.

"Of course." In just a few moments, the little boy is inhaling. He's still wheezing but then, after a minute, I see that he's able to breathe more deeply. His mother is crying slightly, saying, "Good job, Brian. Good job. Breathe slowly, *sl-ow-ly*, that's it. Take the air all the way down to your tummy." A few minutes later his breathing is calm and even. I realize I've barely taken a breath during the whole episode, I was so nervous. I suggest to the woman that she return to the doctor's office immediately, let him know that her son has just had an attack. She readily agrees and I walk both of them to the front door. "Thank you so much," she says.

"I'm just glad he's doing better." I watch as they walk off, the little boy holding his mother's hand. The boy is probably about four, not yet in school. A real cute little guy with bright red hair. Please keep him healthy, God, I pray. Let him grow up strong.

It's a beautiful day, sunny but not blinding, and there's even a little breeze. I stand for a moment with the door open enjoying the fresh air. Inhaling deeply, I think how difficult it must be to have asthma, how just breathing, what most take for granted, can be heavy work for others. But now the summer air feels as if it's whispering over my skin and I linger at the door. For a moment, I close my eyes, enjoying the warmth of the sun on my face. Buffalo winters are hard, but the summers are great. Hot, but not too hot, and often breezy because of the lake effect. I open my eyes as a young man in a Saint Martin's t-shirt jogs by. He too is clearly enjoying the weather. There's a look of contentment on his face, his brown hair lifted in the back with the breeze. To be that young and have that much energy, it must feel great.

Suddenly Mary is behind me, pushing the door wider and stepping around me. She calls, "Joe! Joe! Can I talk to you, Joe?" She steps outside and continues to call the boy's name. Now she's running and calling, "Joe!" over and over. For just a second he turns his head, but he continues to run. He hears her voice but hasn't spotted Mary yet. As he runs into the street, his eyebrows lift as he recognizes her and there's a screeching of car breaks and a sickening thud that seems to rock the store. The scream from Mary is something inhuman, like the cry of the banshee in the Irish ghost stories. She's in the street next to the boy as the driver of the car leaps out as well.

A woman approaches the store, reaching to put her hand on the door handle. "I'm sorry," I tell her, "I have to close for a while." In the store, I call the emergency number and hear myself giving the location of the accident. My voice is odd, too loud, and I'm shaking as I replace the receiver.

I should be moving more quickly, but I can't bear to. I can't face the scene outside. Just a minute ago, I saw a young man in the prime of his life sprinting down the street as if he didn't have a care in the world. Now it's an effort to walk out the door and start down the street. I'm ashamed of myself for not running to Mary's side, but I'm stuck in slow motion. It's as if I'm trying to move through honey and my limbs are paralyzed by the thick syrup.

Now I see the ambulance, the two police cruisers and a young officer who is trying to restrain Mary. Her screaming sorrow echoes up and down the block. "JOE! JOOOOOOE! NOOOO! NOOO!!!" There's a rip in her voice, a ragged edge to her screaming. I force myself to run the last steps and approach the officer who's holding her by both shoulders to keep her from running to the boy. "LET ME GO! LET GO OF MMEEE!"

Gently, I hold her face in my hands and she collapses onto me. I look out at the wreckage and then I see the motionless body on the stretcher. There is still a look of pleasant surprise on the young man's face. It seems that at any moment, he will turn and speak to us. That he will push himself up with his arms and assure us that he is okay. That I will softly turn Mary around and whisper, "Shh, shh. See, he's all right. No need to cry. He's all right." I want so much for all of this to happen that I believe it will happen. I wait for it to happen. I will wait forever if I have to, anything to bring back the moment I just witnessed of this boy running with boundless energy, running as if he'd never stop.

Sheila

Kevin calls me on the phone. I should hang up on him, but I've missed him so much. There's pain in his voice, a quiver when he talks, like he's trying to catch his breath between sobs. He tells me that he barely survived Mary's leaving him, but that Joe's death makes him want to die too. He sounds like a little boy, young and scared, and something maternal blooms in my chest.

"I'm coming over," I tell him. "Stay right there." When I see him so pale and thin, I hold him in my arms and tell him I love him. He doesn't answer, I don't expect him too, and I say it again, "Kevin, I love you." Slowly,

I rock him in my arms; we sway side to side. It's almost like dancing, and the hurt I felt when I first learned he was taking Mary to the prom pounds at my chest. That pain was slight compared to what I felt weeks later when I heard about the pregnancy, the wedding. But Kevin's in my arms now, and despite how he's treated me, I wouldn't dream of abandoning him.

We go to the funeral together. South Buffalo is not that big and everyone is here grieving together. The firemen who bring the casket down the aisle of the church have stoic expressions, but there are rivers of tears running down their faces. Joe's older brother and his wife look shell-shocked, like they've just come from a war battle. Surprisingly, Mrs. Gleason looks the strongest of all. There's a sense of resignation about her, as if she somehow knew that Joe would be taken from her. She's able to comfort Eileen, thank goodness, because Eileen looks as if she's been whipped within an inch of her life, her face so pale and drawn, she's barely recognizable. She stumbles in the church aisle and clutches the back of a pew to keep from falling. Her father puts his arm around her and half-carries her to a seat.

Kevin can't stop crying. At first, I pull tissues from my purse and hand them to him, but finally I put my arms around him and lay his head against my chest. His breathing is hard, short huffs of air. Softly, I smooth back his hair and stroke the side of his cheek.

Father Gibbon says, "I don't know why Joe had to die early. Life is full of mysteries, things we don't understand. That's where faith comes in. We have to believe that this was God's plan for Joe. Maybe God called Joe home so he could look over the rest of us." There's a fresh outburst of wailing and Kevin presses even deeper into my chest.

With small circular motions, I rub his back and gently kiss the top of his head. "Shh, shh. I'm here. It's going to be okay. You'll see." We make it through the rest of the funeral like that, Kevin sobbing while I do what I can to comfort him. He's so broken right now, so fragile, I forgive him everything. *I pray, God, please help me to get Kevin through this. Please help me know what to say and do.* I know it's too much to expect, that I shouldn't hope that Kevin and I will be together, that he'll recover from all this. I think I've been disappointed too much to have faith, but praying is a hard habit to break.

Eileen

It's lilac season again. Lockey's Hill is covered with the lavender and white flowers, the dark green leaves swirling through the blossoms. I pick a large bouquet and cross to the other side of the hill where the cemetery begins. Joe's marker is in a newer area where there aren't as many trees and the sun isn't blocked by shadows. His grave simply says:

Joseph Michael Gleason
Beloved Son
1957—1975

With my forefinger, I trace the "B" of "Beloved." Yes, beloved, Joe is beloved. He wasn't my son, he wasn't my husband, but he is and will always be my beloved. I arrange the lilacs around the words on his marker and close my eyes. It's here that I can see Joe best. I feel his shining green eyes on me. Once again, I run my finger over the scar on his chin. He moves closer and we are kissing. I will sit here for at least an hour and feel his love the entire time. And I know he feels mine.

Right after the accident, I couldn't comprehend what Mary was saying when she told me that she caused Joe's accident; she had to explain to me four times that she wanted to wish him good luck before he went to college. Finally, I shrieked at her, told her she murdered him by chasing him down the street that day. I was even angrier when she agreed with me, when she told me that she'd hate herself until the day she died for causing Joe to step in front of that car. But hate won't bring Joe back; nothing will.

On Sundays, I have dinner with Mrs. Gleason. We don't say much, but it helps us to be near each other. She has kept Joe's room exactly as it was and doesn't mind that I always go in it after supper. I open the closet door and slip on Joe's denim work shirt because that's what he was wearing the last time I saw him. The fabric still carries his scent, a mixture of Ivory soap and something else that is just Joe. I look around at his awards, trophies and ribbons from track, his name engraved on tiny plaques that hang on the wall. After I've absorbed everything in the room, I lay down on his bed and close my eyes. We never laid in a bed together but I don't feel as if I'm laying alone now. I can feel his arms around me, the pressure of his lips on mine. Sometimes I think I hear his voice, that it's not coming from inside my head but from somewhere outside. He says, "You know I'm here. I'm always here."

Mother is still drinking and Dad is urging me to go to college, to do something for myself. I guess I will. I don't have anything else to do. Dad tells me I'll fall in love again, but I'm not ready to hear that. I'm still in love. Just because Joe isn't here doesn't mean I don't love him more every day. My heart could burst with all this love I feel for him. There are days it threatens to suffocate me, and I realize what Mother went through after Jimmy's death. But I'll never drink to dull the pain. This pain I have is mine and I have so little else left.

So I trace the "B" of "Beloved" on his grave, pushing my finger into the groove of the script. The ring of lilacs comforts me, but it makes me ache as well. Maybe next spring the pain won't be as heavy, but I have so many days to live through before that time.

Mary

I didn't go to Joe's funeral. How could I? I didn't get out of bed for two weeks. Nausea took hold of me much worse than when I was pregnant, my stomach seeming to swell to the bottom of my throat. Who knew that grief has a taste as vile as acid that fills your mouth in your first waking moments and is there long after you fall asleep? After Joe died, grief poisoned my entire body, as if my heart had ruptured and was spilling something toxic throughout me. No matter how many times I vomited, I couldn't get rid of that bitter liquid that pumped through me.

Of course, grief lodges itself in your chest too. Every drop of blood your heart pumps carries that sorrow into your arms, your legs, your whole body. The very thing that keeps you alive throbs with despair. And my grief was made worse by knowing I'd ruined Eileen's life as well. I had wreaked such destruction by running down the street that day, by calling Joe's name. Mother and Dad told me over and over again not to blame myself, that it was an accident. I'll never believe that.

I almost lost the modeling deal with Ford, but they signed me once I got to New York. I was so thin from having eaten next to nothing for so long that my eyes looked oddly huge and photographers went wild for me.

During my first year, I did some cosmetics ads and was on screen for a couple of seconds for a shampoo commercial. Things moved faster my second year. I walked the runway in Paris and Milan and was in every New York show. The Casablanca Agency tried to steal me from Ford, but Ford promised to push me hard. If you look through Vogue and Cosmo, you'll see me modeling hand bags, shoes, clothes, everything. This year, there's talk of a Vogue cover before the year is out. I've made it. Not in record time, but almost.

I make enough money to afford my own little apartment in the east eighties, and I'll be able to move to a bigger place soon. I send my father a nice check every month, although lately he hasn't been cashing them. "Use the money for a trip home," he tells me. He's got to be kidding. As if anyone in South Buffalo would want to see me. Sure, I bet there are people who buy magazines and scan them for pictures of me, but then they probably talk about the baby and Joe's death. Now and then, I wonder if Kevin ever thinks of me, if he's forgiven me. He and Sheila got married last year and maybe he's happy. My hope is that I never even cross his mind and that he doesn't privately look at our wedding photos. But knowing Kevin, I'm sure he does.

Every model has a trademark look. Patty Hansen has a great backside and landed that major Calvin Klein jeans campaign. Roseanne Vela has a face that makes her look like a sweet waif. She was recently photographed in a loose Peter Max t-shirt, her long hair tumbling over her shoulders. Industry insiders say I have a tough, confident look, that my eyes could bore through steel, that the set of my jaw is as strong as any man's. They think my ads appeal to female executives, confident women after the same top salaries as men. These are the women I see walking to work in navy blue suits. They wear Reebocks and carry fancy shoes to slip into at the office. There seems to be an army of them walking up and down the avenues. You can't distinguish one of them from another, they look like clones. I shake my head when I see them and think, *These are the women I appeal to?*

When I look at myself in the magazines, I know I look arrogant, haughty. My hair is blown straight back away from my face and there's something insolent about my forehead, that naked expanse of skin. My eyes are icy blue crystals full of determination. And I'm so thin now, my high cheekbones are very pronounced. Yes, arrogant and haughty, that's how I look. It's the way I act here in the city because it's the way I feel or, more truthfully, it's the way I act because I *don't* want to feel. One photographer affectionately calls me, "the aloof bitch." That makes me laugh. I've become exactly what South Buffalo always thought I was.

I don't read anymore except for brief blurbs in magazines. I'm just too busy, but even if I weren't, I'd still avoid the bookstores and the libraries. Reading makes me think about life too much, and I can't do that any more. Obsessing about your life can drive you mad. You just have to live it and forget about it.

Lots of men ask me out and there are times I disco the night away. There are plenty of places more exclusive than Studio 54, and I never deign to wait in line. Inside, my blood jumps with the disco beat. Actually, I hate the music, long for the rock of the sixties, but I move with the simple, incessant throb of the music and think how easy it is to block everything out. There's only the lights, the music and me. Oh, and whatever man I'm dancing with at the moment.

If a guy gets too serious, wants a monogamous relationship, I tell him sorry. Time to move on. I don't stay with anyone long enough for my heart to be involved. Looking back on the men I've gone out with these last two years, I realize I hardly know anything about them other than their names and maybe where they work. Sometimes, very rarely, I allow myself to remember standing at my window and watching Joe run down the street. I remember how it made me happy and sad at the same time. Then I call myself a fool for letting the memory surface, for being sentimental when there's nothing left to feel that way about.

I want things to keep changing, to never let anyone or anything stick around long enough to become familiar. As long as I don't feel anything, love, grief, guilt, I won't get hurt. On the disco floor, one song ends and the next one starts. I keep moving and life does too.

Mr. Harrigan

I usually enjoy these late summer evenings in the pharmacy. About 8:30, the sun is going down, and the light through the store window is a hazy gold. The late sunshine seems to stop time, to make you take a moment and count your blessings. Tonight, though, the sun's behind a bundle of thick clouds; I might not make it home before it rains.

Buffalo is changing. It's not the same. My youngest son, David, graduated from college with a degree in marketing but he can't get a job. There are no jobs left. Every generation is supposed to do better than the one before it, but our children are getting the short end of the stick. This last year, he's just been moping around the house and working at odd jobs. I could have given him a part-time job at the pharmacy, but he wouldn't hear of it. Marie and I want him to go to graduate school and get his MBA. Maybe the economy will be better by the time he graduates, and he'll be able to find something.

A year ago, a little punk with a gun walked in right before closing and made me hand over the day's cash. I was more surprised than scared while I was pulling the bills from the register. A robbery right here on Abbott Road in South Buffalo! You've got to be kidding. I had to install security mirrors and cameras, pay a fortune for a fancy alert system. Receipts have been falling too. People will always need prescriptions, but they don't have as much money any more for all the extras we sell. Marie and I can't take a vacation this year unless we dip into our savings, and I'm hoping our car lasts a long time. I shouldn't complain; we're much luckier than most. The layoffs at the Bethlehem Steel Plant have been steady. I'm afraid it's the beginning of the end for the city.

I'm not superstitious, but there are times I think our luck changed when Joe Gleason died, that his death ended our era of good fortune. We had been so happy for so many years, and now we have such hardship. Heartache too. Timmy Corcoran died in a boating accident on Lake Erie last summer. His father took it so hard, people say he's going to die of a broken heart. That's a saying in South Buffalo for when someone takes to drink. Poor man;

I'd be drinking myself if I lost a son.

We were all shocked when Father Gibbon died of a massive heart attack on Ash Wednesday. He was rubbing ashes on the school children's foreheads when he fell right over the communion rail. The parish doesn't have a replacement yet since so few young men are going into the priesthood. Yes, it's all been bleak and folks are feeling down. The best thing for morale has been this fashion magazine with Mary Connolly's picture on the cover. Mary's done as much for civic pride as O.J. Simpson. If she came back to visit, she'd be handed the keys to the city. But she hasn't come back. My guess is she never will.

It's funny; a few years back my wife didn't want me to hire Mary Connolly, and now she thinks we should put the fashion magazine with her picture on the cover in the window. "She used to work here!" Marie says, excited. "Now she's famous. It kind of makes us famous too!"

Ridiculous. Well, the magazines sold fast. We normally remainder a bunch of the women's magazines, but after three days, there's only two left. I expected Mrs. Connolly to come in to buy a stack, parade them all over the neighborhood, but my wife heard that Mary had already sent her several advance copies. No doubt Mrs. Connolly has framed copies in her living room. It's a triumph for the woman who took so much pride in her daughter's beauty. Now Mrs. Connolly has everything she always wanted except Mary herself.

I look my watch. Ten minutes until closing. After I lock up, I have to make sure the security system is set up for the night. It's tricky; twice I've set off the alarm and the police came. I think I finally have the hang of it now, but I miss the old days when I just turned a key in the front door and exited out the back door with the bolt lock.

I'm just about to turn the lights off when Kevin Walsh walks in and says, "You closing?"

I smile and shake my head. "Not yet, but you have to be quick. How's it going?"

He seems startled by the question, swinging his head to take in the whole store. "Good, good," he says, his hands burrowing further into his pockets while standing in the same spot. He looks so young in that Buffalo Bills football jersey, one of the sleeves partially ripped.

"What do you need?"

He closes his eyes for a moment, like he's thinking, and his skin goes pink. I smile, thinking he's here to pick up condoms. Even though he's a married man, it's still not an easy request.

But he stammers and finally blurts, "Uh, that magazine, you know, um, Sheila wants it, the one with Mary on the cover?"

His face is scarlet, and he starts tapping his right foot rapidly. I don't want to add to his embarrassment so I try to sound as business-like as possible. "Aisle three. This way."

We walk over to the magazine stand display and I pick up the latest issue of *Vogue*. The heft of the magazine surprises me; it's much thicker than *Time* or *Newsweek*. Does a fashion magazine really need to have so many pages? The slick, shiny cover feels like satin under my fingers. The headlines scream messages about designer collections, new trends in cosmetics, hair-dos for summer. In the center of all of it is Mary Connolly. I'd know her anywhere. I've heard young women exclaiming over the magazine in the store, saying how different Mary looks, how they probably made her eyes bluer in the photo and air brushed out some freckles. "She looks too perfect," one girl said, "you can tell the picture is fake." It was all I could do not to interrupt and say, "She was perfection. This photo hasn't been altered in any way."

Mary's wearing some ridiculous outfit in the picture, some garish purple dress with small straps made from what appear to be peacock feathers. Her lipstick matches the dress, and the lids of her eyes are smudged dark. It's more like a Halloween picture except that it's not. It can't be because it's Mary. No matter how they tried to make her look shocking or like some pop art piece, her beauty penetrates the camouflage. The perfect skin, the delicate nose, the sapphire eyes, everything that makes Mary who she is.

I hand it to Kevin and try to sound joking when I say, "Why women need a magazine to tell them how to dress is beyond me."

"Yeah," Kevin agrees readily, happy that I'm not talking about Mary. At the cash register, he pulls a wad of singles from his pocket and I give him change. I usually just slip the receipt in the magazine and hand it to the customer, but it occurs to me that Kevin may not want Sheila to see him bringing the magazine into the house. Despite what he said, it's clear he's buying the magazine for himself. I pull out one of our white plastic bags and pick up the magazine. Kevin and I look at the cover at the same time and then our gazes lock. For the merest second, I consider saying something to him, but what? How do you offer comfort to someone who's been through what he has? He senses my hesitation and turns his head, pretending to cough.

Quickly, I turn the magazine over before putting it in the bag. For just a second, I see the back cover. A bottle of beige-colored make-up appears over the words, written in a fancy script, "Fix your flaws and flaunt your face!" For heaven's sake.

     "Here you go." I hand over the bag to him and Kevin tucks it under his arm. The poor kid's cheeks are still flushed and he's swallowing nervously. He looks like I caught him trying to rob the store. Well, he needn't worry. I'll never breathe a word.

ACKNOWLEDGEMENTS

The majority of these stories originally appeared, in slightly different form, in literary magazines.

"Makeover" originally appeared in JMWW.

"The Comet" originally appeared in *Cimarron Review*.

"A World Transformed" originally appeared in *West Branch*.

"Trying So Hard" originally appeared in *Fireweed*.

"Man Talk" originally appeared in *The Seattle Review*.

"Memphis, Tennessee" originally appeared in Rosebud and was reprinted in *Literary Mama*.

"Eternal Youth" originally appeared in *Thema* and was reprinted in the anthology, *Families: The Frontline of Pluralism* (Wising Up, 2008)

"The Marshall Islands" originally appeared in *Phantasmagoria*.

"Citizen" originally appeared in *Eureka Literary Review*.

Grateful appreciation to our photographers:

Cover photo: Richard Hogan with Kerry Hughes.

Author photo: Bob Geitz

Kerry Langan was born in Buffalo, New York, and completed her undergraduate and graduate education there. She had a career as an academic librarian before becoming a fiction writer. Her short stories have appeared in dozens of literary magazines in the United States, Canada and Hong Kong and have been anthologized often. *Only Beautiful & Other Stories* is the first book-length collection of her short stories. She lives in Oberlin, Ohio, with her husband and daughters.

To order *Only Beautiful & Other Stories*
and other books from Wising Up Press go to:
<www.universaltable.org/bookstore.html>

www.ingramcontent.com/pod-product-compliance
Lightning Source LLC
Chambersburg PA
CBHW030319020726
47493CB00004B/1080